EVERYBODY LIES

B.M. Hardin

Dedicated to Kita, Brenda, and Angela

EVERYBODY LIES

CHAPTER ONE

"Ahhhh!"

Kelli rolled her eyes. "What in the hell is Coco screaming about now? I swear, she's like the worst drunk ever! She's so damn dramatic!"

"Somebody! Help me! Help!"

We heard her scream again, just as the next song started to play. No one else seemed to be paying attention to Coco's pleas.

"Girl, let me go out here and check on her ugly self," Kelli yelled over the music as she stood up.

"Stop it. Coco is not ugly."

"Shiiiit! You know you lying! That bitch looks like a chewed up Slim Jim," she laughed.

I spit out my drink.

"A what?"

"A chewed up Slim Jim," she spaced out her words. "Pep, you know that woman ugly. Hell, we all know she ugly. Humph, and she's the one with a husband while we're over here lonely as hell," Kelli let out a jealous sigh, and then she trotted towards the direction of the screams.

Once she disappeared out the back door, dizzy, I sat my empty glass on the table and attempted to stand.

I was drunk. Too drunk and I didn't like the feeling.

We were at my sister, Olivia's, bachelorette party.

And what a party it turned out to be! I'd gone all out to make this night special. I wanted it to be a night she would never forget. I rented this overpriced mansion, hired a bartender, paid for strippers, both male and female, and spent three times my mortgage on food and alcohol. If Olivia didn't go all out for me, when it was my turn, *again*, I was going to be pissed!

Finding it hard to take my first step, suddenly, Kelli reappeared and started running towards me. She looked scared. Or shocked. I couldn't really tell the difference.

It seemed as though it took her forever to reach me, but once she did, she caught her breath and said:

"The bride…your sister…Olivia…is dead!"

My heart stopped beating for a second too long, and I lost my balance. I hit the floor, hard, and it seemed as though my entire body had gone numb.

Did she say dead?

I felt Kelli tugging at my arm, but I couldn't move.

The music ended abruptly, and I looked up to see Coco with her hands in the air.

"The Bride is on Fire! The Bride is on Fire!"

On fire?

What does she mean *on* fire?

I felt Kelli pull at my arm again and this time I allowed her to help me to my feet.

Everything was a blur.

Everyone was running.

I ran too. With Kelli still holding onto me, drunkenly, we ran together.

The chilled breeze took me by surprise, but once I adjusted my eyes, I saw it.

The fire.

The body.

It was on fire, literally, on the far end of the pool.

Olivia?

No. That can't be her.

In unison, everyone around me either started to scream or started to cry. Some did both at the same time.

Everyone but me.

I was stuck. Frozen. Maybe even a little confused.

My eyes were locked on the tiresome yellow and orange flames. My chest was tight, and my heart was heavy. It felt as though it was a pound away from exploding, but still, I just stood there.

"I came outside to throw up and---and---that's when I saw her," Coco started to explain. "She---Olivia---was already spinning around in flames. By instinct, I screamed for help as I ran towards her. I couldn't get but so close to her. It was too hot. I tried---I tried---to tell her to fall into the pool, but she was in a panic. She was shrieking in turmoil and---and---she wasn't listening to me! She just wouldn't listen to me!" Coco stuttered her way through her explanation.

I heard her, but it was as though my mind refused to retain the information. It was as though my ears were rejecting the words and telling my heart not to accept them.

"The water was right there. All she had to do was fall in the pool. I kept screaming for help, but no one could hear me. I knew it was because of the loud music, but I kept screaming anyway. I wanted to help her. I really did. She fell to the ground, and then…she stopped screaming. She stopped moving. I called her name over and over again, but she didn't answer me. She couldn't answer me. So, I ran back towards the house and started to scream for help again," Coco was in tears as I pulled away from Kelli.

"Pepper! No! Wait!"

I ignored her and hastily, my feet pushed me towards the flames. My feet were moving, but it was as though I was in a daze. As though time had stood still.

Seconds seemed to last forever, but finally, I reached the end of the pool. I walked as close as I could to the flames and desperately, I peered through the smoke just as the sirens started to wail in the distance.

The only thing left visible was the very end of her six-inch gold heels. The ones that I'd gone through hell to find for her today.

It's her.

The burning body belonged to her.

My sister.

My Olivia.

She was disintegrating right before my eyes, underneath the flames, and there was nothing I could do about it. There was nothing I could do to stop it.

I couldn't save her.

Still, my emotions refused to surface because my mind wouldn't stop running. It was running from the truth. Racing to find some kind of explanation because this just doesn't make sense.

How?

Why?

What?

What was she doing out here?

The last time I saw Olivia, she was getting a lap dance and having a drink. It was her fault that I was drunk in the first place. She told me that I didn't have to be the chaperon. She'd said that everyone was grown and responsible for themselves, so she demanded me to relax. I tried to decline, but Olivia was bossy, almost mean whenever she was drunk, so she basically forced me to take shots of tequila with her just to loosen me up.

I remember the stripper, the one in the catsuit, smiling as she rolled her booty around in Olivia's lap. Olivia squealed and covered her mouth, as though she was ashamed or embarrassed. As though she didn't like it, but I was almost certain she did.

I could tell.

That's the last time I saw her.

That's the last time I saw her dashing smile or her pretty face.

That's the last time I would ever see her...

There it is.

Shock, sorrow, sadness.

Finally, all at once, my emotions slammed against my heart like a category four hurricane, and I started to break down. I wasn't sure who caught me before I hit the ground as I began to cry and scream out Olivia's name.

"Noooo! Olivia! Olivia! Noooo!"

This can't be real.

This can't be happening.

She can't be dead.

Seconds into my breakdown, firefighters rushed past me. I watched them through blurry eyes, as they immediately started to tackle the flames, but I knew, I knew in my heart there was nothing they could do.

She's gone.

They're too late.

The bride, my sister, had succumbed to an unbelievable, unimaginable, and undeserving tragic fate.

~***~

"You have to come downstairs Pepper," my oldest sister, Honey, demanded.

She was a little over five months pregnant and hadn't come to the bachelorette party that night. She'd planned to attend, but when I called to tell her that I was on my way to get her, her husband answered the phone and said she'd fallen asleep on the couch.

I told him to let her sleep.

"No. Just leave me alone," I whined.

It's been four days since the bachelorette party.

Four days of pain.

Four days since Olivia had been found in flames; dead. And I just couldn't get the images of her out of my head.

I'd forced myself to look at her once they put out the fire. I just wanted to make sure. I had to be sure it was her.

It was.

It wasn't much left of her, but I knew it was her. And the horribly tarnished gold necklace with the letter "O" that was around the body's neck confirmed that.

Olivia and I had a strong sisterly bond.

Actually, all three of us had been extremely close.

Our relationship as sisters was a lot stronger than most.

We had our lovely mother, Grace, to thank for that.

Growing up, she made sure that we understood the importance of family, and she always reminded us that in life, we were going to need each other.

She taught us to be there for one another.

And we were.

Always.

Olivia is…well, she was the smart one.

The one that succeeded in everything that she did. She was ambitious, confident and spontaneous. It was no secret that she was well on her way to becoming our family's first millionaire. She was definitely almost there.

She was a die-hard entrepreneur, and she loved every minute of it. I've always admired her drive and her dedication to her many crafts. I didn't want to be like her, but watching her strive, accomplish and achieve, made me want to figure out my own goals and dreams. She made people want more out of life. She just had that effect on people. And she was such a people-person too. So friendly and sweet. Everyone wanted to be around her. Everyone loved her; especially Greg. Her fiancé.

And one of my best friends, I guess I should say.

Greg adored her and treated her like a princess. He did whatever she told him to do. He gave her whatever she wanted. Had it been up to him, he would've married Olivia years ago, but she'd wanted to wait. She wanted to get herself together, crush her goals and chase her dreams, first, before she made that type of commitment.

None of us understood it.

But she did.

And then, about five months ago, she popped up with a new ring on her finger and told us to start planning a wedding. She'd wanted something small and intimate. And since money wasn't an issue, it hadn't taken us long to pull everything together.

It would've been just one week away.

Her wedding day.

She was going to be such a beautiful bride.

And now…now she was…

"I can't imagine how you feel, after seeing what you saw, but you're the strong one. You're the tough one. And mama needs you. Hell, I need you too," Honey confessed.

That's me.

The tough one.

The "don't take no shit" one.

The backbone.

The protector.

The one who has always been just a little rough around the edges. Mama always said I had middle child issues, and perhaps she was right. I was a handful growing up, and I was always getting into trouble. And the trouble didn't necessarily stop as I got older. Throughout the years, I've had some challenges, and I needed a major attitude adjustment. But I was dependable. Loyal. Sometimes to a fault. If someone needed someone to hold their hand and tell them that they were going to get through the impossible…they called me. And if someone needed someone to flatten a tire or two, bust out a window, down to catch a charge, you know shit like that; they called me too. I was always right there.

I've always had a wild and crazy side, but over the last few years, I've calmed down tremendously. I started to get my priorities in order; especially after my daddy died.

He left me his dry-cleaning business and becoming a business owner overnight sparked a different type of fire in me. And although it wasn't my dream, it helped me to focus on something bigger than myself.

Finally, I was headed down the right path. I just never would've guessed one of my sisters wouldn't be walking down it with me.

Honey reminded me of her presence once she started to run her fingers through my short curly hair.

Honey is and has always been the nurturing one.

She's just like Mama. So cool, calm and collected. She's the responsible one. The crybaby one. The one who rarely raised her voice or got out of character. Honey was born with an old soul, as some would say. So, it was no surprise to me that she married young and married a man that was about fifteen years older than she was. Now, at thirty-three, Honey had two kids, another one on the way, a fifty-year-old husband and an old blind dog, who was named after her husband, Joe.

"Come on, sit up."

I whined, but I sat up anyway.

"You have cried your big ass eyelashes off," Honey chuckled. "Look," she pulled off the fake eyelash and showed it to me. "Why do you wear them so big anyway? You don't even need them. You're beautiful without them."

I was brown-skinned and average-looking, I guess.

We all had different fathers, so none of us looked alike; but we all had a thing or two from mama.

Honey was chunky, fluffy, and golden brown like jiffy cornbread, just like mama.

I have mama's eyes. Perfectly shaped and daring brown. Honey was right. I didn't need the fake eyelashes, but I loved how much attention they drew to my best assets. I've always been tall and shapely, just like the women on my father's side. And mama always said that I acted just like them too.

Thinking about Olivia, she'd had mama's lips, nose, and her long beautiful hair. Mama's hair nestled right above her butt crack, and Olivia's hadn't been too far behind. Olivia had never even worn a weave.

Honey and I hadn't been so lucky.

Until she was about ten, Honey was so bald-headed you could roll her hair with rice. And my hair never seemed to grow past my neck. So, for the most part, unless I was in one of my hair weave or wig phases, I kept a low, curly pixie cut.

"Baby! Are you okay?"

Honey's husband called up the stairs to her.

"I'm fine, Joe!"

A husband would've been nice to have at a time like this.

I'm divorced.

My marriage only lasted about six months.

It was years ago, and I haven't seen him, Rodney, ever since we signed the divorced papers. We were on and off for a while before we decided to take vows. In the back of my mind, I knew he wasn't the one for me. I guess I just thought no one else would put up with me. But even he got tired of my loud and obnoxious ways.

I'm not afraid to say that my marriage failed because of me. If I had been then, who I am now, maybe we would've worked out.

Maybe.

Rodney tried though. He tried to love me. He really did. But once our marriage started to feel like one roller coaster ride after the other, agreeably, we decided to go our separate ways.

And I've been single ever since. A couple of regular sex buddies, here and there, but I always remained unclaimed.

And I was okay with that until we started planning Olivia's wedding. Seeing her, and Greg, and how perfect they were for each other, reminded me of what love was supposed to be.

"Is Greg down there?"

"Yeah. He isn't doing too good. They were trying to get him to eat something, but he wouldn't."

That night, I was the one that called him to give him the horrific news. It was one of the hardest things I've ever had to do.

Greg and I had a *weird* history.

We dated---first.

Well, sort of. We went on three dates.

He was a good guy.

Too good for me.

I would've ruined the fuck out of him!

We were introduced by mutual friends, literally only a few months before I went back to my ex-husband Rodney, for like the third time, and soon after that, I married him.

Greg wasn't my "type" at the time. Back then, I was into the steady job, with a little *hood* in him, six-pack, skinny with a long dick, been to jail at least once type of guy.

That wasn't Greg at all.

He was funny and slightly attractive. Tall and a little on the husky side. Ambitious and optimistic. He almost gave me the nerdy guy vibe, but a little more entertaining. Nevertheless, I just wasn't interested.

Who knew that seven years later he would lose seventy-five pounds, grow a beard, get some abs and become the CEO of a flourishing engineering company.

Greg was sexy as hell now, and he knew it too.

Anyway, all those years ago, I enjoyed dinner with him for the third time, and then at the end of the night, I "friend-zoned" him. I told him that we would make great friends. And then, I told him I knew a woman that would be perfect for him...my sister.

So, I gave him Olivia's phone number, and the rest is history. They fell in love, and Greg and I developed a strong friendship. He was my go-to for advice, my male perspective when I'm confused, and the sense of humor that he possessed was priceless.

I was proud to call him my friend.

But the night of the bachelorette party, I almost wished it was someone else that had to break the news about Olivia to him. Someone other than me.

I was crying so hard as I called him. I called him at least ten times before he finally answered his phone. It was the night of his bachelor party too. It was Olivia's idea to have the gatherings a week or so out from the wedding. She refused to be hungover on her wedding day. And since drinking was something she loved to do, she wanted to get drunker than she'd ever been before and take a whole week to recover.

Greg's words slurred in my ear that night, and the only thing I could make out was that he couldn't hear me. So, I hung up and texted him. I said that something terrible had happened to Olivia and that he needed to call me back immediately. It took a few minutes, but when he called me back his background completely quiet.

And that's when I told him the news.

His reaction...

The way that he cried...

I'll never forget it.

"Come on," Honey said.

Everyone had gathered at our mother's house.

Greg had Olivia cremated, of course, and it was the day before the memorial service was set to take place.

Slowly, I took steps behind Honey.

I stopped in front of the mirror in my old bedroom to pull off my other fake eyelash and examine my face.

I've been staying here, at mama's house, since the fire. I was barely, eating and if it weren't for mama raising hell if I didn't bathe, I probably wouldn't have been doing that either.

I could tell that she was hurting, but she was trying to keep it all together. She was trying to be strong for me.

And for Honey.

Honey and I walked down the stairs, and the entire room fell quiet. All eyes were on us. Well, they were mostly on me.

Everybody had so many questions.

Everybody wanted to know what happened and what I saw. I didn't see anything, except for the unimaginable.

I didn't have the slightest clue as to what else had taken place before the fire.

Before…

All of my friends greeted and hugged me, and then finally, Honey and I stood in front of mama.

She kissed Honey, and then she kissed my cheek.

"How are you feeling, baby?" she asked.

Mama, Grace Honey-Kaye Wilson, was everything that a mother was supposed to be, and then some. My mama was all that and a bag of chips. And she always has been.

She loved us, unconditionally. And she raised us with such grace and dignity, all by herself. She hadn't been so lucky in love, obviously, since we all had different fathers, but for her, that was okay. She was always the one to leave the relationship and with no hesitation. She always told us that when a man stops showing you that he loves you, wants you or respects you…then it was time to go.

And she always did just that.

The last man mama dated was a man named Bill.

He was the man she started seeing, after she left Olivia's father. But Bill and mama didn't work out either. And on the day that he left, I remember mama saying that she had all the love she needed in the three of us; in her daughters.

So, for over twenty-plus years, I've never seen mama with another man.

And she always seemed happy about it.

"Baby, you need to eat something."

"I'm not hungry," I said to her.

I scanned the room for Greg. Once he noticed me looking at him, he stood up from his chair and immediately headed in my direction. As soon as he reached me, he embraced me.

"Hey Pep. How are you?"

I nodded at him. "I'm okay. You?"

"I miss her."

We all did.

Honey and mama smiled at us, and then they walked away, leaving Greg and me to continue our conversation.

"I called you a few times."

"I don't even know where my phone is," I confessed. "I haven't spoken to anyone, since that night, except for Mama and Honey. And that's because they make me. But everyone has been calling mama, asking questions and trying to get answers. Answers that I don't have."

"Well, I'm here for you. If you need anything."

"I know that, Greg." He exhaled. "Have you heard anything? From the police? Have they figured out what happened to her? You know, other than the obvious?"

"Some. But not much. Why did you have the cameras turned off at the mansion?" He asked.

"I wanted us to have privacy. We didn't need our actions being videotaped. Before renting the place, that was one of the requirements. Who knew that turning them off…"

"Was going to be a huge mistake?"

I nodded.

"The owners said that the cameras would've covered inside of the house as well as the outside. We would've known exactly what happened to her," Greg cleared his throat. "What do you think happened?"

"Greg, honestly, I don't know. I just don't understand how or why or who…I just don't know."

"I spoke to the cops. Although Olivia's body was burned…" Greg paused. I touched his hand, and he continued. "There were still some things left behind on the scene. Enough to make some assumptions. She was drunk. They found a shattered glass with traces of vodka not far from the body. Her fingerprints were on the broken pieces of glass, as though maybe she'd dropped it before the fire. They found a book of matches. One match was missing, but they didn't find it at the scene. They also found a cigarette."

"Olivia didn't smoke."

"I know that. We know that. But the DNA around the butt of the cigarette matched hers. And her fingerprints were all over the book of matches. They matched the prints and DNA with what was in the system for her, from an old shoplifting charge in her teens. She never told me about that. Anyway, the cigarette hadn't been lit, but from what they are telling me, it had definitely been in her mouth. It was found right near the shattered glass. But the book of matches was a few feet away."

Olivia hated cigarettes.

I couldn't even imagine her with a cigarette in her hand, let alone, in her mouth.

"Twenty-two people, including you. The police have spoken to twenty-two people. Sixteen of those that were either guests or "workers" at the party that night; Mama Grace, Honey, my best man and the bartender of the bar we were at that night when you called me. And then they spoke to you and me. And out of twenty-two people, no one saw or knows anything."

"What does that mean?"

"I don't know Pepper. For now, all we know is what they've found. The broken glass, the cigarette, and the matchbook with one missing match. Other than that, no one knows what happened. No one knows how Olivia ended up on fire or dead." Greg's voice cracked.

Immediately, I wrapped my arms around him.

I was tall, so we were almost the same height, and he rested his head comfortably on my shoulder.

I could feel people staring at us.

I held my breath until Greg finally pulled himself away from me. He sniffled, and then he pulled out his cellphone. He showed me a picture of the cigarette and the book of matches that were found at the scene. The photos had been sent to him as a favor from one of the detectives investigating my sister's death.

Immediately, I recognized the name of the store on the matchbook. It had come from the store right around the corner from Olivia's house.

Olivia refused to live with Greg before they were married; even though she basically lived with him for years, whether she'd wanted to admit it or not. But she wouldn't officially move into his house or put her house on the market until they were husband and wife. Olivia had this crazy rule of staying at home, at her house, two days a week. And she would only allow Greg to sleep over on one of those nights. The other night she said was just for her.

Olivia was a complicated woman. Not only was she a boss; but she was the Queen of Being Bossy. A woman of rules and structure, but somehow, Greg loved her for exactly who she was.

"One of the detectives pitched a scenario to me," Greg started. He touched my arm, pulling me towards the dining room table. I could tell that he didn't want anyone to hear what he was about to say. "They are wondering if maybe Olivia did this to herself."

"I don't understand," I asked confused.

"Olivia was drunk and went outside because she decided to have a smoke."

"She didn't smoke."

"Again, I know this. But this is just one of the detective's scenarios. Olivia goes outside. She's heavily intoxicated. At some point and time, she drops her drink. Then, they suggest that she puts the cigarette in her mouth. Her prints are all over the matches. One match is missing. They're suggesting that maybe she lit the match, and instead of lighting the cigarette, she could've accidentally dropped the match on herself. Possibly catching her dress on fire. Since the match is missing, they're proposing that it was somewhere on her and completely burned with her…"

"What? Are you fucking kidding me right now? You know how stupid that sounds, right?"

"I'm only telling you one of the possible scenarios that were given to me. Do I believe Olivia was so drunk that she accidentally set herself on fire? Hell no. But to believe that someone else did this to her, on purpose…" Greg stopped his sentence short. After a second or two, he opened his mouth again. "The backyard of the mansion is surrounded by trees and a fence. No one saw anyone out of place. No one saw anyone around Olivia, around the time of her death. They haven't found anything that suggests foul play. The only prints on anything are hers."

"How did she get the cigarette? Someone must've given it to her, right? She didn't smoke, so she had to have gotten it from somebody. Whoever gave her the cigarette is probably the last one to see her alive. And where did she get the matches? Why not a lighter? I mean come on, who the hell still carries matches these days?" I questioned aloud.

My thoughts were all over the place, but I refocused my attention on Greg once he started to mumble.

"Unless she had the book of matches long before the party. The matches came from that store right around the corner from her house. Their logo is on the front of the matches. Maybe she bought them for whatever reason. You know how much she loved candles, and she always lit them with a match."

"Yeah, but she used those big boxes of matches. The ones from the hardware store. And she keeps them over the fireplace. We both know this. Why would she get matches from a convenience store?"

"I don't know, Pepper. I'm trying to figure this out too. I'm still trying to see her with a cigarette. We both know she hated smoking for her personal reason. And she knew how I felt about women smoking cigarettes. I can't stand it either. So, I'm trying to see it. I'm trying to imagine her last moments and the possibility of her dropping the match on herself. If she did, maybe that's when she dropped the glass of vodka, and the cigarette out of her mouth to search for the match. At that point, did she notice that her dress is on fire? Did she try to put it out? Coco told the police she was spinning around in a panic when she saw her. Maybe that's how the fire spread so fast. There was a big ass pool right there. And she was too drunk to think about jumping into it. That's the craziest part of all. But I'm trying to see it. I'm trying to see what the police are seeing."

"I don't see it at all," I shook my head. I wasn't believing for a second that this was some kind of accident. There's no way that Olivia did this to herself.

"They questioned the bartender that was there that night. He couldn't remember how many drinks he made for her, but he said that it was a lot and that she only asked for tequila shots and vodka."

I shook my head again. "Yeah, but Olivia could *drink* her ass off! She could drink with the best of them. I just can't believe that they think this could be an accident."

Greg shrugged.

"The police asked me if she had any enemies or if she was in any kind of trouble. Or if I knew anyone that would've wanted to hurt her. I said no. She was the most loving person that I've ever known," Greg cleared his throat.

"The cops asked me that too. They asked me a lot of things that night. I told them that everyone loved her. And it's the truth," I let out a long sigh. "I don't know of anyone that would want to hurt her or want to do something like that to her. But I refuse to believe that she did this to herself; or that she caused the fire that killed her. No. Someone had to see something. I just can't believe that."

I've been known to be stubborn. People often told me that I could sometimes be overly persistent. And I could hold a grudge like nobody's business. But in this case, I felt the need to be stubborn. I felt the need to express my thoughts and concerns and standby them.

I was trying to see the situation from an officer's perspective. I was trying to see Olivia with a cigarette in her mouth. Like Greg, I tried to see her dropping a lit match on her dress. The dress she wore that night was made of all kinds of sheer, polyester and tons of other shit that I'm sure could easily catch fire.

But still, she did this to herself?

She was the reason that she was dead?

For the life of me, I just couldn't see it.

"Is there anything that you can remember about that night? That may have seemed wrong or out of place? Anything different about Olivia?"

Shaking my head again, "No. Everything was perfect. She was happy. She was having the best time of her life. Nothing was wrong. Nothing was out of place. I still can't believe this happened! This wasn't supposed to happen!" I tried to steady my breathing, but Greg's loud panting only made me breathe harder.

We both looked at each other without saying a word for a while. Finally, Greg opened his mouth.

"What if we never find out what really happened to her?" Instead of waiting on my response, Greg walked away from me.

I watched him until he was out of the front door. I noticed mama staring at me, but I turned my head. I inched towards the window just in time to see Greg get into his truck. He slammed his hands against the steering wheel and then he dropped his head.

He's crying. I think.

And watching him, my heart started to break all over again.

Before our conversation, I'd been filled with so much sadness, that I hadn't really thought much about the facts. I hadn't really weighed the different scenarios of what had could've taken place that night. I hadn't thought much about how the fire actually started or if someone had done something like that to her on purpose.

All I had been able to think about was that she was gone.

But now, now I didn't know what to think.

Now, I was wondering.

Wondering if the police are right, but more importantly, wondering if they are wrong.

Is there something that they missed?

It has to be.

What if it wasn't an accident?

Then what?

Then who?

Who would've wanted to hurt Olivia?

And why?

The more and more I thought about it, the more my head started to spin. I started to blame myself. I should've been watching over everyone; especially her. I just wanted her to have a good time. I should've never let her talk me into having a drink.

I had one job to do. And that was to protect her and give my sister a night that she would always remember. But instead, it turned into a night that I would never forget.

~***~

"Rodney?"

My ex-husband approached me.

It had been years since I'd seen him.

He looked good. He was still slim, but his shoulders were broader than I remember. His dreadlocks were long and neat. And the facial hair looked good on him too.

"Pepper. I heard about what happened. I wanted to reach out to you but…I reached out to Mama Grace. She told me the time and the place. I just came to show my respects."

The service for Olivia was over.

It was as beautiful as she had been. There wasn't a body to view, but the urn, the flowers, and the speeches from so many people who looked up to her; it was all so beautiful.

I eyed Rodney.

I was surprised that mama hadn't mentioned speaking to him.

"How are you holding up?"

I shrugged.

I noticed the gold band on his finger.

"And you? I see…" I nodded my head at his finger.

"Yeah. For about four years now. And I've been better, but I won't complain. I have a beautiful wife. And four kids. Ages three, two, and we just had twin boys," he said to me.

Why am I jealous?

Rodney and I met at a bar a long, long time ago.

I was twenty-one, and he was there, having a few drinks with his friends for his twenty-fourth birthday.

I stood beside him at the bar. He looked at me, and the first thing he said to me was: "Damn, girl. I've always wanted a tall woman. What's your name? Or can I just call you "Legs"?"

And it started from there.

He was a decent guy. We had good and crazy sex. Some of the best sex I've ever had to be honest.

But after a while, I would want and need a little space. I was just made that way. So, I would push him away. And then when I would want him back, I would force myself back into his world again.

That's kind of what happened after the dates with Greg. A week or two later, I reached out to Rodney, and he took me back. Years of my back and forth little game, but he always took me back. I wasn't sure why. And then once we got married, he tried to change me and calm me down a little. He wanted me to focus more on the future. He wanted us both to make all of these life changes and he started talking about kids. He tried to make me something that I wasn't ready to be. So, for months I pushed back. We were always arguing and disagreeing.

It was always love and war.

Until finally, one day, the war was over.

And so were we.

Now, he was married to someone else.

And he looked happy.

"I know how close the two of you were. I'm sorry this happened. And I'll keep you in my prayers."

Fuck you and your prayers.

I thought. But what I said was, "Thank you. And good luck with everything," I mumbled as he started to back away.

"Yeah. Same to you. Goodbye Pepper."

I watched him until he disappeared.

"I forgot to tell you he called," I heard behind me. My mother touched my shoulder. "What now? She asked.

"I don't know mama. I don't know."

She held the urn with Olivia's ashes close to her chest as we made our way to the parking lot.

In the far distance, I noticed a woman in a black pants suit, leaned up against her car. She looked like some kind of cop or something. And since I didn't recognize her face, I was sure she was.

Speculations were all over the news and internet about Olivia's death. Everyone had their ideas of what they thought happened.

But no one wanted to know the truth more than I did.

Since talking to Greg, it was all that I could think about. It was the only thing on my mind.

"I can stay mama," I said to her after everyone left her house later that evening.

It had been a long, emotional day and even though I felt like crap, I wanted to make sure that she was okay.

"No. Go home. Go home so I can grieve just for one night, without being worried if you'll hear me."

Her words made me shiver with heartache.

"I'll be okay, baby. Just go home," mama demanded again, as she walked towards her bedroom with Olivia's urn still in her hands.

After standing there for a while, I did as I was told.

It was early summer, and almost eight o'clock in the evening. I drove home in complete silence.

My house was a charming, split-level house on the corner of Edgar Street. My dream home. The house that I always said I wanted to come home to. I guess I was hoping that it would be filled with a husband and kids by now, but I hadn't played my cards right.

Last December, I turned thirty-one.

Luckily, I still had time.

Sitting in the car, I thought about Olivia.

I remembered her smile and her laugh.

I remembered how she glowed that night and how she'd run me half to death looking for that long white dress and those expensive ass gold shoes.

And then I remembered…

A few ladies were passing around a cigarette. It was at the beginning of the party, once everyone had a drink or two. I remember them reaching the cigarette towards Olivia, and she shook her head no. She pinched her nose in hopes of blocking out the smell, and when she couldn't, she started to fan the space around her until eventually, she stood up, took a sip of her drink and walked away.

I was right.

Olivia didn't smoke.

She hated cigarettes.

So, why would a cigarette have been in her mouth?

Maybe one of the ladies who was passing around the cigarette ended up giving her one. They could've been the last one to see her alive. They could've seen her make her way outside.

I recalled the faces of the women. Two of them I knew personally. They were childhood friends of ours. The other two were friends of Olivia's that I'd become acquainted with and even quite fond of over the years.

After making a mental note to mention my memories to Greg, and to the police, I decided that I was also going to contact the women and ask a few questions on my own.

Everything still felt surreal.

I still hadn't accepted Olivia's death, and I was sure that I wouldn't be able to until I knew exactly what happened to her.

Forcing myself out of my car, I made my way inside. I frowned once I entered my house.

It looked exactly how I'd left it.

One big mess.

There was shit all over the place. I haven't been home since the day of the bachelorette party. While I was sleeping over at mama's, Honey would come by my house, every other day, and grab me a few things. I was surprised to see that she hadn't tried to clean. She was the definition of OCD, just like mama, but considering everything, I guess she just wasn't in the cleaning mood.

Making my way to the sofa, I laid on top of the pile of clothes and gift-wrapping paper. Spotting the remote, I grabbed it and turned on the T.V.

By default, it was already on the news channel, so I left it there. And for a long time, I stared at it. My mind was somewhere else until I saw her photo on the T.V. screen.

Olivia.

Speedily, I turned up the volume.

"We've been looking at everything about this case very closely. We've spoken to a lot of people, and sadly, we are leaning towards the conclusion that this case ends with it being a tragic accident."

I sat up.

"A night of fun, gone wrong. No evidence points to foul play. The deceased was heavily intoxicated, and we think she may have accidentally set fire to a piece of her clothing. She panicked, started to run and the fire started to spread. Again, we will keep looking, and nothing is official as of yet. We can assure you that we're still investigating and gathering all of the facts. Thank you."

What!

Where the fuck is my phone?

I looked for my purse. I had to call mama to see if she'd seen the news. After realizing it was still in the car, barefoot, I ran to get it.

I had 27 missed calls.

Some from earlier that day and six from Greg, in only a matter of minutes.

But none from mama.

I called her, and she immediately clicked in Honey who was on her other line.

"They think it was an accident," mama said.

"Pepper, do you? You were there that night. Honestly, do you think that it was all an accident?" Honey asked.

Loudly, I exhaled.

I thought about what I wanted to say.

And although there was no evidence of foul play, although no one saw anything strange, and although I didn't have the slightest clue as to who would want to hurt or furthermore, kill her…

Something just didn't add up.

Something, a lot of things, just didn't make sense. Olivia was dead.

And my gut told me that someone knew something. Someone saw something.

Maybe someone even did something.

I couldn't be sure, but something just wasn't right.

"No," I finally answered the question. "No. I don't think it was an accident. I think someone knows something. I think---I think someone did this to her. Someone killed Olivia." I paused. "And if it's the last thing I do...I'm going to figure out who."

****

CHAPTER TWO

"I wouldn't advise you to run around accusing people of murder or looking for evidence that isn't there. If it were there, we would've found it. We're very good at doing our jobs," one of the detectives who worked Olivia's case proclaimed on the other end of the phone. "I know this must be hard for you. Seeing what you saw. But I can assure you, we explored every possibility, and there was nothing that would suggest that someone was out there with her that night. She was out there alone."

Now, it had been over two weeks since Olivia's death. And the police were calling it quits. They hadn't been able to find any evidence of foul play, and they were officially ruling Olivia's death *accidental*.

Accidental my ass!

"If you find anything new, sure, you can let us know. But I don't think you will. My advice: Focus on healing and letting go."

I would never just *let* this go.

How do you let go of your sister's death, without being sure of what really happened to her? If you weren't sure if she was killed?

After hanging up the phone, I knocked on Kelli's front door.

I'd questioned the four ladies that were smoking cigarettes around Olivia at the bachelorette party:

Deb, Shakira, Valerie, and Brenda.

They all assured me that they didn't have a clue as to where Olivia got the cigarette. As a matter of fact, without telling them, I asked them to show me their packs. Three of the four smoked the same brand, but neither brand was the same brand as the cigarette that had been in Olivia's mouth.

She didn't get the cigarette from any of them.

After a few more questions, Deb, who is one of mine, and was one of Olivia's, closest friends, admitted that on a few occasions, while drinking, Olivia had actually taken a few puffs of a cigarette, which is why she offered her a smoke that night.

Still, even coming out of Deb's mouth, I was finding that hard to believe.

Mainly, because of Olivia's father.

Olivia's dad had lung cancer, twice, as a result of years of smoking cigarettes. He beat it both times, but now he is having problems with everything else. According to Olivia, he has so many health issues that she'd lost count. So many that his doctor wouldn't give him clearance to fly into town for Olivia's memorial service.

Phillip, Olivia's father, moved to California a long, long time ago. He was a truck driver. After he and mama split, he found love out there on one of his driving trips. He married her and moved thousands of miles away from good ole' Winston Salem. He would still come to visit Olivia though. And every summer, he would fly her out there to spend a few weeks with him, his wife and step kids. Olivia was his only biological child and she loved her daddy. His cancer devastated her. She was always so worried about him, and she said she would never smoke cigarettes after seeing what he was going through. She'd been flying out to California, at least once a month for the past year. And she'd been on pins and needles wondering if he would be able to make it to walk her down the aisle for her wedding.

She would've been so disappointed.

He couldn't even make to her funeral to say a proper goodbye.

So, that's why I couldn't believe that she would ever smoke a cigarette. But Deb swore that she had. And all four ladies swore that they didn't know what happened to Olivia; well, other than the obvious, of course.

"Hey hun," Kelli said once she opened her front door.

Kelli was also one of our best friends.

She grew up with my sisters and I. Along with Deb, Shakira, Jai, and Crystal. We all lived on the same street for many, many years. Some of our parents still lived on that exact street; including mama.

Deb and Kelli were both an only child. Shakira only had all brothers. And Jai and Crystal were sisters. I hadn't had a chance to speak to Jai and Crystal yet. I did notice them all at the funeral. Almost everyone was in tears, but Crystal was crying hard and loud; like a hungry, newborn baby. And next to her, Jai, sat there with a strange look on her face. And surprisingly, she wasn't shedding a tear. You couldn't help but notice how awkward she looked.

Then again, we all knew how much Jai hated funerals; especially since she had to bury the love of her life. But even before then, she never wanted to go to them, and I'm sure if it hadn't been Olivia's, she wouldn't have.

Maybe that's why she seemed uncomfortable.

Anyway, Kelli and I talked all the time and we hung out quite often. We had an incredibly close friendship, and the fact that we lived right around the corner from each other didn't hurt either.

"How have you been?"

"I'm okay, I guess. Taking it day by day. Worried about mama."

"How is she?"

"She keeps saying that she's fine, but I know she isn't. She won't let me be there for her. She's too busy trying to be there for me."

"After what you saw...after what we saw...can you blame her?"

I shook my head.

Kelli poured herself a glass of wine.

"It's too early to be drinking wine, Kelli."

"Mind your business. And don't lecture me, okay? I *need* this wine. I can't go to sleep at night without drinking a whole bottle since "it" happened. I'm a mess. I took my whole four weeks' vacation, and hell, I feel like I'm going to need another four. I barely have two weeks left, and I don't want to go back. I just want to stay in the house and drink my wine," Kelli took a sip of her drink.

Kelli was so attractive.

Just looking at her made you want to kiss her.

Or lick her. Or touch on her…or maybe even touch yourself.

Kelli has always been pretty, but in our mid-twenties, she really started to settle into her features, and now, in our early thirties, she was absolutely gorgeous!

She was like this exotic or erotic kind of pretty. It was hard to explain. She had dark, mahogany-colored skin. High cheekbones, hazel eyes, and perfect lips. If I were batting for the other team, I would be all over her like a dog on a bone. Or more like a dog in heat; just like every other man in this town seemed to be. Kelli being single was definitely by choice. She could have any man that she wanted, but let her tell it, the right man hasn't come her way yet.

"This wasn't supposed to happen."

"I know," Kelli gulped another sip of her wine.

I noticed a card from one of the detective's from Olivia's case on her coffee table. I picked it up.

"That card has been sitting there forever."

"Do you really think it was an accident?"

Kelli swallowed hard. "Honestly…no."

I exhaled. "So, it's not just me? I'm not the only one who was there and thinks something doesn't make sense?"

"I get that she was drunk…very drunk…hell, super drunk! We all know she loved to drink. But how do you accidentally set yourself on fire? I guess you could. I mean a lit match, touches her dress, causes a fire. I guess it's possible. Remember that story where that house burned down from a single match? So, I get how it *could* happen.

But I don't know. And who still uses matches? Why not a lighter? Where in the hell did she get the matches from? I guess the same place she got the cigarette. Something just seems…I don't know."

"See! I said the same thing about the matches! And the matches came from the store around the corner from her house. At least that's the label that was on the front of the box. You know that store is family-owned, and they brand every damn thing. But I know exactly what you're saying. Something doesn't seem right."

I thought back to the night of the party.

Kelli and I were lying on the oversized furniture, laughing and drinking, and then we heard Coco's screams.

"Have you spoken to Coco?"

"Everyday. She's not doing so good."

Initially, Coco was a friend of Kelli's.

They both worked for a huge Fortune 500 company. Kelli started to bring her around, and she just sort of stuck. I really like her, and we definitely had a good time with each other whenever we were together.

"I haven't spoken to her since the day of Olivia's memorial service. I'm wondering if there's something she forgot to mention."

"Like what?"

"I don't know. Anything about that night."

I was sure that Coco was all talked out; especially since she'd probably had to explain what happened over and over again. Not just to the police, but also to her husband.

Pastor Troy.

He had no idea that Coco was at a bachelorette party. Actually, if you ask me, he had no idea who Coco really was at all. She was a totally different person whenever she was around him.

Wholesome. Calm. Covered-up. Innocent. And she was the complete opposite of all of those things whenever he wasn't around. She was loud and silly. She would dance to just about anything, and she loved apple martinis.

I'd asked her once, why she'd married him when clearly, she wasn't ready for the type of lifestyle he was living. I asked her why she would become a preacher's wife, when she still wanted to drink and party. She simply said that he was a good man and one day, she would be ready. And when she was, he would be right there.

"She said her husband flipped out on her because she lied about where she was going that night."

"Obviously."

"And when he came to pick her up, did you see how mad he was?"

"No. I think I was still talking to the cops when she left."

"Girl, that mother---, oops, I can't call him that, can I? I'm pretty sure calling a pastor a motherfucker is the quickest way to get me a first-class ticket to Hell. Sorry," Kelli looked up towards heaven.

I giggled.

"But girl, that man was pissed! He was cursing her out in scriptures! And then he invited the half-naked strippers to church, chile."

"Girl, no he didn't."

"Yes, he did. And the gay bartender too."

I laughed so hard tears came out of my eyes.

I hadn't laughed in over two weeks.

"I've missed you."

"I missed you too," Kelli smiled.

"I have to find out what happened," I got back on the subject of Olivia.

Kelli looked at me with concern in her eyes. "Are you really gonna' look into all this?" Kelli asked.

Exhaling, I answered her. "I have to. I have to know the truth. Only then will Olivia be able to rest in peace. Hell, I need peace too. Well, more like a peace of mind."

Kelli nodded, as she poured herself another glass of wine. "Well, if anybody is going to find something, it's you. Girl, we both know you mixed with Black and FBI. Girl, you can find any damn thing!"

I laughed, but deep down, I hope she was right.

I hope I could find out what really happened to my sister.

Kelli held her glass full of red wine in there air.

"To Olivia." She smiled as I echoed her words.

"To Olivia."

After leaving Kelli's house, I headed to the dry cleaners. My employees were doing just fine without me, but I still tried to show my face every few days.

After texting Coco to see if she could meet me for a late lunch, I pulled on the door handle of *Pep in Your Step Dry Cleaners.*

I changed the name of the cleaners after daddy died. I absolutely refused to say "A Broke Man's Cleaners" every day.

What the fuck was he thinking with that name?

Maybe it was because he'd had all of his services so underpriced. His idea of trying to be "inexpensive" almost cost him his dream.

He was behind on pretty much everything when I got the place. Every bill was late. The books were horrible. He was barely bringing in enough to feed himself. I wouldn't be surprised if stress from the cleaners contributed to his heart attack.

Nonetheless, I'd had my work cut out for me, but I did it. I actually turned the place around and brought in a ton of new business---even with my higher prices. His loyal customers decided to stick around too.

"Hey, Jordan, how are you today?"

Jordan was one of my full-time employees. I only had two. And one part-time.

"Aww, hey sugar plum."

Jordan walked around the counter to hug me.

"I'm fine. How are you? I told you I got this. You don't have to come all the way over here."

"I know you do. I just like to drop by. I know you and Drake have been covering the hours that I'm usually here. Has little Ms. College asked for more hours?"

"Nope. She says she can't pick up any extra hours. She's tutoring too, and those folks pay her a pretty penny to get access to all that information in that girls' brain."

"I bet they do. That girl is gonna' be somebody one day."

"Yeah. She is."

After small-talking a little while longer, and looking over the finances, I headed across the street to the deli.

Coco was meeting me there.

Just as I took a seat, I laughed aloud as she walked towards me.

She was wearing a skin-tight, white dress, that buttoned from top to bottom. A silk white and black scarf, six-inch black heels, and a big ass black church hat in 90-degree weather.

"Girl, why the hell you dressed like an usher and a prostitute? All at the same damn time?"

"Fuck you, Pepper," she laughed as she took off her hat. "I'm coming from a church meeting. Since I've been staying out of work, Troy thinks I'm supposed to be around him 24-7 at the church."

"Was he mad about you being at the bachelorette party?"

"Was he? Girl, we argued all damn night about it. I guess the issue was that I lied about where I was going but had I told him the truth, he would've given me the 3rd degree about it. All that "a pastor's wife shouldn't do this or go there" mumbo jumbo. And girl, at the time, I didn't want to hear that shit. I wasn't in the mood. And I just wanted to have a good time." Coco paused. "Wait. I'm sorry, how are you?"

"I'm making it."

Coco nodded. "I wanted to call you...I just didn't know what to say."

"I don't think any of us do."

"I especially wanted to call when I saw the news. When police ruled what happened to Olivia as an accident."

"Yes. Well, that's what I wanted to talk to you about. I'm not sure I think it was an accident."

The waiter came over, and after we ordered our food, we continued our conversation.

"Why?"

"I don't know. Olivia going outside to have a smoke doesn't make sense to me; especially since she didn't smoke. And no one seems to know where she got the cigarette from. No one at the party admits giving it to her. And she didn't have a pack of cigarettes in her purse. I had Greg check. So, that's one thing. And dropping a match on herself, setting her dress on fire...now that's the other. Does it all seem and sound crazy to you? Like it does to me?"

"Well, listening to you say it, yeah it does. But no one else was out there or around her."

"Are you sure?"

"Yes. When I saw her..."

Coco hesitated, as she closed her eyes to reminisce.

"It all happened so fast. She was trying to pat herself as she screamed. I kept shouting, "Jump in the pool! Olivia the pool!" But she couldn't hear me. She was screaming. The fire consumed her. It spread fast as though she had something flammable all over her. And then...she just fell."

My stomach was in knots.

"Is vodka flammable? They said that it looks like she dropped a glass of vodka. I wonder if she spilled some of it on herself."

"Maybe. I don't know. All I know is if I hadn't been so drunk, if I'd been thinking straight, I could've thought of something else to do. I don't know, maybe I would've been able to save her. I could've gone from behind her and pushed her into the pool. I probably would've gotten burned too, but who knows, that probably would've saved her life. I just wasn't thinking straight. She was panicking. I was panicking. I swear, I'm never drinking again."

I touched Coco's hand.

"It's not your fault. You know that, right? No one blames you."

"I know. I just wish I could've done something. I was right there."

The waiter sat our drinks down in front of us.

"And you were outside throwing up?"

"Yes. I don't know how long it took me to realize that she was screaming. All I remember is coming outside, in the backyard, to puke. And then I remember looking up and seeing her. And then trying to get to her. I was running, but it was like I wasn't running fast enough."

"And you didn't see anyone? You didn't see anything out of place?"

"Not that I can remember. If it was someone else out there, if we're being honest, I wouldn't have noticed them unless they were right in my face. I was so focused on Olivia and the flames."

Coco took a sip of her water. Her hands were shaking.

"Seeing her, like that, reminded me of all the sermons my husband preach about on Sundays. About Hell. After watching her, burning, in so much pain, and hearing her screams, I know for a fact that Hell is one place, that I don't want to go. I plan on getting my life together. Sometimes, we just need a wake-up call. And Olivia's death was mine. I'm ready to change."

And from the look on her face, I could tell that Coco would never be the same.

~***~

"Ma!"

I could smell the food as soon as I walked through the front door. I headed for the kitchen.

"Dang, are you having company?"

I sat my purse on the counter as mama smiled at me.

"No. I just felt like cooking."

"All of this?"

There was enough food to feed at least ten people. Steak. Sweet Potatoes. Stuffed Bell Peppers. Apple Pie. Pound Cake. Chocolate Cake.

Wait.

These are all Olivia's favorites.

"Mama?"

She started to hum.

"Mama?"

She ignored me as she mixed something in a blue and red bowl.

"Mama?"

"What!" She shouted while slamming the spoon down against the counter.

"I'm sorry. I'm sorry. I know. I know it's all her favorites. Just let me be, chile. Okay? Just let me be," she mumbled. She didn't even look at me. She just started to hum again and resumed mixing the contents of the bowl with aggression.

After I realized that she was refusing to look at me, finally, I mumbled the words *I love you*, and I walked away. I held my breath until I was back inside my car. And as soon as I shut the car door, I screamed.

I know that we all grieve in our own way but seeing my mother in so much obvious pain was killing me.

And there was nothing that I could do about it.

Though parents aren't supposed to have favorites, I'm pretty sure that I'd always been mama's favorite. She used to tell Honey and Olivia that she felt like I needed her more. She always checked up on me just a little bit more. She always made sure I was okay and made sure my head was on straight. Yet, she loved us all and would've given her life to save any one of ours. So, I could only imagine how she felt or what she was going through.

I couldn't say that I understood because I didn't have a clue as to what it felt like to lose a child.

I just wish she would let me help her through it.

With my family on my mind, finally, I made up my mind to go to the one place we've all been avoiding since her death.

I headed towards Olivia's house.

Ten minutes later, I was passing by the store. The same store that was on the front of the book of matches found near Olivia's body.

I wondered if the police had gone by the store to request or watch the surveillance footage. I'm sure they did. I'm sure that was a part of their investigation.

A minute later, I was pulling into Olivia's driveway.

Her garage door was still open, and her car was still inside. I'd picked her up from her house to take her to the bachelorette party. We had a forty-five-minute drive to the mansion, and in a rush, she'd forgotten to close her garage.

The bright red Range Rover was a gift to herself for her 29th birthday this year. She always said that she would have one before she turned thirty. And she did. She always did everything she said she would do.

Using my spare key, I entered Olivia's house.

It still smelled just like her.

I couldn't believe that none of us had been come by here since her death. Not even Greg.

Olivia's house was stunning.

She'd had it professionally decorated.

Her theme colors were canary yellow, light gray and off-white. And she had the colors throughout her entire home. Those were also going to be the colors of the beautiful wedding that she would never get to have.

Walking around the house, everything was so clean.

You could tell that she was hardly ever home.

I stopped in front of the fireplace. And just like I knew there would be, there were three candles and a big box of matches. She always bought the same kind, from the same hardware store. She was just systematic like that. She rarely strayed from her routines. Olivia was the most disciplined woman that I've ever known. And she used to get on my last nerves with her habits and schedules. But now that she was gone, I missed them.

I missed her.

The box of matches was almost full. The candles were barely used. Greg's theory about the book of matches was wrong. But I'm sure he knew that all ready. He knew Olivia just as well as I did.

After pondering why Olivia would've gotten matches from the convenience store for another minute or so, I finished walking around the living room, touching everything in my path as I made my way to her bedroom.

I was surprised to see that her bed was unmade.

And her laptop, iPad, and what looked to be about a hundred papers were all over it.

Olivia was a workaholic.

She'd always been that way.

She would get an idea and just go with it.

She wouldn't care if it seemed impossible and she didn't care if others thought that she couldn't do it.

She always did it.

She always proved them wrong.

Every. Single. Time.

Picking up one of her pillows, I sniffed it. Instantly, so many memories of our last days together flooded my mind. I was reminded of the day that she asked me to be her maid of honor. She said her sisters were her first best friends, so it only made sense to have me as the maid of honor, and Honey as the matron.

She was so dramatic. She got down on one knee in the crowded restaurant and asked me with a candy ring in her hand. Everyone laughed and thought it was the cutest thing. Everyone except for Crystal.

Olivia's closest friend from our crew was Crystal. They cliqued together similar to the way that Kelli and I did. And if I had to say which friend was closest to Honey; I would say our friend Deb.

Anyway, Olivia and Crystal shared the same drive and ambition. They were both serial entrepreneurs, so naturally, they spent a lot of time together. Most of the time, if you saw Olivia…you saw Crystal. Or she was on her way.

So, I guess I can see why Crystal had a problem with Olivia making me her maid of honor; at least that night she did. During Olivia's silly sister-proposal, Crystal walked out of the restaurant. Once Olivia was on her feet, and everyone told her that Crystal stormed out, Olivia went after her, but she was gone.

Crystal didn't stay mad long though.

In about a week, she got over it. She said no matter what, she couldn't miss Olivia's big day.

And though I offered to let her take my place as maid of honor, she declined and agreed to play her role as a bridesmaid. She said it was Olivia's day, and no matter what, it should be her way.

Crystal did agree to help me with the wedding plans though. Her and Deb helped me out tremendously. And I'd needed all the help I could get. Planning a wedding was one thing. Planning a wedding for Olivia…was something else!

She was such a headache, yet we ended up having so much fun at the same time. It was hard to explain.

I laughed as I continued to scroll down memory lane.

Making space for me to sit down on her bed, I clicked a button on Olivia's laptop. Nothing popped up.

Duh, Pepper.

Olivia has been gone for weeks.

Of course, it's dead.

Next, I picked up the iPad. Seeing that it was turned off, I turned it on.

She'd had the same password, for everything, since she was eighteen. And after typing it in, I started to look around.

So many notifications started to chime and pop up all at once.

Updates.

Emails.

And surprisingly, text messages came flooding in too.

Her cell phone was connected to her iPad. I didn't even know where her phone was, but I tapped on the blue message icon.

Immediately, I touched the contact *Hubby*; which was Greg, and started to read their messages.

My eyes filled with tears to see that he was still texting her, even though she was dead. I wondered if he had her phone with him. Yeah, I'm sure he did. He got her purse after the cops went through it for evidence.

And starting only two days after Olivia's death, Greg had been sending her text messages.

"I miss you. What am I supposed to do without you?"

Four text messages in, I had snot dripping from my nose and tears racing down my face.

This was probably a major invasion of privacy, but I couldn't help myself. I knew how much Greg loved her. Even when she drove him crazy, he always told me that she was worth it.

I continued to read the messages, and from the deepest part of me, I bawled uncontrollably.

I tried to stop reading, but I couldn't seem to look away until...

At the sight of the dick picture Greg sent Olivia, the day before the bachelorette party, I gasped and dropped the iPad in a hurry. I looked around as if someone was watching me.

Damn!

Who knew Greg was packing like that?

Don't look at it again, Pepper! Don't look!

Ignoring my inner thoughts, I picked the iPad up again, and took another look.

Turning my head to the side, I looked at that *monster* with a smile. This was so wrong, on so many levels, but it was harmless. It's just a dick.

A big, thick…

Shaking my head, I closed out of Greg's messages. There was no telling what else was in them, and I convinced myself that I didn't want to find out.

I scrolled through random text messages until a particular text message caught my attention.

"Fuck You!"

I clicked on Honey's name and started to read.

I read.

And I read.

And I kept reading.

Huh?

I read the argument between my sisters, in their voices, inside of my head.

They'd been arguing for about a week before Olivia's death, and neither of them mentioned a thing to me about it.

Honey and Joe were having problems.

Financial problems, from what I could tell.

I never knew that.

No one ever told me.

They'd borrowed money from Olivia, what looked like a few times. About a week before the bachelorette party, Honey texted Olivia and asked her if she could loan them another $1500.

Unlike the other times, this particular time, Olivia said no. She said that they hadn't paid her back all the money that she'd let them borrow the last time and that it wasn't her job to keep giving them money for Joe to gamble away.

Olivia said that she wouldn't lend her any more money until they repaid what they owed her.

Honey got upset.

Honey hardly ever got upset. I mean, I can't remember the last time Honey was mad, that's how rare it was for her to get angry. I remember when we were younger, I always had to stand up for her and fight her battles. Even though she was the oldest, Honey was so passive that you could probably spit in her face, and she wouldn't do a thing. And people knew that about her. So, they tried to bully her and take advantage of her niceness all the time, but they had no idea that she had a little sister that was hell on wheels.

She had me. And when it came to her, I always came through swinging. Blows first. Questions later. That was my motto.

But reading through the text messages, Honey was cursing and calling Olivia everything but a child of God!

Wow!

This is so unlike her.

It's probably the pregnancy hormones.

Honey told Olivia that they needed the money for bills and that Joe was going to get help with his gambling problem. I knew he liked to gamble, but damn, I didn't know it had gotten that bad. So bad to where Honey had to beg for and borrow money.

No matter what Honey said, Olivia continued to say no. And still yet, Honey kept trying to explain to her that the bills were behind and she started to name things that the kids needed. Olivia offered to take care of the kids' needs, instead of giving Honey the money.

That pissed Honey off even more.

She called Olivia a bitch.

For days leading up to the bachelorette party, Honey texted Olivia every day with something rude to say or cursing her.

Olivia never responded.

Bachelorette party day, Honey said their lights were going to be cut off if they didn't pay by the end of the day. She told Olivia that she didn't understand why she wouldn't just give her the money. She reminded Olivia that she knew she had it to spare.

Olivia finally responded: "See you tonight."

And that's when Honey responded back: "Fuck You."

I looked up from the iPad.

Sisters had arguments.

But they were rare for us. And never like this.

I was surprised that Honey hadn't mentioned the fight to me since Olivia's death. I couldn't imagine how Honey must feel knowing what her last words to Olivia were. And knowing that she would never get the chance to apologize.

After e-mailing some of Olivia's pictures to myself, I glanced through her e-mails and her bank accounts. And then I placed the iPad back where I found it.

We hadn't discussed what to do with her money, her house or her car. Greg handled the payments for her cremation and everything else for the memorial services. I was sure that he was in charge of whatever insurance policies she had out there. And I'm sure mama figured that Greg would be the one to handle her other assets too.

Forcing myself to take my first step, I was headed out the bedroom door when suddenly, Olivia's iPad chimed again. Curiosity made me turn around to go see what it was.

It was from Greg.

I clicked on the message.

"It took me forever to figure out where you kept the nail clippers. I'm losing my mind over here without you. It's just not the same without you here."

Throwing the iPad back on the bed, this time I made it out of her bedroom, and out the front door.

Greg needed a shoulder.

Greg needed a friend.

Every few days, we were reaching out to each other, just to check on each other, but he was always pretending to be okay when clearly, he isn't.

After closing Olivia's garage door, I lingered for only a second to look at her house. And then I forced myself to turn away from it. I didn't look back. I didn't even look up at it as I backed out of her driveway.

As soon as I reached the stop sign at the end of her street, my gas light popped on. Knowing that I wouldn't make it to Greg's without getting gas, I stopped at the store.

The "matchbook" store.

Walking inside, I looked around. I noticed the cameras in the corners of the store, and one right behind the counter. As I got closer to the counter, I saw the matches. The matchbooks came in three different colors. The one found at the scene was red, with the white and green store logo on the front of it.

"$40 on pump 4," I said to the clerk as I picked up one of the red matchbooks.

The clerk asked me to insert my card.

"Did the police look at the tapes from the store?"

"Excuse me?"

"My sister. Uh, she's the lady that was found on fire almost three weeks ago. I'm sure you've heard about it. One of these matchbooks were found at the scene."

The clerk nodded her head. "I remember seeing her story and her picture on the news. I'm so sorry. And my boss said that they came in for footage but..." She leaned across the counter. "The cameras inside the store don't work. Only the ones outside. They're just in here for show. But I do remember seeing her, your sister, a few times." The lady asked me if I needed a receipt and after shaking my head no, I walked out of the store annoyed.

I wasn't sure what I would've wanted to see on those tapes. But they didn't have them, so in a sense, there was nothing to see. There was no way of knowing if Olivia was the one to actually purchase the matches or why.

With a tank full of gas, and minutes later, I arrived at Greg's house.

He opened the front door before I got a chance to knock.

"I just wanted to come by and check on you."

He stepped to the side and allowed me to come inside. "I'm okay."

"Boy, stop lying! No, you're not."

I sat on the sofa. Greg plopped down beside me. *Oooh.*

At least he's bathing. He smelled so good.

"I uh, I was at Olivia's house, not too long ago. And I saw your text message. All of them," I admitted to him.

Greg stared at me. I noticed the pink phone case that used to belong to Olivia on his coffee table.

"Her phone is still connected to her iPad."

"Oh. Damn," Greg said.

"Look, you don't have to fake the funk with me, and you don't have to go through this alone. I'm here. I'll always be here. You know that, right?"

"I don't know why I text her. If..."

"You don't have to explain. Do what you need to do. But you can text me too, you know. Anytime. And I'll respond. If you need to talk, I'll listen."

"What if I just need a hug?"

I opened my arms. "I give pretty good hugs too."

Greg made himself comfortable inside my arms. He nestled his head right above my breasts. I inhaled and exhaled loudly.

"Why are you sniffing me?" Greg laughed.

"Shit, you smell good. I can't help it."

Greg somewhat buried his head in between my breasts. "Dang!"

"Sorry. You smell pretty good too," he said.

"I bet I do. You bought the perfume I'm wearing for my birthday last year, remember?"

Greg nodded. "Damn. I got some good taste."

"Greg...shut the fuck up!"

We both chuckled and once Greg was comfortable on my chest again, he spoke.

"We need to set up a time to meet with the lawyer. We need to go over her insurance policies. She had a few policies that will be paying out. She even had an AD&D policy. She was always one step ahead," Greg muffled.

"What about them?"

"You do know that you and Honey get everything, right?"

"What?"

Greg lifted his head. "She never changed her beneficiaries on her life insurance policies. Neither of us did. It was something that we were going to do after we were married. My mother is still my beneficiary. Her sisters were hers. You didn't know? I'm surprised. Honey knows."

"Honey knew that we were Olivia's beneficiaries?"

"Yeah."

Greg stood up. He disappeared and came back with some papers in his hand. "Everything for the cremation and the service I took care of out of pocket, but here's what she has. See. With all of her policies together, you and Honey will split about $300,000. Though her death was ruled accidental, I called, and these three will be paying out for sure. We added each other to our house deeds about a year ago. I'll sell her house and give the money to your mother. Whoever needs her car, can have it."

I was still stuck on the $300,000 insurance part.

I knew she had policies, but I guess I assumed that Olivia would've left everything to Greg. They were together for so long. It was only right for him to be her beneficiary. Not me. And not Honey.

"I don't need the money."

Greg hung his head, and I stood up. Rubbing the back of his head, I told him that everything was going to be okay.

He didn't believe me.

"You'll get through this. We all will. I promise you that. And I'm going to get us all closure."

"You're going to drive yourself crazy, just like I've been doing," Greg confessed. "There's nothing there. Vernon, my inside man, has given me every detail, and everything else they found at the scene. Every possible scenario, and there's nothing there, Pepper. Nothing out of the ordinary. Nothing that says anything other than..."

"What do you mean he *gave* it to you?"

"As a favor."

"Can I see what you have?"

Greg nodded and disappeared again.

He returned with a folder.

"I'm *not* supposed to have this. Understood?"

"Yes."

Greg reached me the folder, and I sat back down on the sofa.

"I've looked at it over and over again, and it's looking more and more like an accident to me."

I skimmed the pages. There were photos and typed statements from everyone that had been questioned.

"Can I take this with me? I won't do anything crazy. I just want to read over it all."

"Yeah."

I closed the folder and placed it on the table.

"But while I'm here," I slid off my shoes and placed my feet in Greg's lap. "Can you rub these *dogs*? I'm like so overdue for a foot rub."

Willingly, Greg started to massage my feet.

"They stink a little bit," he laughed.

"My feet don't stink!" I kicked him, and after spatting a few curse words at him, I asked him a question. "So...what's your favorite memory of Olivia?"

Though I was eager to get home to read the contents of the folder, I'd come over here for a reason. I'd come over to make him feel better. And that's what I planned to do.

So, for the next two hours, Greg and I talked about everything under the sun. We shared memories of Olivia. We talked about the future and the past. And we made jokes and laughed.

This is what I do. I was playing my role. I was being his backbone and a good friend.

"Thank you, Pep," Greg said as he walked me outside.

"No problem, big head," I hugged his neck. "I love you boy."

"I love you too."

Greg stepped in close and pulled me close to him by my waist. He didn't say anything. And neither did I. But the longer he held me, the more his hug started to feel less and less like a best-friend hug and more and more like ...

Finally, Greg let me go and stepped back. "I'll, uh, I'll see you later," he said.

"Okay."

"Okay." Greg watched me walk towards my car, and once I reached it, he shut his front door.

After starting my car, I checked my cell phone. I had a few missed calls. One call was from Honey.

I started to think about her text messages to Olivia.

I wondered why she never told me that they were having money problems. I wasn't as financially stable as Olivia used to be, but I would've helped her if I could.

It was strange that she never mentioned the argument between her and Olivia. And she never mentioned anything about us being Olivia's beneficiaries. And being that she and Joe need money, I'm sure it crossed her mind.

The moon was full, and it followed me as I drove in silence down the quiet street. Once I finally arrived home, without getting out of my car, I turned on the interior light and opened the folder.

I cringed at the evidence photos, and when I got to the one of Olivia's burnt body, I gagged.

Feeling sick to my stomach, I opened my driver's side door and stuck my head out.

Inhale. Exhale. Inhale. Exhale.

After waiting to see if I would vomit, once I didn't, I took a deep breath and closed the car door.

I never should've looked at the photos.

Visions of that night attacked my mind and my heart, but I forced myself to pick the folder back up again.

I need to know more.

I need to know the truth.

Slowly, my breathing steadied, and after turning all of the photos face down, I put them at the back of the stack of papers and picked up a witness statement instead.

I read Coco's statement aloud.

"I came outside to get some fresh air. I heard screaming and ran around to the back of the house. That's when I saw her. That's when I saw her on fire."

Huh?
This can't be right.
I reread the statement.

What Coco told the police was completely different from what she told me. She said, repeatedly, that she went outside to throw up and that's when she saw Olivia.

But her statement says she was getting some fresh air and ran *around* to the back of the house.

So, she wasn't already in the backyard?

That's not what she told me.

And if she wasn't throwing up, was she really outside just getting some fresh air?

Or was she doing something else?

Hmmm...

If she lied to me, does that mean that she lied to the police too?

I read her statement, for the third time, and still, I couldn't understand why.

Why did Coco lie?

****

CHAPTER THREE

I watched Honey as she acted surprised to learn that Olivia had named her a beneficiary. She grabbed her chest when the lawyer explained to us that we would be getting about $150,000 a piece.

Greg and I looked at each other. And then together, we looked back at Honey.

The lawyer continued to talk about Olivia's other assets. Greg made his suggestion to sell the house and give the proceeds to mama. He also handed mama the keys to Olivia's car, and told her that since he was an authorized user of Olivia's bank accounts, he would be transferring all of the money into her bank account; which in total, including Olivia's savings, was almost $130,000.

Greg had plenty of money of his own. He made in the upper six-figures a year, so I wasn't surprised that he didn't want anything. He only wanted a few pictures and items from her house, and then he told us we could sell or split everything else amongst ourselves.

The signing of the paperwork made everything official, and then Greg and I waved at Honey and mama as they drove away.

"Honey is hiding something," Greg said.

"Funny, I was thinking the same thing. Are you sure Honey knew about the life insurance policies?"

"I'm sure. She borrowed money from your sister a few times. Once, Olivia had her stop by my house to pick up a check. It was months ago. Even before she found out she was pregnant, I think. I know it was before Olivia and I decided that we were going to get married. We were having a conversation about our life insurance policies when Honey knocked on the door. Olivia continued the conversation as she wrote the check. She stated, in front of Honey, that once we decided to get married, she would remove the two of you as her beneficiaries from her current life insurance policies. And Honey was right there. She heard the entire conversation. She even joked around and said: "So, if you *kicked the bucket*, like today, how much will I get?" Olivia told her that it was none of her business."

Greg's words concerned me.

And so did Honey's actions, as well as her reactions.

Why would she pretend to be surprised about the news if she already knew?

And I couldn't help but think about Honey and Olivia's argument and how Honey had been acting towards her up until she died.

"You knew Honey was borrowing money from Olivia? Do you know why?"

"Yeah. I knew. And no. I don't know why. I stayed clear of asking Olivia about "sister" business. And she never mentioned what Honey needed money for to me either. All she said was that she needed to borrow it."

Of course, Honey wasn't responsible for what happened to our sister. She wasn't even there that night. But something was definitely going on with her. And I didn't like how it was making me feel.

"I gotta' go. It's my first day back at work, and I have a one o'clock meeting. I'll see you later," Greg half-smiled. I watched him until he was out of sight.

"Excuse me, Miss," I turned around.

Good God Almighty!

My knees buckled at the sight of him.

Goddamn!

This man is *fine*! And I wasn't exaggerating!

He was "old school R&B" fine! The "You can live with me rent-free, with no job" fine! The "Fuck up my credit, drive my car without a license" fine! Shit, he was even the "You got thirteen kids, and they can all call me step mama" fine!

He was all that and just a little bit more!

He was probably the sexiest man that I've ever seen in person. My vagina agreed.

He had dark milk chocolate skin, deep brown eyes, perfect white teeth, and a beautiful smile that was surrounded by a well-kept beard. It was something about the shape of his nose and his juicy, bronzed lips. He reminded me of an oil painted canvas that was still slightly wet, and I was just dying to touch him.

Perfect height, with an even better body, dressed in a suit and tie, and he wasn't wearing a wedding band.

Good God, where have you been all my life?

For a moment, and for the first time in weeks, Olivia was the furthest thing from my mind.

"Sorry to bother you, but I've seen you before. At the dry cleaners on Mahoney Drive."

"Yes. I own that place."

He smiled. And my clitoris throbbed a little bit.

"I told myself if I ever saw you again..."

He extended his hand. "I'm Brian."

"Pepper."

He looked down at my hand.

"Are you single, Pepper?"

"Hell yeah!" I cleared my throat. "I mean, yes. I'm single."

Brian chuckled. "Good. That's good. So, can two single people perhaps get dinner or a drink..."

"When? Where? Today? I'm there!"

Calm down, Pepper!

I was sure that I seemed desperate, but I hadn't had sex in months, and no matter how hard I tried, I couldn't stop thinking of all the freak nasty things I could do to him.

"I'm sorry if I seem a little..."

"Crazy? Dramatic? Loud? Direct?"

I sucked my teeth and placed my hands on my hips.

"Oh, and I see you got a little attitude too. Don't worry about it. I can handle it. I like my women *medium-ghetto* anyway," he said.

"What in the hell is medium-ghetto?"

Brian walked closer to me. "Sexy, oh so sexy, beautiful, and classy. But just enough attitude to put a bitch in check if she needs to."

I was *not* expecting those words to come out of his mouth! Maybe it was because of how he looked or the way he was dressed. I'm not sure, but just like him, I too like a man with a little *edge* to him.

"Does that sound like you?" He asked.

"Maybe. Maybe not," I laughed as he handed me his cell phone. I put my number in it and then pressed call so I could have his. Once my phone vibrated twice in my purse, I pressed the end button and gave his phone back to him.

"So, Brian, I guess I'll be expecting your call."

He nodded as he started to back away from me. He must've come out of the same building I was just in.

I wondered if he was a lawyer too.

"And I'll be expecting you to answer," He flashed his million-dollar smile at me one last time, and then he opened the door of the building and disappeared.

Well damn!

My phone started to vibrate, and I grinned from ear to ear, assuming that it was Brian already.

But it wasn't.

It was Coco.

Since discovering that she lied to either me or the police, about why she was outside the night of the bachelorette party, I've been calling her like a crazy person.

I wanted to talk to her about it, but for whatever reason, I was having a hard time getting her on the phone.

"Hello?"

"Hey, I was wondering if we could meet up. I want to talk to you about something."

"Sure. Something like what?"

I started to walk towards my car. "It's about that night. The bachelorette party."

"Oh, okay. You found something?"

"Well, not exactly. Not yet. But I noticed that you told the police a completely different story from what you told me and everyone else."

"What are you talking about?" Suddenly, the tone in her voice changed.

"I thought you said that you went outside to throw up and that's when you saw Olivia."

"That's right."

"But in the police report, you said you went outside for some fresh air and ran around the house. So…"

I moved the phone away from my ear.

"Hello?"

She hung up.

Coco hung up before I could finish my sentence.

I called her back, over and over again, but she never answered.

She knew what I was going to say.

She knew that I knew…she lied.

Whether it was to me or to the police, for whatever reason, she was lying. She was lying about what she was doing outside that night.

Why?

What if she lied about other things too?

What if she saw something else? Something more?

What if she knows what really happened to Olivia?

Coco could hang up, even run, but she damn sure couldn't hide! Sooner or later, she was going to have to look me in the face and tell me the truth about the night my sister died!

~***~

"Aren't you the sweetest," Honey squealed as I reached her lunch from her favorite restaurant. I followed her into her house and closed the door behind me.

Honey and Joe's house was nice and cozy. He'd lived there before they were married. If I wasn't mistaken, the house used to belong to his parents, and then he remodeled it once it was passed down to him.

It was charming and full of character. And it was the kind of home that after you entered it, you never wanted to leave.

"What are you doing on this side of town in the middle of the afternoon?"

"I came to see you."

Honey took a bite out of the parmesan crusted chicken.

She closed her eyes as she chewed and with her free hand, she rubbed her belly.

"Umm, so good."

I thought about baby-stepping her into the discussion, but I didn't have the time.

"Why didn't you tell me that you and Joe are having money problems?"

Honey stopped chewing.

"I saw all of the text messages between you and Olivia. It's not my business that you were borrowing money from her…"

"No. It's not," Honey snapped.

"Why didn't you ask me?"

"Olivia had plenty of money to lend out. It only made sense to ask her."

"Why did you guys need money in the first place?"

"Look, business has been slow at times for Joe, and sometimes we have more bills than we have cash. That's all. So, I asked my sister to borrow money. No big deal."

Honey was lying.

It was a big deal to her when Olivia told her no. And I read where she said they were struggling because of Joe's gambling problem.

So, why was she lying to me?

"And it has nothing to do with Joe's gambling problem?"

"Gambling problem? Who's gambling problem?" Joe entered the kitchen with a smile. "Your sister gambles way more than I do these days," Joe gave me a hug. "Hey, Pepper. How are you?"

"I'm doing just fine Joe," I smiled at Joe and then looked at Honey.

So, she'd been lying to Olivia too?

Why did Honey need the money?

Was it her who was gambling all of their money away?

"So, you guys have enough money to get by, until you get the life insurance settlement?"

"What settlement?" Joe asked. "And enough to get by? Sis, business has been booming like never before! I've had so many new contracts. We have been bringing in more than enough money these past few months."

And the plot thickens.

"Yes. We're doing fine, sister," Honey finally spoke up.

I gave her intense eye contact. She did the same. Her eyes almost warned me not to say anything else.

"What settlement, baby?" Joe asked.

"We're Olivia's beneficiaries."

"Really? Wow. Baby, why didn't you tell me?" Joe asked Honey.

"I didn't know until the other day." Honey lied again.

Joe asked a few more questions about the settlement, and then he continued to talk like he didn't have a care in the world.

"That's fucked up how they just closed Olivia's case like that. They could've looked into it a little longer. I feel like they didn't give it a real effort, you know? I keep telling your sister that it seems like there's more to the story, but she thinks I'm crazy. I wish she had gone that night. She would've been sober since she's pregnant and all. She could've been the eyes of the party."

"Yeah. She could've," I said, still staring at Honey.

"I felt bad about us lying to get her out of going."

Honey looked at her husband with an attitude.

I could tell that she was frustrated that he was running his mouth.

"She wasn't asleep that night, were you baby? Olivia's not around anymore. She just didn't want to go. I think she and Olivia were mad at each other, for whatever reason. Honey complained about going to the party all damn day. So, I answered the phone and lied for her. Sorry. Don't be mad at her. She didn't tell me to. It was my call to do it."

Joe kissed Honey's cheek, and then he walked out of the kitchen.

"He talks too fucking much," Honey mumbled.

My eyes widened when she cursed.

She was definitely a 'different' Honey.

"Honey, what's going on? Why are you lying to me? To everyone? Tell me what's going on?"

Honey took another bite of her food.

"Thanks for lunch, Pepper," is all that she said.

And in silence, she stood there, continuing to eat and ignoring my questions until finally, I decided to leave.

"Ma, something is going on with Honey," I said to our mother, Grace, a few hours after leaving Honey's house.

"She's been going through something for months now, but she won't tell me what it is."

"She was borrowing money from Olivia."

"I know. Olivia told me. Something about Joe."

"That was a lie. Today, Joe said they are doing well. He doesn't seem to have a clue about Honey borrowing money. Like, no clue at all!"

"Hmm," mama said. "Well, maybe whatever she has going on is private."

Maybe.

Mama and I talked continuously as we placed Olivia's things in boxes.

"Did you know that we were Olivia's beneficiaries? And not you?"

"Of course I did. I'm an old lady. Never did I guess I would be burying one of my children. It wouldn't have done me any good to be her beneficiary. Now, let's just focus on getting as much packed as we can. I have church tonight," she said.

For the next hour, we didn't speak.

Mama sang random hymns, and I thought about Olivia. I also thought about Honey and Coco and how they both seemed to be telling one lie after the other. I thought about Greg. And then finally, I found some time to think about Brian.

We met three days ago, and we've spoken five times since then. At six o'clock on the dot, he called me the other day, and I was waiting just like he told me to be.

It's been a while since I've dated or even talked to a man over the phone, so I was nervous. But he was so easy to talk to that about twenty minutes in, I forgot that we were basically strangers. I damn near told him my whole life story that night. We talked for hours and hours. On purpose, I didn't talk about or mention Olivia's death. Actually, I didn't mention her or Honey, specifically. I only mentioned that I had two sisters, but that was it.

I ended up falling asleep with the phone on my ear and woke up to a warm and fuzzy text message from him.

He was basically everything I've ever wanted in a man.

Kind.

Sincere.

Attentive.

A good listener and an excellent communicator.

And I won't get started again on his looks.

To be honest, I wasn't sure if it was the right time, or if I was in the right head space to get to know someone new. I wanted love and a relationship, but I wasn't sure if now was the best time to go for it.

But Brian made it impossible to turn him away.

If I *had* a list, he would be everything on it. He was amazing. And I could tell that he was a man of his word. He was a man that did exactly what he said he was going to do. And we all know how hard it is to come across a man like that these days.

So, for now, the best thing for me to do was to go with the flow and see what happens next.

I checked the time on my cell phone.

Tonight, Brian and I were going on our official first date. He was taking me to eat crab legs and shrimp, per my request and I couldn't wait.

"What are you smiling about?"

Mama's words caused me to remember that she was there.

"I don't know yet."

"That's a new man or some new dick smile. Which one is it?"

"Mama!"

"What? You know I'm right. Hopefully, it's a new man, with hopes of becoming a new husband, smile. It's about time for you to spit me out a grandbaby or two. In case you didn't notice, I'm getting old, you know. So hurry up!" She beamed. I changed the subject.

"I've been looking into Olivia's death…"

"Baby, just let it go. Let her rest in peace. Let us all just move on and have peace. Peace is hard enough to come by these days as it is. And as hard as it has been on me, on all of us, we all have to accept it, move on, and find some peace."

I didn't say another word.

Mama was in better spirits.

That made me happy.

It's been over a month now, so I was glad that everyone seemed to be trying to move forward with their lives. And in a way, so was I.

But I wasn't just going to let it go.

Not now. I couldn't.

Not after finding out about Coco and Honey's lies. Not after discovering that they either involved Olivia's last days alive or were told about the night she died.

I felt like searching for the truth wasn't a choice anymore. This was something I had to do.

Finding out the truth is my destiny and my duty.

Mama and I left Olivia's house a little after four o'clock, and we went our separate ways. I had plans with Brian at seven, but I'd arranged to meet with the strippers and the bartender from the bachelorette party.

I'd hired two female strippers, two male strippers, and the bartender was male; at least he was by birth.

If you know what I mean.

I didn't know any of them personally, so reading them wouldn't be easy, but still, I wanted to speak to them face to face. So, I'd reached out, and they all agreed to meet me for a little chat.

"Hi guys, sorry I'm late," I apologized as soon as I saw them at the bar. The restaurant was crowded. I couldn't believe how many people were already having drinks this early in the day.

The five "workers" from the party, all greeted me at the same time as I sat down my purse and pulled out a notepad and pen.

"So, I know you guys were questioned by the police already, a while ago, but my family and I don't believe the fire was an accident," I explained. Truthfully, my family didn't seem as concerned anymore about the truth as I was, but it sounded a lot better than saying I was doing this on my own.

"Is there anything that any of you can remember now, about that night, that you couldn't remember back then?"

"I was dancing with the lady in the purple wig, when it all happened," one of the male strippers started.

I saw that in both his and Tina's, one of Olivia's entrepreneur friends' statement.

"And we were in the bathroom---together," one of the women said, pointing to the other male stripper.

I saw that too. They were being paid to dance, yet they were in the bathroom screwing each other, while my sister was outside on fire.

According to both of their statements.

"And you?"

This stripper was a part of the last memory that I had of Olivia. She was the one that was wearing the catsuit that night. The one that was giving Olivia a lap dance the last time I saw my sister alive.

"Like I told the cops, it's all a blur. And I was very drunk. Thanks to the bride. She made me take so many shots that I could barely dance. All I remember was dancing. And then the fire."

I stared at her.

She was pretty. And she had one of the biggest asses that I've ever seen. And the way that it juggled, that booty was real too.

I can see why Olivia was drawn to her.

Olivia never walked on that side of the fence, not that I know of, but she loved a big butt. She was always booty watching in public. Once, she asked a lady if she could touch her ass. The lady told her yes.

"I do remember giving both of them shot after shot, honey!" The bartender spoke up. "Especially, your sister. God rest her soul, but she was wasted! I kept trying to get her to slow down, but she told me it was her party, and that I worked for her. And she followed that with: "Pour me another shot of tequila!" And so, I did as I was told. And vodka too. She liked that vodka," he nodded his head and placed his hands on his hips.

He was so handsome. And though he acted feminine, he didn't dress that way. He was dressed nice and casually as if he worked a professional day job. Nice build. Nice teeth. A full beard and a fresh, low fade.

Too bad I wasn't his type.

"You were sober?"

"For the most part. I had a beer or two. The music was loud, and I was serving drinks. Between getting my dance on, and keeping everyone cups full and souls happy, I didn't notice anything strange. If I'm not mistaken, the last time I saw your sister, she was asking for a glass of vodka. I told the cops that too!"

Well, at least I asked.

None of them were saying anything other than what was in the police reports.

And I believed all of them…except for the stripper that was wearing the catsuit.

She barely made eye contact with me, and every time I looked at her, she looked somewhere else. And she fiddled with her keys as though she was nervous.

"Thank you all for meeting me. I really appreciate it."

I walked away from them, unsatisfied. I was also a little frustrated knowing I had to get through traffic, make it home, and prepare both mentally and physically for my date with Brian.

I was definitely going to contact the big booty stripper again. I was hoping that on a different day, in a different setting, maybe she would have something different to say.

Something more.

As soon as I walked through the front door of my house, I started to strip. I showered and got fully dressed, before sitting on my bed with the evidence folder.

I'd gone over the statements so many times that it was all starting to look the same.

I haven't spoken to everyone yet. And other than Coco, so far, of the people I talked to, their stories were the same from the night of the bachelorette party.

No one saw anything.

Some of my closest friends were still left on the list to talk to. I planned to speak to each one of them alone.

Going by the mansion was on my to-do list too. The owners were still out of town, but they gave me permission to go by and have a look around.

They were in Paris, but their son was in charge of looking after the property while they were away. The day before the bachelorette party, he met me there, gave me the rules, turned off the cameras, per my request, and left me with the key.

That night, he'd had to drive over an hour and a half just to get back to the house, once the police got in touch with him. Greg and I were the last to leave the scene, so I was there when he arrived. In my opinion, he seemed bothered by what happened more than anything else. He asked just as many questions as the police did. And he was almost emotionless to what was going on around him.

My phone chimed, interrupting my thoughts.

"I can't wait to see you beautiful. And I hope you're showing off those sexy ass legs. See you soon."

The butterflies in my stomach rustled around.

Brian was continuously finding ways to make me blush and smile, and it almost frightened me.

In a way, it feels like whatever this is, with him, may be happening at the worst possible time. Or maybe he was meant to be my sunshine during this terrible *storm*. Perhaps the Man above sent him to me, to be a pleasant distraction, while I travel this investigation road alone.

The police had closed the case.

No one else was trying to get answers.

It was just me.

After looking at the contents inside the folder for a few more minutes, I rushed to the closet to find something shorter. Something that really showed off my legs. I haven't dressed up in a while. Usually, whenever I went into the cleaners, I dressed the part. I made sure I looked like I owned the place. In my opinion, it made new customers trust me, and my business, just a little bit more. But, lately, whenever I stopped by, I looked a mess. I haven't dressed up since the day of Olivia's memorial service, but it felt like home as I slide my foot into the thick wedged shoe.

I admired my new attire and my curves in the full-length mirror, and baby, I was loving every inch of me! Tonight, I was going to show off these greasy long legs, eat, drink, and then hopefully, these legs would be up in the air or around somebody son's neck.

At least, that's what I was hoping for.

I'm just saying, I'm too damn old to "wait" and all that other stuff. I didn't mind screwing on the first date. Shit, actually, I prefer to. I need to know what I'm getting myself into from the very beginning. I tried that whole making a guy wait for a few months thing, before giving him the goods, and needless to say, it was the worst mistake of my life!

He got me all hot and bothered, and then he pulled out a baby mouse dick.

What the fuck was I supposed to do with that?

I asked him with a straight face who stole the rest of his dick. I absolutely refused to believe that God had only given him three inches of dick. Somebody had to have stolen a piece of it.

Of course, he got offended by my comments, and he ended up pushing me, and he called me a bitch.

So, I had to get all crazy on him. By the time I tried to stab him with a pair of scissors, I had that damn man running out of my house with his pants still down. And then he had the nerve to try and take out an assault charge on me!

Three months of my life---gone down the damn drain! That's how long I talked to him and made him wait.

Never again!

Since then, if it felt right, and if I wanted the dick on the first night or after the first date...I got it.

Hell, either it's gonna' be meant to be, or it isn't. That's just the way I see it. Either way, I may as well get something out of the deal.

After playing around with my face, finally, I was out the door and heading for the restaurant.

When I arrived, Brian was standing outside waiting for me.

"Blue. I love blue. And I love how it looks on you. Hello beautiful," he smirked at me and grabbed my hand.

"Hey."

Brian looked and smelled so good. I just wanted to put him in my purse and take him back home with me.

He led the way, and after checking for our reservation, we were seated.

It was an upscale seafood restaurant, the most expensive one in town and it was always crowded.

"Ms. Pepper, how are you?"

At the mention of my name, I looked behind me to see that it was Coco's husband.

Pastor Troy.

"Hey Pep," Coco said dryly.

I could tell that she was worried about what I would say to her.

"Hello, Pastor. How are you? I thought there was church tonight. Mama said she had to go to church when I saw her earlier."

Mama switched to Coco's husband church a little over a year ago. The pastor of our home church, the church we grew up in, passed away. Mama wasn't too fond of the man that had taken the deceased pastor's place, so one day she went to visit Pastor Troy's church, and that's where she's been going ever since.

"She must've been mistaken. We didn't have a church service tonight."

"Hmmm. Oh."

Brian pulled out my chair, and I took a seat.

"Brian, this is a friend, Coco, and her husband Pastor Troy," I introduced him. "This is my date, Brian."

They greeted each other as I got comfortable at the table.

"Coco, I've tried calling you a few times since the other day."

She glared at me. "Really? I've been a little busy." She looked at her husband as though she was looking for approval. Or maybe she was hoping he didn't say something that would contradict what she'd just said.

"Maybe we should let them enjoy their dinner. And we should get started on ours," Brian interrupted.

Coco and I shared a smile, and then I turned my attention to Brian.

"It's obvious there's some kind of bad blood between the two of you. It was in her voice. And all over your face."

Relaxing my face, I exhaled. "I wouldn't say bad blood. She's cool. It's just our last conversation was a little strange. That's all. But anyway…"

The waiter took our drink orders, as I eyed Brian in lust. He did the same.

"You look good enough to eat tonight," he complimented me.

"Oh, I do, huh? Well, I got something you can eat," I semi-whispered so the pastor at the table beside us couldn't hear me. Brian coughed.

"What?"

"You heard me."

"That I did," he grinned mischievously.

I opened my mouth to say something else inappropriate, but before I could, my phone started to vibrate. I checked it just to make sure it wasn't mama or Honey; it wasn't.

It was Greg.

Once the phone stopped vibrating, seconds later, he called again.

I held up a finger at Brian and answered my phone.

"Hello?"

Greg was whimpering.

"Hello? Greg? Is everything okay?"

He continued to sob. "I found Olivia's wedding vows. I read them. I shouldn't have read them."

"Aw Greg," I said.

He started to sob louder.

Hearing a man cry, or maybe it was just hearing Greg cry, made me want to curl up in a corner and cry too. It just did something to my soul.

Greg didn't say anything else, so I did.

"Greg…I'm on my way."

I hung up my phone and looked at Brian.

He was staring at me.

"I'm so sorry, but…can we…"

"Sounds like "Greg" has a real emergency."

I hadn't mentioned much about Greg to Brian, other than calling him one of my best friends. Since I hadn't told him about my sister's death either, I wasn't sure how he was going to react to what I was about to say.

"Remember I told you about him. He's my good friend. And he's going through something horrible." I stood up from the table.

I'm not sure why I didn't tell him that Olivia recently passed away, or that Greg was her previous fiancé, but now just didn't seem like the right time.

I don't know. I guess in a way I didn't want his sympathy.

"I'll explain it all to you later, okay? But I need to go. I'm so sorry. Can we…"

Surprisingly, Brian seemed unbothered. "Go on."

I couldn't tell if he was upset or not. I didn't know him well enough to decipher the tone in his voice, but I do know if it had been me, on the other end of that table, watching him run out on a date to go comfort a "friend"….uh, yeah, he would never hear from me again!

But I had to go.

Greg isn't just my friend. He's my family.

And as I hurried out of the restaurant, I vowed to tell Brian all about Olivia later.

It took me fifteen minutes to arrive at Greg's house just to find that he wasn't there. I called his phone over and over again, but he never answered it.

Really!

You mean to tell me…

Suddenly, the headlights shined bright in my rearview mirror. Greg pulled up beside me.

We both got out of our cars at the same time.

"I ran out of alcohol. I had to make a run to the liquor store before they closed," Greg mumbled, as I followed him inside the house. I could smell the alcohol on him. He was already drunk, or very close to it. He didn't need anything else to drink.

"The vows are on the table."

I headed to the living room and picked up the folded piece of paper. Olivia was wordy, so I could only imagine what her vows said.

"You know what, nope. I'm not going to read them."

"I wish I hadn't," Greg said behind me. He reached a glass towards me. I shook my head.

"I bet I sound like a little bitch, don't I?"

"No. You sound like a man who lost the woman he loved. Or loves. I'm sure you still love her."

Greg took a sip of his drink.

"Nothing feels right anymore. When I can't find something, I wish she was here. She always knew where everything was. After a long day, I'm used to..."

"Trust me, I get it. Things won't ever be the same without her."

Greg swallowed the contents in the glass, then poured another drink. I texted Brian to apologize again. I thought he was going to tell me to go to Hell or ignore me, but he didn't. He told me to call him whenever I could.

I haven't seriously dated in a while, but I damn sure don't remember men being this understanding.

"Sooo,"

I said to Greg as he sipped. I figured I would change the subject to get his mind off Olivia.

"I think I met someone."

He looked at me.

"I don't know yet. We've only been talking for a little while, but he's nice. He's different."

Greg just looked at me. He swallowed the rest of the alcohol in the glass, and then he attempted to pour more, but I touched his hand.

"I think you've had enough, Greg."

He didn't say anything. Instead, he poured himself another drink.

"Okay...anyway, I was actually on a date when you called me."

I waited for Greg to make a joke or apologize for interrupting my date, but he didn't. He didn't say anything at all.

"Greg?"

He cleared his throat. "Yeah, so uh, you like him?"

"I think so. I don't know. I have a lot going on right now. And with me trying to look into Olivia's death…"

"You ever wonder what things would've been like if we'd gone on a fourth date?" Greg interrupted me.

Whoa!

Where the hell did that come from?

Now, Greg was drinking straight out of the bottle. He was going to have one hell of a hangover tomorrow.

Greg moved the bottle away from his lips.

"Have you? Have you ever thought about it?"

"Greg, at that time in my life, you were just the type of friend that I needed. Trust me, I did you a favor. And besides, you were perfect for my sister. That's why I introduced you two."

Greg sipped from the bottle before he spoke. "Maybe I could've been perfect for you too."

"You are. My perfect friend."

Why is he talking about this?

Where is this coming from?

"And this dude…this new dude…you don't want to be his friend?"

"It's too soon to really say what I want. I don't know. All I know is that he's different."

"Different," Greg repeated, still drinking.

"What's up, huh? What…you don't wanna' be my friend no more, huh?" I joked with him and nudged him with my right arm.

Greg's eyes were glassy, and he frowned before speaking his next words. "What if I never wanted to be your friend? What if I just accepted what you made me be?"

Huh?

Still holding the bottle, Greg exhaled and closed his eyes.

I glanced down at the almost empty bottle.

Greg was definitely drunk. He had to be to say something like that.

Greg and Olivia were a match made in Heaven, thanks to me. They were soulmates, and Greg knows that. Hell, everyone else knew it too. There was no denying it. They were the perfect couple.

Never before had he questioned it.

And never before had he questioned me.

Greg breathed heavily, but he never opened his eyes. Once he started to snore, I took the bottle out of his hand and sat it on the table.

Reading her vows had him in his feelings.

That's all.

He was just feeling some type of way.

Tip-toeing, I headed down the hallway to the bathroom. Greg still had Olivia's shit all over the place; as though she was coming back. Her bathrobe was still hanging behind the bathroom door and everything.

After I finished using the toilet, I hurried to the kitchen and found a trash bag. Once I was back in the bathroom, I put all of Olivia's toiletry items, her robe, and anything that so much as looked like it'd belonged to her inside of the bag and tied it in a knot.

The reminders of her everywhere and every day were a part of the problem.

It's funny.

I could see what he needed to do to move on and move forward, but I couldn't make myself do the same.

My mission was different.

My mission was about justice.

I placed the bag at the bottom of the linen closet, all the way at the back.

And then curiously, I headed into the bedroom that Olivia and Greg once shared. I'd been there, to his house, plenty of times, but I never went past the bathroom.

Turning on the light, the bedroom had Olivia written all over it. Honestly, it looked almost identical to how her bedroom used to look at her house; except instead of using off-white at Greg's, she'd used black.

Greg spoiled her, and always let her have her way. But she was gone. So, now he was going to have to find his own way.

A manlier looking room would be a good start.

I walked around, grabbing stuff of Olivia's that hadn't been touched since she's been gone.

With my arms full, I flipped off the light switch and started to back out of the bedroom.

"Whooo! Greg, you scared me!"

Greg was standing behind me.

He didn't say anything. He just looked at me.

"Uhhh, I'm just cleaning some stuff up, okay? Don't be mad, but you have to start small so that you can move forward."

Greg didn't say anything. He just stood there, somewhat zombie-like.

"What Greg? What is it?"

Finally, he touched the side of my face, but still, he didn't say a word. Instead, he brushed past me and as soon as he reached the bed, he threw himself on top of it.

I stood there, watching him until he started to snore again. And with my arms still full, I made my way back to the kitchen. After putting Olivia's things in a bag, I grabbed my keys and purse, and took the bag with me out the front door. I threw the bag into my back seat, and once I was in my car, slowly, I backed out of the driveway, with thoughts of Greg on my mind.

Hmmm.

What was that about?

~***~

"Heyyyy Biiitttcchh!" Kelli sang.

"We have to get back to our routine of seeing each other at least two or three times a week. It's been too long."

"I know---right. What are you up to?" She said reaching me a cup of my favorite raspberry iced tea. She'd grabbed it from the deli across the street.

I'd stopped by the dry cleaners, just for a second. Now, I was about to head over to the mansion where Olivia died.

I was nervous. Light-headed, and I felt like I was going to have a panic attack or something, but I had to go back.

"I'm glad you're here. Ride with me somewhere." Kelli agreed and after she flirted with my employee, Drake for a few minutes, I damn near had to drag her out the door.

"Girl, you are a mess."

"No, girl, I'm horny. That's what I am," she buckled her seatbelt. "So, where are we going?"

I waited until I pulled off to tell her so she couldn't change her mind.

"To the mansion."

"What? What mansion? *The* mansion? Why?"

"I don't know. Just to look around. Just to make sure the police didn't miss anything. I don't know. But I've been contacting everyone and looking over all of the evidence. I'm just trying to find out what happened. For real."

Kelli didn't respond.

"Now, I've spoken to everyone other than Jai and Crystal. And I wanted to talk to Deb again, about those cigarettes. And Coco, did she tell you that she hung up on me?"

"No. I haven't spoken to her, lately. And she quit her job."

"Why?"

"I don't know. And when I called to ask her about it, she didn't answer her phone."

"She hung up on me, after I discovered that she lied. Coco told the police a completely different story than what she told us."

"What? What do you mean?"

"She told us she was outside, in the backyard, throwing up that night. But she told the police that she'd gone outside to get some fresh air, heard Olivia scream, and ran to the back of the house. But something tells me that she wasn't doing either of those things."

"Damn. Maybe she's just confused."

"Was she confused every single time she told us the story? If she'd just said it that night, okay, maybe, but days after, a week after, a month after, she was still saying the same thing. She isn't confused Kelli. She's lying."

"Well, Pepper. *Everybody lies,*" she said.

She's right. We all do.

But if Coco knew something about Olivia's death, her best bet was to tell me. If I find out she knows something else, or that she could've saved her, I'm not sure what I would do.

Kelli and I discussed our friends and our lives the whole car ride to the mansion. I told her about Brian. I told her that I'd never met anyone like him before and that it scared the shit out of me.

Surprisingly, Brian called me, the night after running out on our date, just to make sure I made it home safely. Finally, and without too many details, I told him that one of my sister's recently passed away and that Greg *was* her fiancé. And his response took me by surprise.

He said he understood grief and how difficult moving on could be. Brian also stated that sometimes it takes others a little longer to heal. He didn't question me about how close Greg and I seemed to be, nor did he complain about me leaving him to go comfort another man. He simply requested that I make it up to him with a nice, homecooked meal for our next date.

I told him it would be my pleasure.

As I pulled into the mansion's wrap around driveway, I started to feel like I was going to be sick.

Kelli breathed loudly, as though she was about to hyperventilate.

"Kelli, are you okay?"

She nodded, but I could tell that she wasn't.

I never planned to see this place again.

Ever.

But here I was.

Almost two months now after her death, I was here.

After giving each other little pep talks, finally, we were able to approach the front door and ring the doorbell.

Almost immediately, he opened the door.

"Hi," he said.

The owner's son, Carlton, was one sexy white man. Okay!

He was tanned, fit, and his inviting blue eyes were so mesmerizing that you found it hard not to stare at them. They were so hypnotic that they took your breath away.

Shoot, he could tell me to take off my panties or jump off a building or something, and if I was staring into his eyes, I just might do it.

"Uh, I'll let you ladies do whatever you need to do. I have to make a phone call, so I'll be outside if you need me."

He closed the door behind him, and Kelli and I just stood there.

"I can't move."

"Me either."

In the beginning, the bachelorette party had been everything it was supposed to be. We were having so fun. We'd laughed until our stomachs hurt and made so many memories.

"I can't be in here Pepper," Kelli started to breathe all loud and crazy again. "I just can't be in here. I'm sorry," Kelli ran out the front door.

So, there I stood.

Not knowing what I was looking for.

The house was clean and effortlessly beautiful.

High ceilings, marble fireplaces, oak hardwood floors, and crystal chandeliers. It had oversized windows that pulled in what seemed like the sun itself and oversized cranberry and ivory furniture.

It was an open floor concept. The kitchen and the bar were visible from the living room. And right in between the two was the back door. The door that led out to the pool.

Finally, I was able to take my first step. I walked towards the front window and peered out of it. Kelli was in my car, and the owner's son was sitting on the steps on his cellphone.

I gotta' do this on my own.

And as if a burst of energy or a strike of lightning shot through my entire body, I was all over the place. I looked in every room of the house. Even the rooms that I'd never bothered to go in before. I checked them too. I wasn't looking for anything in particular; I just had to see for myself that there was nothing there.

I crawled around on the living room floor, went upstairs to check underneath the beds, checked all the cabinets in the kitchen. I'm not sure why. The house was spotless. If something had been there, it was long gone by now.

And then there I was, standing in front of the back door, almost terrified to turn the knob to get to the other side. I could see the calming blue water inside of the decent sized pool. The pool that probably could've saved my sister's life.

My hand turned the doorknob before my mind was ready. Still, I stepped through the door and onto the freshly-cut green grass.

Time stood still, as I walked towards the spot where my sister took her last breath. Where she'd experienced one of the most horrific deaths that someone could ever imagine.

The lawn was neat, and everything was in its place. And the spot where she once laid had been redone.

It looked as though nothing had ever happened. There wasn't a single trace of tragedy.

After staring at the ground for a while, I looked back at the house. I was about 100 steps, if not more, from the back door. As drunk as Olivia had to have been, I was surprised that she would've made it this far by herself.

Why would she have walked all the way out here in the first place?

Even if she'd come out to smoke, which I still didn't believe, but if she did, why come all the way out here towards the end of the pool?

She'd skipped over the beautiful patio set-up that was full of available chairs. She'd walked past the lawn chairs that were lined up along one side of the pool.

Why would she walk so far out?

What was on this end of the pool?

Or who?

There was nothing behind the pool except for a tall fence and bushes. No one would've been able to jump over that fence. And if they could, there's no way that they wouldn't have been spotted trying to get away.

Still, I walked towards the bushes and the fence, just to inspect them up close.

Nothing seemed out of the ordinary.

The fence went all the way around the backyard.

There was only one small opening in the fence; which led out to the driveway on the left side of the house.

I thought about the evidence pictures from the folder.

I tried to pinpoint where the broken glass, cigarette, and book of matches would've been found.

I wondered if she'd dropped her drink on accident, because she was drunk, or if something else caused her to drop it. Maybe someone approached her from behind and frightened her.

My head was spinning.

I felt hopeless because whatever I was looking for, wasn't here. I wasn't going to find anything.

This was a waste of time.

Slowly, I trotted back towards the house, but not before stepping through the part of the fence that opened into the driveway. There was a walk space, a small path, that if you went straight, you ended up on the concrete driveway, but if you went to your left, you ended up at the separate four-car garage.

As I inched up the path, I could see my car, but from the bushes, I wasn't sure if Kelli could see me.

Coco's statement to the police came rushing back to my memory. She told them that she came out for some fresh air and then she ran around to the back of the house, once she heard Olivia's screams. If that's true, this is the way she would've come.

My instincts told me to look around, so I did.

For what seemed like forever, I looked around on the ground. At first, I didn't see anything.

And then...

Behind the garage, on the furthest side from the house, in the grass, I noticed a piece of red and white ribbon.

For the bachelorette party, I'd given the ladies individual handmade pins, that were laced with ribbon and a wig.

They were supposed to wear both the wig and the pin all night. Once the drinks started to flow, most of them took off the wigs, but not many of them bothered to take off the pins.

The pins were a part of a bachelorette party game that I'd found on the internet. Each pin was made out of cardstock paper, ribbon and tulle. I made them myself. Well, Kelli helped me. In the middle of the pin, on the cardstock, there was a fake name and a city or country. I picked exotic names and places, just for the fun of it, and the women were to tap into their inner sexy and create an alter ego.

For example, Coco's name that night was "Ziggy from Morocco." So, all night, well before she became too drunk to keep up with it, she wore a red wig, and spoke with a fake Jamaican accent for whatever reason. And she wouldn't answer to "Coco". You had to call her "Ziggy".

The purpose of the game was to loosen everyone up and allow them to be someone else for just one night. Someone without restrictions, reservations or hell, even morals. I thought it would be a fun game and I swear it was. Some of the women took the game to the extreme. And I'd loved every minute of it.

I rubbed the piece of ribbon around between my index finger and my thumb. It had to come from one of the ladies' pins, but which one?

If Coco came running, down the small path at the sound of Olivia's screams, then how would a piece of her ribbon end up all the way over here?

I looked at the distance from the path to where I was standing on the far end of the garage.

The wind could've blown it over here, I guess.

Or maybe Coco was already over here, and not in the front of the house like she'd said.

Hmmm.

Olivia's pin had been all white. Mine and Honey's were blue, though Honey didn't get to wear hers. Everyone else's pin was red, with two red and white strings of ribbon dangling from the ends of them.

This ribbon came from one of the pins.

I looked around for a little while longer, and when I didn't find anything else, I put the piece of ribbon in my back pocket and followed the path to the driveway.

"Are you done?" Carlton screamed behind me, as I made my way to my car.

"Yes. Thank you," I half-smiled at him just as I opened my car door.

"I'm so sorry. But being in there…"

"It's okay," I said to Kelli, as I hit the gas and made my way towards the street.

"Did you find anything?"

Someone was behind that garage that night.

Was it Coco? Or someone else?

What were they doing over there?

What did they see?

What did they hear?

From behind the garage, you couldn't see *over* the fence, but if you walked close enough to the fence, you could see through the bushes. You could see the pool.

If someone was back here that night, they could've seen what happened to Olivia.

Perhaps I was overthinking this whole thing.

After all, it's just a piece of ribbon. And there's no way to know how it ended up over here.

But I couldn't help but wonder if it was a clue.

A clue that the police missed. And one that I'd found.

A clue to finding out what really happened to my sister.

"Pepper? Did you hear me? Did you find anything?"

Blinking away my thoughts, I looked at Kelli.

"Nope."

I lied.

****

CHAPTER FOUR

Coco still wouldn't answer my calls, so I decided to show up at church.

Since inspecting the mansion, all I could think about was whose bachelorette pin the ribbon had come from.

I figured it was probably from Coco's pin, but I was going to make sure.

The church service was long as usual. And not to mention, it's baptism day.

Everyone applauded once first lady, Coco, appeared in a white robe.

"My beautiful wife has decided that she wants to be baptized again. This journey is personal. And to continue her personal walk with the Almighty God, she would like to be cleansed once again. Amen Somebody!'

"Amen!" The church cheered.

I watched Coco as she closed her eyes and allowed her husband to dip her into the water. Once he brought her back up, with her face drenched, she smiled.

The church rang in applause, but all I could do was stare at her. I wondered if Olivia's death was the real cause of her turning over a new leaf.

Or if it was because of guilt.

After church, Mama chatted with some of the elders, and I stood by the front door, waiting for Coco.

"Hey," she said, once she noticed me.

"Can we talk outside?"

She was dressed more like a preacher's wife than I'd ever seen her dressed before.

She looked good.

Relaxed, relieved and renewed.

I thought about how I wanted to approach the conversation. After all, we were at church. I wondered if it was better for me to tell her I found something behind the garage and see if she admitted to being back there. Or if I should just ask her the same questions, again, and hope with her newfound spirituality, she would give me a different answer.

Hopefully, this time it would be the truth.

"So, Kelli and I went back to the mansion, and I found…"

Coco pulled me by the arm, leading me far, far away from the crowd. She looked around her and then she looked at me.

"I lied. Okay?"

Nerves attacked me like a swarm of hungry bees. I held my breath as I awaited her next words.

"I was outside that night. But…"

"But what?"

"But I was doing something I shouldn't have been doing."

Uh oh. Here we go.

"The stripper; the one that was wearing the black catsuit," Coco started. "She and I kind of…"

I thought about how uncomfortable the stripper seemed when I met them at the restaurant to ask a few questions.

"I was drunk, okay. And we kind of hooked up."

"What do you mean hooked up?"

"I mean, one minute we were laughing, drinking, and she was rubbing and dancing all over me. And the next minute, we were outside on the side of the house, kissing and touching," Coco whispered. She rechecked her surroundings. "And no. I'm not gay, at least I don't think I am. It was just fun. Different. That's why I was outside that night. We were fooling around, and then I heard Olivia scream. At first, I thought she'd screamed just to be screaming, so I ignored her. When she screamed again, I still didn't think much of it. We just kept right on doing what we were doing. But when I heard Olivia scream for the third time, I knew something was wrong. So, I told the stripper to go around the front, and I made my way into the backyard. I had no idea that she was going to be spinning around in flames on the other side of that fence. That's why I was too late. That's why I couldn't save her. I didn't see her until it was too late. If I'd gone back there, the first time she screamed then maybe…I don't know. All I know is that I was too late. By the time I ran towards her, it seemed like it was only a matter of seconds before she fell to the ground." Coco had a single tear rolling down her left cheek as she exhaled.

I knew right then that finally, she'd told the truth.

"I didn't want to tell anyone what I was doing. It was wrong on so many levels. That's why I lied. I was ashamed, I guess. I didn't want anyone to know that I'd been out there kissing a stripper. I am a preacher's wife and all. I didn't want that to get back to my husband. But most importantly, I didn't want anyone to know that I ignored her. I ignored Olivia's screams…twice. I took too long to come to her rescue," she sobbed. "But that's the truth. I promise you, that's the truth."

After swallowing the lump in my throat, I opened my arms, and Coco damn near threw herself inside them.

"She was my friend. And I couldn't save her. But in a way, she saved me. I will never be the same."

I squeezed her tightly, but in a hurry, I let her go.

"Wait, you said that you were on the side of the house."

"We were."

"You weren't behind the garage?"

"What? No. We snuck out the front door and made our way to the side of the house. Why? What about the garage?"

I stared at her.

"Did you keep that pin that I gave you that night? The red one from the game? Do you know where yours is?"

Coco shrugged. "No. It's wherever that red wig is. I remember taking both of them off inside the house. Long before the fire. I was hot. I remember taking off my top shirt, which had the pin on it, the wig, and then I took my bra off too and just kept on my tank top. You know, I'm a part of the itty-bitty-titty committee so I can go braless without anyone noticing. Why?"

If she took off her shirt that had the pin on it, before she went outside...that means someone else was outside that night. Yet, Coco was the only one who admitted to being outside before Olivia was seen on fire.

And though she was with the stripper, the stripper wasn't wearing a pin.

"I'm sorry I lied to you Pep," Coco apologized.

Shaking my head, "Don't worry about it." I knew in my heart that finally, she told me the truth and that she didn't have anything to do with or know anything else about Olivia's death.

"I heard you quit your job," I said to her.

"Yeah. I'm on a different path right now. No more drinking or partying. And right now, I just couldn't handle going to work every day. I'm right where I belong---with my husband, by his side. At this church. Maybe I'll finally give him that son he's been asking me for."

I stepped back from her, and she laughed.

To hear her say those words...

Yeah, the old Coco is gone.

She was someone new. The old Coco was sneaking and taking birth control pills so she wouldn't get pregnant by her husband. She'd said something about not wanting to be tied down yet. But now, the new Coco was considering it. And I was happy for her.

Genuinely, I smiled at her, and after talking to her for a little bit longer, we agreed to do better with keeping in touch. After we hugged again, First Lady Coco walked away.

"What's on your mind baby," Mama asked on the car ride home from the church.

"Nothing."

"Chile, I'm your mama. I know when you're lying."

I didn't reply.

"You know, some days I still call her cell phone. Greg always answers it and says "Hey, Ma." He reminds me that she's gone."

I swallowed hard.

"You need…we all need closure. I think that's why processing what happened to Olivia is so hard, for a lot of us. We need the truth," I proclaimed.

"Pepper, have you ever stopped to think that maybe we already have the truth? It could be that you just don't want to accept it. You've always been a little stubborn."

"Ma, I can't accept it because it doesn't make sense. How can they not feel like there's a possibility that someone did that to her? Instead, they just wrote it off as an accident. Like she was nothing."

"She was a whole lot of something, to a lot of people baby. Police believe the evidence. That's their job. Now, I've never been a drinker, so I can't tell you what state of mind she may have been in, or how drunk she actually was, but accidents do happen. And sometimes they're terrible, terrible accidents. And sometimes they're painful. And sometimes they're deadly. Matches catch things on fire all the time. Houses have burned down to the ground because of something as small as a match. Now, don't get me wrong, I'm still grieving. Some days are harder than others. I miss my daughter. You know, a mother isn't supposed to bury her child, but I still have two daughters left. I have two daughters that still need my love. Two daughters that still need me to be their mother, until my days on this earth come to an end. So, every day, I focus on healing just a little bit more than the day before. And baby, you need to focus on healing too."

"I am, mama. I can do both. I'm trying to heal, but I can't ignore the fact that something doesn't feel right." Internally, I debated whether or not to mention the ribbon to her. Unfortunately, I decided not to. "And if I find nothing, then no harm is done. But if I find something, something that says that night wasn't just some crazy, horrible accident, then it'll all be worth it, mama."

"Okay baby," was all she said. It was as though she knew there was no changing my mind.

"I promise, I won't let it drive me crazy. Besides, I have a little something else to help take my mind off it all sometimes."

I was referring to Brian.

We were still talking regularly. We hadn't been able to schedule another date, but he was still my small escape from reality. The hours I spent on the phone with him at night, I can't say that I completely forgot about Olivia, but Brian always had my undivided attention.

"I knew that smile had something to do with a man."

"I guess you can say that. We've been talking over the phone. And we attempted to have a first date, but Greg needed me, and I had to go."

"You and Greg have always been close. Some might say a little too close. It's good that he has you as a friend. He definitely needs it. I'm worried about him."

"Me too."

Lately, Greg and I have been playing phone tag. Either I would miss his call, or he would miss mine. We would text here and there, but that's about it. In a way, I felt like he was avoiding me. Maybe he remembered the awkward questions and statements he made towards me the last time I was at his house.

Once I dropped mama off at home, I told her I would be back once she was done with Sunday dinner. Honey and her family were coming over, so I wanted to be there to talk to her.

Hopefully, she was in a better mood than the last time I was at her house. Maybe I could get some answers to my questions.

For now, I was meeting Brian at the park.

"This Greg guy ain't gonna' call and steal you away again, is he?" He smiled at the sight of me.

"Hey," I hugged him, without answering his question.

"I've been waiting all day just to see you."

Aww!

We started to walk side by side.

"So?"

"So?"

"I want to be honest. I wasn't expecting you…us."

"Oh, we're an *us*?"

I nudged him. "Not like that. Just talking to you has been easy. Refreshing. And I like it."

"I like you too."

I grinned at him catching what he said.

"That's not what I said."

"No. But that's what you meant," Brian answered cockily.

Maybe I did.

I like him.

I really, really like him.

It was now late summer, but it was as hot as early June. Still, Brian and I walked around the park, having another amazing conversation, hand in hand.

And the conversation ended with me inviting him to mama's house for Sunday dinner. I owed him a homecooked meal anyway. He never said I had to be the one to cook it.

Of course, mama said it was okay for him to come, so after sharing our first kiss, Brian followed me towards mama's house.

"I haven't brought a man home to meet my mama in years," I admitted to him.

"Well, I must be special."

"You must be."

I led the way, and after using my key to let myself in, I announced myself.

"Ma!"

"We're in the kitchen.

Brian followed behind me.

"Hey everybody. This is…"

"Brian?" Honey answered and dropped her glass.

"Honey?"

Confused, I looked at her and her facial expression. And then I looked back at Brian.

"Wait…y'all know each other?"

The tension was so thick that you could cut it with a knife. Honey and Brian were both quiet as they stared at each other in…what is that?

Is that anger?

"What---what are you doing here? And why are you with my sister?"

"I didn't know you had a sister. I guess that's something else you conveniently left out of our conversations."

"Excuse me, can someone tell me what's going on here?"

Honey grilled Brian for what seemed like forever and then finally, she looked at me. "Brian is…was…my therapist," Honey admitted.

"Therapist?" Both Honey's husband Joe, who had just entered the kitchen, and I said at the same time.

Before either of us could say anything else, Brian spoke instead. "I'm also the father of that baby in your stomach too," he said.

What!

~***~

"Honey? Your sister Honey? Sensitive ass, reserved ass, wouldn't hurt a damn fly, Honey? Of all people, was having an affair?"

"Apparently so."

I still didn't know the full story.

All I know is that after Brian's comment, all hell broke loose.

Joe was older, but that day, he moved faster than a speeding bullet to get to Brian. Joe took a swing at Brian, missed, and Brian took a swing back. He knocked the damn dentures out of Joe's mouth.

But Joe was back on his feet within seconds.

By then, I was in between the two men, trying to get them to calm down. For a while, it seemed as though they were going to fist fight whether I was in the middle or not, and then Honey's sudden scream somehow managed to distract both of them.

Both men looked at her in concern. Honey started to cry, and at the sound of her loud sobs, Brian apologized to me and stormed out of the house. And right behind him, Joe did the same.

Then, Honey claimed to have sharp stomach pains. So, she and mama rushed out of the house to go to the hospital, leaving me to tend to her other kids.

They didn't come back until that next morning.

Honey and the baby were okay, but she was exhausted, so instead of questioning her or trying to get the full story, I let her rest.

I'd tried calling Brian a few times. He only answered once to say that he didn't know that Honey and I were sisters. And then he said that he was sorry, again. When I tried to ask him more questions, he told me that he had to go.

I tried to remember all of our conversations. I couldn't remember if I'd ever said Honey's name. I know when I told him about Olivia, I briefly explained to him that one of my sisters had recently passed away. I didn't tell him how. And being that her death was all over the news, purposely, I didn't mention her name. I didn't want him to question me about her death. I liked the fact that he was the only person that I could talk to that wasn't talking about or mentioning Olivia. He was my small break away from thoughts of her.

And now he's gone.

And Honey was in therapy?

Of course, I knew that Brian was a therapist, but I had no idea that Honey was seeing him. And she never mentioned her sisters to him. Remembering his comment, he said that he didn't know Honey had sisters at all.

"I was really starting to like him, Kelli. Like, so much. Now that I think about it, during our first over the phone conversation, he told me that he'd just gotten out of something complicated. He loved a woman, who didn't love him back. For the life of me, I couldn't understand who wouldn't want him. What woman in her right mind wouldn't want the type of man that he seemed to be? I guess a married woman wouldn't, huh? Who would've guessed that he was talking about Honey?"

"Girl, I damn sure wouldn't have guessed it. Who knew Honey had it in her? Honey out here getting her freak on! Joe old self must not be getting the job done no more," Kelli laughed. "Oh, and I'm sorry about Brian."

I heard a car alarm beep and glanced out the window. Seconds later, our friend, Crystal knocked and I told Kelli that I would call her back later.

"Hey, girl."

"Hey."

I've been meaning to call Crystal and her sister, Jai, to talk to them about the night of bachelorette party, but I never got around to it. And these past few days, I'd taken a much-needed mental break from everything and everyone.

After the whole Brian and Honey situation, I just needed a few days to myself.

So, for three days, I didn't answer any calls, texts, or leave my house. I didn't look at the evidence folder or obsess over Olivia. I didn't check on Honey or Mama. I didn't check on Greg. I just laid around, watched my favorite shows, and ate popcorn and ice cream all day.

I just needed to clear my head.

Now, I was recharged.

And I was ready to finish what I started. I was more determined than ever to find out the truth so I could move on, and work on finding the one thing I was still missing.

Love.

Crystal hugged me, and I inhaled her scent.

She smelled familiar.

Crystal texted me a few times, while I was ignoring everyone. She said that she needed to talk to me about something, and since I wanted to talk to her too, finally, today I told her to come by.

As she stood in front of me with a smile, I stared at her. Suddenly, I was able to put a name to the fragrance she was wearing, and I couldn't help but notice her overall look.

She smelled like and looked like...

Olivia.

Not feature-wise; but in every other way possible.

She was wearing her hair the same way Olivia used to wear hers. She was dressed like Olivia used to dress. Crystal was even wearing the same shade of lipstick Olivia used to wear and she was carrying the purse that Olivia always begged her to return.

"So, I wanted to talk to you about one of Olivia's online stores. Since she isn't around to carry on the brand anymore, I figured I could. I helped her with orders all the time, and I'm very familiar with her audience. I'm sure she would want me to take it over."

I shrugged. "Sure. I haven't even looked at her business stuff."

"Don't worry. I've been doing everything, since a few days after her service. I've been fulfilling the orders online and going to the warehouse to ship them. I switched a few things so that I would have access to the payments, and everything has been going just fine. And since I've gotten all the back orders caught up, I figured now was a good time to discuss it with you."

Crystal let out a slight chuckle as she checked her phone. She had the same pink case that Olivia had on her phone. The same case that was still on her phone and in Greg's possession.

"I know all of her passwords and everything, but I think it's best to rebrand. I'll be the new face. I think I should change the name from "Oh Olivia B!" to "Cuttin' Up with Crystal." What do you think? And I remember with this store, she did it as a sole proprietorship, instead of an LLC, because she wasn't sure if it would take off or not. But it did. So, it'll be easy to switch everything right on over to me. Shouldn't take much time or money to do at all. I just wanted to run it by you first. What do you think?"

"Sounds like you might want to be her."

"I could never be her. No one could. Maybe I could come pretty close but..." Crystal stopped her sentence short and smiled. "I don't want to be her. I just want to continue what she started."

"Have at it."

Crystal smiled. She was jumpy. Full of energy and flipping her hair. She was different. Nothing at all like her usual self. And everything like Olivia used to be.

And quite frankly, it was creeping me out!

"Can I ask you a question?"

"Sure."

"Did you go outside that night? The night of the bachelorette party?"

"No. Not before…you know, not before Coco told us what was going on. Why?"

"Oh. Just one of the strippers said they saw one of the ladies wearing a blonde wig go outside. You were wearing one of the blonde wigs, right?" I was probing. And I was lying. None of the strippers said anything about seeing someone in a blonde wig going outside. I just used that to see if Crystal would say something that I might need to know.

"Uht, uht, remember I wore the blonde wig for a while, but it didn't take long for Olivia to get tired of wearing the blue wig. You know she never wore wigs or weave. So, when she took that wig off, I put it on. I switched wigs towards the beginning of the party. Remember? "

Oh yeah.

That's right. She did.

I don't know why I didn't see her obsession with Olivia before, but right now, it was crystal clear.

"I don't know who picked it up or who put on the blonde wig after me. And it was what, two or three other ladies in blonde wigs too? Maybe they saw one of them going outside because it definitely wasn't me."

"And you don't remember anything else?"

"Nope. Not that I can think of. All I remember is that Jai and I were taking Jell-O shots and then I remember Coco standing there, screaming that Olivia was on fire."

"No. I think Jai's statement says that she was watching videos on her cell phone right before Coco ran in and announced the fire. She said she was watching videos, and then when she heard about Olivia, at that time, just like the rest of us, she ran towards the back door."

I noticed the sisters difference in stories a long while ago. I just hadn't had the time to speak to them. I'm not sure why the cops didn't catch that they'd said different things as to what they were doing at the time of the incident. Or maybe the police did notice it, and it just didn't seem like a big deal.

But to me, possibly, it could be.

Either one of them is confused about the timeline. Or…one of them is lying.

"Hmm, you may be right. All I know is that I was swallowing Jell-O shots. I remember Jai being at the end of the bar with me. I don't know. I guess she could've walked away, and I didn't notice," Crystal shrugged.

I studied her body language.

She didn't seem nervous.

Maybe she was telling the truth.

"Well, I'm going to get on out of here. Time is money," Crystal blurted out. "I'll handle all the paperwork of switching over the business in my name, and if I need you to sign anything, I'll come by. Oh and, I wasn't going to say anything, but…"

She dangled her finger in my face. For the first time, I noticed the ring.

"Haji proposed! So, I'll be next up with planning a wedding!" Crystal squealed. "You'll be a bridesmaid, of course. And I called the bridal place, the one that had Olivia's dress. Remember, buying her dress was a gift from me. So, since I'm getting married now, there's no need in having the dress go to waste. I'm going to have them adjust it to my size so I can wear it on my big day."

Okay, this bitch has officially lost her damn mind!

"Let me guess, yellow and gray will be your wedding colors? Just like Olivia's?"

"Girl, how did you know? You know those were both Olivia and my favorite colors!"

"Crystal, you are not…"

"Whoops! I'm late for a meeting! I'm going to get all of you together soon. Love you girl!"

Crystal opened my front door, and I followed her outside. From the window, I hadn't been able to see her car, only her, but imagine my surprise to see her getting into a brand-new red JEEP. It wasn't a Range Rover, like Olivia's, but it damn sure wasn't the little white sedan that she was driving only a month or two ago.

Crystal beeped the horn, and I stared at her new car until it was out of sight.

She was trying to become my sister.

And that...that shit just ain't right!

~***~

"Honey isn't answering my calls."

"She's probably embarrassed."

I huffed. "Did you know that she was in therapy?"

Mama shook her head. "No. I don't think anyone did."

"Do you know why she might've needed therapy in the first place?"

"Possibly. No. You'll have to ask your sister."

"I can't believe that she was cheating on Joe. And that the baby isn't his."

"Well baby, sometimes people get good at living a lie," Mama examined herself in the mirror.

"Where are you going?"

"Church."

"Again? You have been going to church almost every day, here lately."

Suddenly, I recalled that night that was supposed to be my first date with Brian. Mama told me she was going to church that night too, but Pastor Troy was out eating and confirmed that church wasn't in session.

"You going to Pastor Troy church?" I questioned.

"Of course. What other church would I be going to?"

Mama put on her pearls and grabbed her purse. She kissed my cheek and then in another minute or so, she was gone.

I checked the time. It was a little after six, so I called to check on the dry cleaners. After discussing numbers and messing around in mama's jewelry box, finally, I decided that I would head home.

"Whoa!"

I placed my hand over my thumping heart.

I'd opened mama's front door to find Greg about to knock. He was holding a bag and a drink tray.

"I rode by after work and saw your car. So, I went down the street to bring you ladies dinner, but I see ma is already gone."

"Yeah. She went to church," I grabbed the drinks out of his hand, and after shutting the front door behind him, Greg trailed me into the kitchen.

"I feel like I haven't seen you in forever," I rummaged through the bag. I smiled to see that he'd gotten my burger with no onions, no ketchup, extra pickles, and mayo.

Just the way I like it.

"Yeah. I've been crazy busy at work."

"So, you're not avoiding me? Since you were talking all crazy that night, while you were drunk?"

Greg sat down beside me at the kitchen table with his sandwich.

"No," he answered. "Whatever I said, I'm sorry."

"It's okay, boy."

Greg and I ate our food and conversed with one another. He was acting ten times better. The sadness in his eyes was gone. He laughed and made jokes, and for a while, everything felt normal.

It felt like it used to.

"Look at you," Greg said. He picked up a napkin and wiped the crease of my mouth. "That mayonnaise on your mouth looks like…"

"Ay now!"

I punched his leg, and he howled in laughter.

Greg finished wiping my mouth and then with his other hand, he touched one of my short curls. Beaming at him, he cleared his throat.

"So, I'm moving."

"Where?"

He hesitated. "To Florida."

"What!"

"Damn, calm down. It won't be for another few months, but we're expanding. And..."

"You're the CEO, you can send someone else."

"I know. But I want to go. Maybe not forever. At least for a little while."

Suddenly, my stomach was in knots.

I wasn't sure what it was that I was feeling. All I know is that it felt a lot like I was losing someone else. I was losing another person that I loved. Someone else that was important to me.

"It won't be until sometime around the end of fall. Or the beginning of winter."

"What if I don't want you to go? I already lost Olivia. Now, I'm gonna' lose you too."

"You won't be losing me, Pepper. I'll be a phone call away. You're my homie. My..."

Greg seemed to be at a loss of words.

And so was I.

All I could do was stare at him.

And he stared back.

There was a strange energy in the room. I could feel it. And I was sure that Greg could feel it too. Still, we both just sat there. Unable to speak or move, until...

Greg's phone started to ring.

We both started to blink, as he found his phone.

He looked at it, but he didn't answer it. Instead, he stood up and asked me to walk him to the door.

"We should get lunch later this week," Greg suggested.

"Deal," I said stepping onto the front porch.

I walked closer to him.

"Come here girl," Greg somewhat tickled me and pulled me in close for a hug. He hugged me, attempted to let go, but I didn't.

I'm not sure why. I just didn't.

Maybe it's because he told me he was leaving.

I can remember when my divorce finally hit home for me, and I was a mess. I couldn't believe that I'd lost the only man that had ever bothered to put up with me. Greg was right there. Olivia told him what I was going through, and every day, he called or came by to remind me of how amazing I was. He told me that I would find love again and that any man would be lucky to have me. Whenever I was down or depressed, he was always there.

Wow.

I always thought I was the one being everyone's rock and shoulder to lean on. It wasn't until that moment that I realized that though I'd always been his, he'd also been mine.

"I don't want you to go."

Greg exhaled. "I think I have to."

"No, you don't. Stay here. I need you."

He pulled me away from him. He wasn't but an inch or two taller than I was, so we were basically face to face. Eye to eye. Mouth to mouth. And then…

"I'm sorry! I'm sorry! I don't know why I just did that! I'm so sorry."

I kissed him.

I kissed Greg.

"It's okay, Pepper. It's okay."

I started to shake my head. "No! It's not. I kissed my sister's man!" I started to shake my hands as though they were dirty or wet, but Greg grabbed them and looked directly in my eyes and said. "Pepper, I'm not anyone's man. Olivia is dead."

He exhaled and waited for me to exhale too.

Finally, I did.

Greg kissed my forehead. "I'll see you later, okay?"

I didn't reply.

"Okay?" He repeated.

Nodding, "Okay."

Greg walked away.

He left me standing there, feeling guilty and confused. I'm not sure why I did it, or why I felt the need to kiss him in the first place. Ever since I forced him on my sister, never had I looked at him in *that* way. I've never seen Greg as anything more than a friend or as a brother.

And you don't kiss your brother!

I rushed back into mama's house to get my keys and my purse. I was embarrassed and ashamed. And I was emotional. Yeah, I didn't mean any harm by it. I just need to get my emotions in check, that's all.

And being that I kissed Greg, and he didn't kiss me back, made me feel even worse. I felt like I'd violated him and our friendship.

What if our friendship was never the same?

I contemplated on whether or not to call and tell Kelli, but I decided against it. I would never tell anybody. I wouldn't want people looking at me crazy or thinking that all along I was after my sister's man.

God knows that isn't the case.

God.

Yeah, maybe I needed to pray.

Or some prayer.

A little Holy water.

Something!

So, I made a U-turn and headed for the church.

Imagine my surprise once I pulled up to find that the parking lot was empty. Immediately, I picked up my phone and called mama, but she didn't answer her phone.

Where the hell is she?

Obviously, she'd been lying about going to church. That's twice now; that I knew of.

Then where is she going if not here?

And why is it such a big secret?

I tried calling her again, and when I didn't get an answer, tapping my thumbs against the steering wheel of my car, I decided that I needed to apologize to Greg.

I needed to apologize for kissing him.

Nervous, I drove towards his house.

Greg's questions that night were harmless. I could tell when I kissed him, that whatever he'd said was not what he'd meant.

I was just his friend.

Approaching Greg's house, I noticed the hot pink Charger, with her custom diamond tag, in his driveway.

Jai.

Crystal's sister.

And my friend.

What the hell is she doing at Greg's house?

I tried to figure out what I wanted to do and after going back and forth with myself, instead of stopping, my foot pressed hard on the gas.

Is she who called his phone at mama's house?

The call that he didn't answer?

I glanced back in my rearview mirror.

Jai and Greg?

Greg and Jai?

She's definitely inside his house with him.

The question is…why?

~***~

"I feel like we haven't really talked at all, in over two months," I said to Jai.

I'd called her and asked her if I could stop by.

Jai was the single mom of our used to be close-knit clique. She was raising triplets on her own, so she was always overworked and exhausted. The father of her three girls: Raliyah, Remy, and Royce, passed away only a day after she gave birth. He was at the hospital with her. He went to sleep on the pull-out couch next to her, and he didn't wake up the next day.

Four years later, she was making it work.

Jai wasn't as friendly as some. She was very quiet and to herself. She only loosened up around people that she knew and she was very overprotective.

Of her kids, of her sister, of her friends...of anyone that she loved.

"I know. Things haven't been quite the same lately."

"Yeah. I rolled by here the other night. Thursday night. I was gonna' stop, but your car wasn't here," I lied.

I was doing a lot of that lately, but I felt as though I had to. I already knew where her car was. She was at Greg's house, but I wanted to see if she would tell the truth.

Jai pretended to think and then she replied: "Oh, yeah on Thursday nights the girls go to ballet practice," she lied.

"Oh. You're gonna' have to let me know when the next performance is. I'll come."

Jai nodded.

"I talked to your sister the other day. She's different."

"By different, you mean she's the new Olivia."

"You noticed?"

"Who wouldn't? I asked her about it, but she pretends that she's not trying to be like her. It's like she's taken on Olivia's entire identity."

"Yeah. It's weird as hell, right?"

"Right. They were pretty close. Maybe it's her way of coping with it."

"Coping my ass? That shit is crazy!"

Jai chuckled.

"Everyone is dealing with it differently, I guess. It's been what, two months and a half, if not longer, and it still feels like it just happened yesterday."

She didn't have to remind me.

"Yeah. Greg is having a hard time too. I need to go check on him. I haven't seen him in a while," I lied again.

"Yeah. I haven't seen him since the funeral," Jai lied too.

Why is she lying?

What is she hiding?

"I've been asking everyone if they remembered anything else about that night. I keep hoping that there's something that the police missed."

"Hmmm. So, you don't think it was an accident? I remember Kelli mentioning that you were looking into it, but she never said anything else about it."

"No. I don't believe it was an accident. I don't know why. It's just a feeling."

"Or maybe you just miss her. I remember when Xyon died, I struggled with dealing with it. I struggled with accepting it. It was so hard for me. And his death changed me. Now, death numbs me. It's not that it doesn't make me sad. I just feel numb."

Is that why she wasn't crying at Olivia's funeral?

"Yeah. You could be right. Still, are you sure you didn't see anyone acting strange? Or see anyone go outside? I know you told the police you were on your phone before Coco came in."

"Yes. How do you know that?"

"I saw your statement. It was a while ago," I tried to throw her off, "The police questioned me about everyone that was there that night since I was her sister and the host."

"Oh. Well, yeah. I was on my phone. I wasn't paying attention to anyone."

"I thought someone said you were taking Jell-O shots."

"No. That was Crystal. She asked me if I wanted some, I declined. In all honesty, I was sober the whole night."

"You were?"

"Yes."

"I thought I saw you with a few glasses in your hand."

"You did. But all of them were filled with water. Not vodka."

Really?

I was surprised to hear Jai say that she wasn't drinking. The only one of us who loves alcohol, more than Olivia, and more than Kelli, is Jai.

"Well, I have to go pick up the girls, but if there's anything you need, don't hesitate to ask," Jai said.

I asked you for the truth. You didn't give it to me.

Maybe I could get the truth from Greg.

I waited around all day for him to get off work, and as soon as I thought he was home and settled, I called him and asked if I could come over.

If he lied about Jai being there too, then I would know that something fishy was going on.

Greg opened the front door before I had a chance to knock.

"I promise I won't kiss you again," I laughed, trying to make things less tense upfront.

Greg chuckled.

"I just want to apologize."

"Really Pep, you don't have to."

"I do. That was out of line. I don't want to make you uncomfortable or lose you as a friend."

"You'll never lose me."

"Are you sure?"

"I'm sure," Greg touched my arm. "You want something to drink?"

"Water is fine."

Water.

Jai.

"I finally saw Jai today. It was weird that I haven't seen her since Olivia's memorial service."

"Oh yeah? Funny you mentioned Jai. She stopped by the other day."

Whoo!

Thank God he wasn't going to lie about it.

"Really? Why?"

"Well, months ago, she and Olivia went out drinking all night, and Jai slept over. She left behind a pair of diamond earrings that she says were a gift from the girls' father. She said Olivia kept forgetting to bring them to her. She just pulled up, knocked on the door and asked about them. As I said, it was months ago that she would've left them here. I'm talking even before we started planning the wedding. Months ago."

"Really? Why did she wait so long to ask about them?"

"I don't know. Jai said she'd asked Olivia about them before she died. But if they were here, I'm sure they're gone. I gave all of Olivia's jewelry away. After I saw that you cleaned her stuff out of the bathroom, I figure you were right. I needed to get her stuff out of sight and out of mind. I found that bag you put in the closet, and along with everything else, I either gave it away, threw it away or put it in the basement. I gave all of her jewelry to her mentee. Remember that girl that she was always helping out? Raven? Olivia used to tell me how much she loved her jewelry. So, I contacted her and gave it all to her. I guess I could reach out to Raven and have her check the box for them."

Greg reached me the glass of water just as he sat down. *Pew! Pew! Pew!*

"Umph, excuse me," Greg farted.

"You nasty mother---"

Greg laughed and farted again.

"Damn, sorry. It must be something I ate," Greg commented as he sat down his glass of what looked like Hennessey. "I'll be back."

"Yes, take your nasty ass on to the bathroom. Ewww! And you stink too!"

Greg scurried away in a hurry.

I exhaled.

I still had my friend.

I heard Greg close the bathroom door just as his phone chimed. And then, it chimed again. And again. And again.

So, I picked it up.

It was a text message. I couldn't see what it said. Only that there were (4) New Messages. The phone number wasn't saved, but I stared at it, and stared at it until finally, it hit me. I knew this phone number.

She's had the same number for years.

I took out my phone and went to her contact.

Yep. That's her number.

Crystal.

What did she want?

Why was she texting Greg?

I looked at his phone. It was passcode protected.

I had to see what the text messages said, so I started to guess. His passcode couldn't be that hard to crack.

I tried his birthday.

Nope.

I tried Olivia's birthday.

No. It wasn't that either.

I tried what would've been their wedding date.

No.

Hmmm…

I didn't want his phone to lock up, and I surely didn't want him to know that I was trying to go through it.

I had one more guess.

After thinking for a second, I shrugged. This probably isn't it, but I tried it anyway.

The code was six numbers, so I typed in the month, day, and last two digits of the year of my birthday and…

Really?

It worked.

Why would Greg have my birthday as the passcode to his phone?

I didn't have time to think about that right now. I had to read the text messages before he came out of the bathroom. I clicked on the number.

And started to scroll.

"Greg!"

"Greg!"

"Greg!"

"Greg!!!!"

For about a week, Crystal had been texting him the same thing over and over again.

What the hell is wrong with her?

I scrolled up to the very first text message. It said:

"Hi, this is Crystal. I need to come by and talk to you about something."

Greg replied: "Okay."

And after that, it was just text messages with his name over and over again.

It was at least 100 text messages of the same thing.

Maybe more.

Crystal has lost her fucking mind!

I guess since she wanted to be Olivia…maybe that meant she wanted Greg too?

I mean, that's the only thing I can think of; even though she already has a fiancé and she's getting married soon.

Glancing to make sure the bathroom door was still closed, and since I was already on his phone, I checked to see if any of my other friends were texting him.

They weren't.

And as he said, there was only one call from Jai.

Maybe she did just come by to ask about her earrings. Then why lie about something so simple?

Scrolling through his text messages again, I smiled at the funny emojis that he still had beside Olivia's name. And there was a beautiful picture of her saved as her contact picture too. He hasn't found the strength to delete her phone number yet.

My contact name in his phone was *Pep*.

Going back down the text log, two contacts down, from Olivia's last text message to Greg, was an unsaved number. It had a different area code, so I clicked on it.

"It's Done."

That's all the text message said.

I looked at the time and date.

It was the same night of the bachelorette party and…

I heard the toilet flush and I clicked out of the text messages, and placed Greg's phone back on the coffee table, just before he opened the bathroom door.

"I had to get that out of me," he smiled. I forced myself to smile too.

The text message.

From the same night of the bachelorette party.

The time. The time on the text message was a little before the fire, but only about an hour or so before.

It's done.

That's what the message said.

Greg started to babble, but I was barely listening to him.

It's done.

No. Pepper. No.

I tried to force myself not to think the worst, but I would be a fool not to consider it.

Could he have arranged…

Would he have arranged…

No. This is Greg.

And he loved her. He still loved her even though she was dead. Still trying to play it cool, I started to shake my head.

Then who sent that message?

Who does that number belong to?
What does 'it's done' mean?
Greg…what did you do?

****

CHAPTER FIVE

"You can't avoid me forever, Honey!'

She rolled her eyes.

I'd stopped by her house, unannounced, and caught her carrying bags inside. She wouldn't answer any of my calls, and her husband hadn't been answering his cell phone either.

I got out of my car.

"What do you want, Pepper?"

"Uh, I want to talk to my sister."

And I truly did. Not just about her situation, or about Brian. But I needed to tell someone about my suspicions, and who better to tell than her?

Olivia was her sister too, and she wasn't there that night, so I know she doesn't know anything.

I know that she didn't kill her.

But now, more than ever before, I was sure someone did.

I couldn't get out of Greg's house fast enough the other night. After reading that text message, it was too hard for me to sit and pretend that I wasn't bothered, so I told him something came up, and I had to go.

I basically ran to my car and locked the doors once I was inside of it.

What's done?

That's all I could think about.

Was the text message confirmation that Olivia was going to end up dead? Was it to confirm that some kind of plan was in motion to kill her?

My heart told me that it wasn't, but my mind was telling me that I couldn't trust anyone around me.

The more questions I ask...the more *everybody lies*.

Crystal.

Jai.

Jai had lied to me for sure.

Crystal seemed to be lying too. Not to mention that she was basically stalking Greg and pretending to be Olivia. She wanted to take Olivia's place.

Greg.

He could be lying about something. I just didn't know what yet.

Coco lied, but she decided to tell me the truth.

Honey was lying to me and to everyone else too.

And shit, now that I think about it, even Mama was lying too. She was still lying about going to church, but every time I went to check, she was never there.

At this point, I was starting to believe that anything was possible.

"How is the baby?"

"Good."

"Where's Joe?"

"Gone."

"For good?"

Honey shrugged.

"Did you get your checks?"

"Yes."

The checks from Olivia's life insurance policies came a few days ago, and they were still sitting on my coffee table. I couldn't bring myself to cash them because once I did, I felt like I would really have to accept that she was gone and she was never coming back.

But looking at all the bags in Honey's hands, she didn't waste any time cashing her checks, and spending the money.

"So, the baby is…" I cleared my throat. "The baby is Brian's?"

"Probably."

Well, there it is.

It's a good thing I didn't get the chance to screw him.

I took the bags out of Honey's hands and followed her inside her house. Waddling, Honey slid out of her shoes and took a seat.

Once I sat down the bags, I did the same.

"I started going to therapy…" Surprisingly, she said.

"Why?"

Honey ignored my questioned. "He made me feel safe. Comfortable. He brought out a voice and confidence in me that I never knew I had."

I could agree with her there.

Brian was so easy to talk to, as he should be. Considering his profession and all. And with the way Honey was acting lately, she was definitely not her usual self. She was someone else. Someone that I've never known her to be.

"One day, during a session, I started to cry, and he comforted me. And then…I kissed him. Immediately, he pulled away."

I had a flashback of kissing Greg.

I'll never tell!

"I leaned in to kiss him again…and…that time, he kissed me back. And that's when it all started. Brian knew all of my secrets, and still, he thought I was beautiful. He still found me desirable. He knows me better than anyone."

"I know you."

"Yeah. But you don't *know* me. The me who is ashamed of a few things. The me who is terrified of being alone. The me who has always wanted to find her own voice and her own way, but for whatever reason, I just couldn't seem to. You know me. But no one knows me in the way that Brian does. Not even Joe."

I didn't know what to say so I didn't say anything.

"I didn't mean to start sleeping around with him. And I definitely didn't mean to get pregnant. At first, I thought it was Joe's baby, but I doubt it. I really wanted it to be his. I do love my husband."

"But you love Brian too?"

"Hell no. I don't love Brian. I never have. He just made me feel like I could touch the sky. It's like I was chasing a high. But once I got pregnant, the high was gone. All I felt was guilt and shame. I cut things off with Brian immediately. And I stopped going to therapy. The crazy thing is that he asked me if I was pregnant; I lied and told him no. But when he saw me at mama's he knew. He knew that I was carrying his child."

"I mean, what are the odds? The one man that I've met, in years, that I could potentially see a future with was *boning* my sister. Just my fucking luck."

Honey looked apologetic and then she started to speak again. "It's a hell of a coincidence, I'll say that much. He never knew I had sisters. I never told him. I always said that I didn't want to talk about my family. I just wanted to talk about me. It was the one place that for once, it was all about me."

Loudly, I exhaled.

"The fight with Olivia was stupid," Honey continued. "Basically, I was sneaking to therapy. I didn't want Joe or anyone else to know that I needed a therapist. So, I didn't use our insurance. Instead, I started borrowing money from Olivia to pay for my sessions, and then I would pay her back out of money that Joe would bring home from work. It was $200 a session; well before I started screwing him. Then the sessions were free. If you could even call them sessions at all once we started to fool around. We didn't do much talking after that."

Bitch!

That man…and that *wood* should've been mine!

"I went to therapy for four months, before we started having sex. We only slept around for about two. In the beginning, I was going three times a month. I'm not ashamed now to say that I needed it. I really did. But that shit started to add up. $600 a month just on sessions. That's why I was borrowing money from Olivia; well, at first. Then, when I found out I was pregnant, I started borrowing the money from Olivia to put in a secret savings account. I haven't worked in over ten years, Pep. Everything we have is Joe's. Joe paid for it. I started wondering what I would do if the truth came out and if Joe left me. So, like a squirrel stashing nuts for the winter, I was in panic mode. I would borrow from Olivia, stash the money, and pay her back little by little with Joe's money. But he started to notice. He started to ask about my spending, and I started to run out of excuses. So, I couldn't pay Olivia back as often as I used to. And then the week Olivia and I had the big argument, it was because Brian contacted me. He said that he'd driven by the address that was on file, which was Olivia's, and he found that I didn't live there. He kept saying that he wanted to see me. And come on, how many people around here are named Honey? I felt like it was only a matter of time before he started asking around about me. Only a matter of time before he found I was pregnant, and then the truth would come out. And I didn't know what his reaction would be once he found out that I had a husband and kids."

"Wait, so Brian didn't know about Joe?"

"I pretended like we were just engaged, and I never mentioned my kids. Ever."

"Damn."

"As I said, I wanted therapy to be all about me. I didn't want to talk about or focus on anyone but myself. So, I lied about the basics. Or intentionally left them out. But with Brian being consistent with wanting to talk to me and see me, I got paranoid. I wasn't sure what Joe was going to say or do. I mean, come on, being pregnant by another man...I expected him to leave me. I figured that he was going to kick me out of here with nothing but the clothes on my back. So, I asked Olivia for more money."

"You could've just told us the truth if it ever came down to it. I'm sure Olivia, myself, and mama would've helped you regardless."

"Blame it on my pregnancy brain. I wasn't thinking clearly. I was on pins and needles, all the time. Worrying. Wondering. Afraid I was going to lose my marriage. I was emotional. Irrational. Some days I didn't know if I was coming or going. I don't know why I got so upset with Olivia. She had every right to say no. I'd been borrowing from her for months. And I had some saved; I guess I just felt like I needed more. I felt like my world was about to come tumbling down, and I just needed more. Just in case."

I listened to her full of sympathy.

"And then you walked in with the same man I'd had an affair with, and my biggest fear came to life. Joe found out the truth about the baby and my indiscretion. And now, I have plenty of money to survive on my own, but all I want is my husband back."

"He will come back, Honey. He just needs time."

"I'm not so sure. One thing I realized during all of this, and with arguing with my sister before she died, was that I put my entire life and fate in someone else's hands. Until now, I didn't have anything for myself. And I only had this money because of someone else. Because my sister died."

"Well, you have plenty of time to change that. If Joe leaves you, and even if he doesn't, you can figure out what it is that you want to do. You have over a hundred grand to fall back on. You can open something, start a business, anything. You can figure out what makes you happy and do it."

Honestly, I needed to be taking my own advice.

"Pepper, I'm about to have three kids."

"And?"

"And...I don't know. I wouldn't know where to start or what I would even want to do."

"Well, figure it out."

I touched my sister's hand. "And Joe will forgive you."

"How do you know that?"

"Trust me, don't nobody want Joe's old ass but you."

Honey slapped my leg as I chuckled.

"It's just the two of us now. You can always come to me. You can always talk to me. You don't have to lie about or hide anything from me," I assured her.

Honey nodded.

"You're going to be okay, sister."

"I hope so."

I wanted to ask her why she pretended to be surprised that we were Olivia's beneficiaries, but we were having a moment, and I didn't want to ruin it.

Clearing my throat, "So...I have to know...was it..."

"Girl...very," she completed my sentence.

"Damn it! I knew it!"

She knew exactly what I was referring to.

Just from the way he walked, I could tell that Brian had that "coma dick". The type a dick that put you in a daze and had you somewhere balled up like an embryo, sucking your thumb, once he was done. He just walked like he was carrying a *monster* in between his legs, and I could tell just by looking at him that his sex was good.

"Pepper, I didn't love him. If you want him, you are free to..."

"Oh hell no. I'm good."

"Why not? You gave Greg to Olivia."

"Yeah. But I never slept with Greg."

"Maybe not. But that doesn't mean he didn't want to sleep with you."

"What do you mean?"

Honey smiled at me. "If you ask me, Greg has always loved you...too."

"What? Girl, I guess you still have pregnancy brain, huh? Because you're talking crazy! Greg loved the hell out of Olivia."

"Maybe. But he loves the hell out of you too. It's always been in his eyes. I've always been able to see it. Olivia could see it too."

"Excuse me?"

"She told me once. That she could see the love Greg has for you."

"Yeah, friend-love. Sisterly-love."

"Maybe. Maybe not."

"We're just friends."

Honey shrugged.

"Do you think they were happy?"

"Who? Greg and Olivia?"

I nodded.

"Yeah. They were happy. They seemed happy. But you can never be sure of what goes on behind a closed door."

"Do you think he really wanted to marry her?"

"I'm sure he wouldn't have proposed if he didn't," Honey answered. "But yeah, I do. Since he couldn't have you."

I rolled my eyes. "Honey, stop it!"

"What? I'm just saying…he's always had a thing for you."

I ignored her comment. "You don't think Greg would've hurt her…right?"

"What are you talking about Pepper?" Honey's stare was intense.

"Since I've been looking into Olivia's death, I've been running across a few things, multiple things, that's just odd. It just makes me wonder about a lot of things and a lot of people in our inner circle."

Honey didn't respond.

"I think someone saw what happened to Olivia that night. I found something that makes me think someone was outside. I can't be sure that they were out there when…you know…but what if they were? What if someone, that we know, like a friend---what if they were out there watching what was happening to her and did nothing to save her?"

"Really, Pepper? Do you really think someone we know would do that? And to Olivia? Everybody loved her."

Thinking about Crystal and her new behavior I replied, "Maybe they loved her a little too much. Enough to want to be her. Maybe even enough to kill her to take her place."

Honey gave me an ear full, and I concluded that it would be best not to tell her anything else. There was no need to fill her in on all the lies told by our friends. And I didn't bother to tell her about the piece of ribbon I found, or the weird text message in Greg's phone.

And after Honey refused over and over again, to tell me why she needed therapy in the first place, finally, we said our goodbyes, and headed to meet our friend Deb for dinner.

"I need a cigarette," Deb grunted before we placed our order.

"You need to give those things up."

"And you need to go to hell," she smiled.

Deb was one of those friends who wasn't around all the time, but she was always there when you needed her the most. She gave really good advice; she was also a good listener, and everybody trusted her. She was usually very open and honest; which is why although I couldn't see Olivia smoking a cigarette, if Deb said Olivia puffed on a cigarette a time or two, then more than likely, it was probably true.

"So...have you seen Crystal?"

"You mean...Crys-Livia?" Deb smirked.

"Girl..."

"That's a hot ass mess! And Haji about to marry her crazy ass."

"You didn't hear it from me...but I think she's trying to get with Greg. I'm not surprised since she wants everything else of Olivia's!"

"Girl, Greg don't want her ass! Especially since he…"

Deb clamped her mouth shut.

"Since he what?"

"Nothing."

"Nothing my ass! Spill it! Since he what?"

"Damn! Damn! Damn!" Deb threw up her hands. "I'm sorry, but it's not my secret to share."

"What fucking secret, Deb?"

She shook her head. "I can't. I can't say."

I glared at her.

Greg doesn't want Crystal. Especially since he…

What?

What the hell did he do?

What the hell does Deb know that I don't?

And about Greg?

"Who does it have to do with? What is it about? Tell me Deb! Tell me!"

"I can't. I can't Pepper."

Deb took a sip of her drink. She was sweating. And she wouldn't look me directly in the eyes.

"So, how is everything? Life? The cleaners? Business?"

"Fuck you," I responded.

Deb laughed hard and loud. "Aww, come on now. Stop it. If it were one of your secrets, you wouldn't want me to tell anyone."

"Yeah, but what you know might help me find out what happened to Olivia."

"I doubt it. What I'm talking about has nothing to do with that night or Olivia's death."

"How can you be sure?"

Deb shrugged.

For a long while, I gave her the evil eye, but knowing that she wasn't going to break, I changed the subject.

"I have been looking into that night for over two months now. I've talked to everyone. The strippers. The bartender. Our friends. And I've met with all of Olivia's friends, who aren't our close friends, and no one knows anything more than what they told the police."

None of Olivia's *other* friends gave me any kind of impression that they were lying about anything.

All the liars were in my inner circle.

"Maybe there's nothing else to know," Deb smiled at the waitress. Once she walked away, she continued. "Personally, I was hoping that you found something. I was just talking to Shakira and Brenda the other week about Olivia. None of us are 100% sure it was an accident, but none of us really know what happened or what she was doing out there that night. Although, while we were all talking about it all, I did remember something else. Something I didn't remember before. Something I didn't remember when the police questioned me."

My heart skipped a beat.

"The last memory I have of Olivia is actually of her on the phone."

"The phone?"

"Yes. I told the police the last time I saw her, she was standing by the bar. But I was wrong. The last time I saw her, she was on her phone." Deb paused. And then she continued. "Valerie and Shakira were trying to teach me one of those new school dances to the song that was playing. Like everyone else, I'd had way too many drinks. Trying to do the dance, I fell. Valerie helped me up, but I remember laughing and looking across the room, for only a moment. I don't know why I didn't remember this before, but Olivia had a drink in her hand and her phone to her ear. That big bright pink case, with the sparkles on it. I can see it clear as day. And she was right next to the back door. I never saw her go out of it, but that is most definitely the last time I saw her. Perhaps she couldn't hear whoever she was talking to. Maybe that's how she ended up outside."

I listened attentively.

Olivia's phone was in Greg's possession.

I'm sure the police looked through it. And I'm sure they checked to see if there was anything suspicious inside of it or anything out of the ordinary.

But what if there wasn't anything suspicious, or strange, because the call came from someone she knew?

If that was the case, then the call would've seemed normal to them and it wouldn't have raised any red flags.

Who was Olivia talking to before she died?

In that moment, something else stumbled into my mind.

If Olivia had gone outside to use her phone, it would've been found outside with her. It would've burned with her, or it would've been somewhere on the ground; like the cigarette, matchbook, and broken glass.

But it wasn't.

If I'm not mistaken, her cell phone was found in her purse.

I think.

"Was it around the time, or close to when it all happened? You know, the fire? When you saw her at the back door, was it right before then?"

Deb shrugged. "I would think so. Then again, I don't really know. I just remember seeing her by the door. It could've been right before, or not. Pepper, I honestly don't know. I just know that's the last time I saw her."

I have to find out.

I have to find out who Olivia was talking to that night, and if they were the reason she ended up outside.

And the only way for me to find out was through Greg.

He's the one with Olivia's phone. And the iPad and laptop too. When mama and I packed up Olivia's house, I took her other devices to him.

So, I was going to have to see him.

Although I'd been trying to avoid him.

Since seeing that text message in his cell phone, whenever he asked me to stop by, I always gave him an excuse.

I know Greg; at least I think I do.

But I also know what I saw.

I saw a text message, in his phone, on the night that my sister died, and it said..."It's done."

And until I know for sure what the text message meant, I have to look at him the same way I've been looking at everyone else around me lately---suspiciously.

"Coco is pregnant," Deb said.

"Is she?"

"Yep. She just found out. She was at the doctor's office two days ago. I was getting a pap smear, and she was finding out her big news. She's only about six weeks, I think."

"Dang, when I saw her a month ago, she said she was thinking about it, but I didn't know she was already trying."

"She said she hadn't taken her birth control since Olivia's memorial service. When you saw her, she was probably already on her way to becoming pregnant. She just didn't know it," Deb suggested. "She's changed so much too. Like a lot. In such a short time. Luckily, she changed in a good way, and not like your little friend Crystal," Deb laughed.

"Girl, don't remind me."

Deb continued to talk, but something...or should I say, *someone* caught my attention.

I stared at him.

He was wearing a pair of dark blue jeans, a nice, striped polo shirt, and a hat.

Is that who I think it is?

"What the hell are you looking at?" Deb looked behind her.

"Look at the man in the striped shirt. Who is that?"

Deb stared. "Wait...ain't that the bartender from Olivia's bachelorette party?"

I nodded. And then Deb noticed what I noticed.

"I thought he was gay?"

So did I.

At least he'd pretended to be.

The bartender was holding hands with a beautiful brown-skinned woman. He kissed her and his body language was different. Everything about him was the complete opposite of how he'd acted before.

"Excuse me," I stood up.

"Pep...wait...where are you going?"

I ignored Deb and followed the couple out of the restaurant.

"Excuse me. Excuse me." I stopped them in the parking lot.

They both turned around.

The woman looked at me confused. And when she noticed that I was looking at him, she looked at him too.

"So, you're not gay?"

The woman's eyes nearly popped out of their sockets.

"Gay? Why would you think my husband is gay?"

"Husband?"

The bartender silently glared at me.

"He was the bartender at my sister's..."

"Wait, bartender? He's not a bartender. He's a cop."

A cop?

"Did you just say a cop?"

"Yes. He's a cop. And has been one for the last five years. Dre, what is she talking about?"

"Baby, go to the car. I'll meet you there, okay," he finally spoke. His voice was deeper, masculine. Nothing like the high-pitched voice he'd used before.

His wife complained for a few seconds, but finally, she strutted off towards the parking lot.

"You're a cop? What the fuck!"

"Yes. I'm a cop."

"Then why were you pretending to be a bartender? And pretending to be gay?"

I glared at him suspiciously.

"Actually, I am a licensed bartender. It was my job, for years, before I became an officer. And before I met my wife."

"Then why were you pretending to be gay? Something isn't right! What were you doing there? Huh? What was the real reason for you being there?"

"You hired me...remember?"

He was right. I did hire him, but that still didn't explain why he was pretending to be gay.

I had a bad feeling about this.

And about him.

"Pretending to be gay was just a part of the act. It was a bachelorette party. I felt it would make everyone a little more comfortable."

Bullshit!

He's hiding something!

"If you're a cop, why didn't you try to save my sister?"

"You saw the same thing I saw. By the time we got outside...it was too late. There was nothing I could do; except call for help. So, I called 9-1-1."

Now that he mentioned it, I never knew who called for help that night. And for some strange reason, it was never mentioned in any of the statements.

Not even his.

"Look, I'm sorry about what happened that night," he hesitated. "To be honest, in a way, I felt responsible for your sister's accident. I'm an officer. It's my job to protect...and that's what I thought I was doing."

Huh?

His words confused me.

"What do you mean by that? So, you weren't just there to bartend? You were there to protect? Protect who? Olivia?"

My head felt like it was about to explode.

He stared at me. "Again, I'm sorry for your loss. I was doing a favor. A job. It's not my place to answer your question. You're going to have to ask *her*."

"Her? Who the fuck is her? Huh?"

The look on his face told me that he wasn't going to answer me. Instead, he said something else.

"And you should watch your back," he said.

"What?"

"I'm pretty sure that someone is following you," he nodded behind me. "I've seen a shadow of someone off and on, the entire time we've been speaking to each other," he said.

I looked behind me.

We were standing in the parking lot. I didn't see anyone and the restaurant was a few feet away.

"Take care of yourself," he said next. And with that, he walked away from me, and never looked back.

I still had so many questions.

I still needed answers.

As I walked towards the restaurant, I eyed the abandoned parking lot. There was no one there.

Whatever shadows he saw, they didn't have anything to do with me. No one was watching me.

After all, why would they be?

~***~

"How are you, Pepper?"

Somehow, Brian and I ended up at the same park.

I was sitting on the bench, watching the children play, as he approached me.

"What are you doing here?"

"Same thing you're doing. Watching. Trying to figure out what to do about the baby."

"You really didn't know that I was Honey's sister?"

"No. I didn't. I didn't have a clue. She never mentioned having sisters. You did, but briefly. And I don't think you ever said their names. You and Honey don't look anything alike. Honestly, I had no idea. Just like I didn't know she was married, pregnant, or that she already had kids." Brian was bothered by Honey's lies. I could tell. And I could tell he had something else to say. "And *if* I'm being honest…"

"Please be. I've had enough of lies. Seems like everyone around me, lately, has been lying to me."

And that was nothing but the truth.

Brian exhaled. "I only approached you because of Kelli."

"Kelli? *My* friend Kelli?"

"Yes. She and I go way back."

Oh really?

When I mentioned Brian to her, for the first time, she never said a word about knowing him.

"She was there that day. At the building where I work and where the office of the lawyer you went to see is located. Kelli was there too."

There are a lot of different offices in that building.

"Why was Kelli there?"

"Oh. She goes to my see colleague. April."

"For therapy?"

"Yes. You didn't know?"

"No. I didn't."

And Kelli and I told each other everything!

At least I thought we did.

"Since she and I have been acquainted for a while, I referred her. Kelli used to associate with my best friend's wife, Candance."

"I remember Candance."

"That's how Kelli and I met. We never had any dealings or anything. But we've been in a few settings at the same time, on several occasions. Anyway, she'd just finished her session, and since I was waiting on my next appointment, I was walking her out. She saw you and your people come out of the lawyer's office and she froze. It was obvious that she didn't want to be seen. She waited until all of you were out of the building and then she looked at me and asked me if I was seeing anyone. I said no. Your sister and I were over. And though I wasn't really interested in getting in something again, so soon, she sold you like an overpriced bottle of wine."

Hmmm…

"She told me that you were a friend of hers. And that you were single. She also said that she thought that you and I would really hit it off. And she told me that you owned the dry cleaners."

"So, you lied about seeing me?"

"Yes. It was a harmless lie. Kelli didn't want you to know that she was setting us up. She said that you would reject the idea of us if you knew it was a set-up. She also said that you were going through a hard time, and you needed someone to take your mind off the situation. I had some things going on myself, so I wasn't going to approach you. But I thought, what the hell?"

"Wow," I huffed. "You only approached me because someone told you to."

"Don't say it like that. As soon as you opened your mouth, I could see why Kelli thought we would hit it off. She pushed me in your direction, but you kept me there. You kept me interested. Call me crazy, but we were going to have something special. I just know it. And if the circumstances were different, I believe we could've been in it for the long haul."

"You mean…if you hadn't fucked my sister."

"The baby is mine, isn't it?"

"She thinks so."

"What should I do?" He asked.

Exhaling, I answered him. "Just let her be."

Though he probably wouldn't, I know that's what Honey would've wanted me to say.

"See you around, Pepper."

Hopefully not.

As soon as Brian walked away, I called Kelli.

I had a bone to pick with her! She could've told me that she set me up.

"Hey, where you at?"

"I'm still at work. I'm working until eight tonight. Why? What's up?"

"Nothing. Call me when you get home."

Honey was going to therapy.

Kelli is going to therapy.

Kelli set me up with Brian.

Honey had sex with Brian.

I felt like I didn't really know anyone anymore.

After the talking to the officer slash bartender the other night, my mind has been in overdrive ever since. He'd said so little, yet so much at the same time.

I just didn't understand it.

I just didn't understand any of it at all.

Forcing myself to get up from the bench, I made my way to my car and headed home.

To get to my house, I had to pass by Kelli's house. Imagine my surprise to see that Kelli wasn't at work.

That lying bitch!

Carlton, the mansion owner's son, held the door to his truck open for Kelli as she climbed inside.

What the hell?

I turned onto one of the side roads, and after making a U-turn, I stopped at a stop sign and texted Kelli.

"Don't forget to call me when you get off work."

I waited impatiently for her response.

Finally, she replied. *"Okay. I'll call you as soon as I'm off."*

Why is she lying to me?

By the time I made my way back up the road, the truck was gone. They couldn't have gotten far. I contemplated whether or not I wanted to find them and follow them, or if I wanted to…

I swerved into Kelli's driveway.

My mind was made up.

Of course, I had a key to her house. We all had keys to each other's home. Most of us did anyway.

I used my key to get inside.

Of all people, Kelli is lying to me too?

I headed to her bedroom and looked around. I wasn't really looking for anything. I was just confused.

She had two empty bottles of wine on her dresser.

And I just found out she's in therapy.

Hmmm.

Perhaps there's another reason why she drinks so much. Maybe she was just using Olivia's death as an excuse.

I moved a few things around on her dresser, and that's when I saw it.

Not far from the bottles was Kelli's bachelorette party pin…and the left string of ribbon was missing.

And I had the missing piece!

So, does this mean that Kelli was outside that night? When?

Kelli was with me when we heard Coco's screams, so, I knew for a fact that she wasn't outside during Olivia's death.

Had she been out there sometime before?

Why wouldn't she tell me that when I asked everyone if any of them had been outside, prior to Olivia's "so-called" accident?

I inspected the pin.

The middle of the pin was a circle and had the name "Onya from Venezuela." That's the fake name I gave her that night, so this was definitely her pin.

The circle was surrounded by red tulle. And at the bottom of the circle, there was a bow. And dangling from that bow, there was supposed to be two pieces of red and white ribbon. There was only one. Her left ribbon was missing.

It had to be the piece of ribbon that I found behind the garage. Kelli must've been back there at some time or another. How else would it have gotten there?

I'm sure there's a possibility that the piece of ribbon came off another pin, but my gut told me it was unlikely.

Kelli was outside.

For what?

With who?

Suddenly, I recalled what I'd just seen.

She was with Carlton.

Maybe she was outside with him.

Maybe he was there.

He could've been there, or still in town the whole time.

They could've met behind the garage.

Did they know each other before that night?

With the ribbon in hand, I headed into Kelli's living room, and I sat there and waited. I waited for her all night.

The sun went down, and no matter how many times I called her, she never answered her phone.

And it was to no surprise to me that she never came home.

~***~

"Damn, I'm surprised to see you," Greg said opening his front door. "You've been avoiding me. What did I do?"

"Boy, what are you talking about? I haven't been avoiding you."

Greg led me into the living room.

Kelli was avoiding me though.

She still wasn't answering her cell phone, and whenever she did reply to my text messages, it was only to say that she would text me back later.

She never did.

"So, what's been up?"

"Nothing. Working. Preparing for this move."

"So, you're still going to move?"

"That's the plan. Why? You wanna' come with me?" Greg offered.

"Boy, I got a business to run."

"Expand. Open another one in Florida."

I shook my head. "I've barely been doing my job with this one. But I came by to ask you something. Do you still have Olivia's phone? I wanted to get a scrapbook of her made and wanted to see what pictures she has of herself in it."

I was lying---again.

Hell, everyone else was doing it, so I didn't feel bad about it. Although a scrapbook of Olivia did sound like a pretty good idea.

"Oh, here, look in my phone. I sent all of her pictures to my phone, before I had her phone and iPad wiped clean. And then I gave them to my niece. I kept the laptop. I needed a new one for work anyway. But I removed her stuff off that too."

Damn it!

I wanted to follow up on what Deb said and see who called Olivia the night of the bachelorette party.

"So, you're just erasing her, huh?"

"No. I'm just trying to move forward. She'll always be in my heart, but every day gets a little easier. I need to make this move."

After taking a deep breath, I decided which topic I wanted to get off my chest first. I felt like I couldn't trust anyone. I needed to know if I could trust him.

"Why is Crystal texting you?"

Greg looked at me.

"I saw it pop up on your phone the last time I was here. I recognized her number."

"Is that why you have been acting strange? Crystal is crazy. Not only does she want to be Olivia...she wants to be with me."

"I figured that."

"Did you know that she and Haji were over? I saw him at the barbershop. He said that they broke up shortly after Olivia died. Her choice. Not his."

"What? She told me they were getting married. She showed me the ring and everything. And she's been planning a wedding. She just sent out an e-mail about it to all of us the other day."

"I don't know. But according to Haji, they haven't been together in about two months. And I just saw him last week."

"Wow!" I was at a loss for words.

"She's bat-shit crazy. I always knew she admired Olivia, but damn!"

"All she's missing on her road to becoming her is you."

"Well, she can't have me. If she knew...she probably wouldn't want me."

"If she knew what?"

Greg looked at me.

"Spit it out!"

First, Deb almost said something about Greg the other day, and now he was trying to hold back something too.

"Say it!"

"Okay, damn," Greg stated. "Olivia is gone, so I'm going to be straight up with you. Olivia was sweet and nice, but she had a wild and freaky side."

"I know that."

"No. I mean...Olivia was intrigued by different, unique, sexual situations and pleasures."

"Look, I don't need to hear about y'all sex life. Please spare me the details."

"No. That's not it. Listen." Greg scooted closer to me. "One night, Olivia and Jai went out."

Jai?

"They both got sloppy drunk. And I'd been at home drinking, watching the game, so when they called me to pick them up, I couldn't go get them. I called you first that night. You didn't answer. So, I called Honey, and she sent Joe to the club to pick them up."

Why was I nervous?

Impatiently, I waited for him to proceed.

"He dropped them off here. Jai was too drunk to drive home, so Olivia told her to stay. At one point in time, we were all sitting here. Them on this couch. Me on the other. Still drinking, talking and laughing. And then Olivia..."

Uh oh.

"Olivia asked Jai if she'd ever had a threesome."

"What?"

"Olivia was always talking about trying one. Jai giggled and told Olivia that she hadn't had one before, and I told Olivia to let the conversation go. But she didn't. Instead, she suggested that we do it."

"Do what?"

"A threesome."

"With Jai?"

Greg nodded. "As drunk as I was, I knew it was a crazy idea. I told Olivia to stop talking crazy, but surprisingly, Jai said yes."

"The same Jai that's very coy, shy and particular? Jai with the three kids? That Jai? She said yes to a threesome?"

"One and the same. I still said no. Both women laughed as Olivia grabbed Jai's hand and walked towards me. Olivia gave Jai permission to touch me. I moved her hand, over and over again. I mean, what man wouldn't be down for a threesome if it's something his woman wants to do? But with her friend? I wasn't comfortable with that. It's supposed to be with someone we wouldn't have to see again. Not with her friend. One of her best-friends, let me add that."

Olivia had always been very sexual, so I wasn't surprised. I always thought that she was a little too intrigued with tits and ass, and not to mention, she didn't mind talking about what she liked to do in the bedroom. But hearing all of this, naturally, was a bit much for me.

"Olivia got upset that I didn't want to participate. She said it would stay just between us. To relax me, Olivia got down on her knees and…she did her *thing*. And while she was doing it, she looked up and told Jai to kiss me. Jai was probably the drunkest of the three of us, but she didn't hesitate to try and kiss me. Olivia got excited and tried to suck the life out of me," Greg cleared his throat. "After a few seconds, I mean, I guess I got into it. It all happened so fast. I'm sure you don't need all the details, but long story short, I had sex with both of them that night. And they did some things friends don't usually do to each other. Needless to say, Olivia got what she wanted. Just like she always did."

"What the fuck Greg!"

He didn't say anything.

I couldn't believe it. I just didn't know what else to say.

"It was fucked up. I know. The next morning, Jai and I regretted the night before, but Olivia didn't. She didn't seem bothered at all. She was singing and shit, while Jai and I both felt ashamed. Olivia didn't care about what we'd done. Until…"

"Until what?"

"Until Jai told us she was pregnant."

"Wait…by you?"

"Yes. That's when things between them went south."

"Oliva and Jai were at odds? Before she died?"

"Somewhat. They were pretending to be okay, but they were in a bad space. I could tell that Jai resented Olivia; especially after the abortion."

"What? What abortion? When was all this?"

"Even before we announced that we were getting married. When Olivia found out Jai was pregnant, she was livid. As if she blamed Jai. She didn't blame herself for wanting the threesome. Hell, she didn't even blame me. Olivia blamed Jai and her fertile uterus. She told Jai to have an abortion. Jai said she didn't believe in abortions and that she didn't want to have one. She said no one had to know that the baby was mine. Olivia told her we would. We would know. So, they went back and forth for days, until Jai finally agreed. Olivia went with her to the clinic, and as soon as she came home, that same day, she told me that she wanted us to get married. She said she was ready. And she said she would never ask me to do anything like that again."

My mouth was hanging wide open. "Did you want the baby?"

"It didn't matter what I wanted. It was whatever Olivia wanted. And that day, I went out and bought her the engagement ring of her dreams and asked her to be my wife---again." Greg paused. "When Jai came by, it wasn't just to ask about some earrings that she left. She asked if I would get her pregnant again."

"Say what?"

"She says Olivia practically bullied and threatened her into having the abortion. She didn't want to have one. So, Jai thinks I *owe* her a baby. She came by here and she wanted to have sex with me. I turned her down. And I turned down Crystal too."

Everybody wanted a piece of Greg.

Everybody but me.

Right?

"So, that's the truth. Olivia isn't here to deny it, but it's the truth."

"And you and Olivia were happy? You loved her right?"

"I loved the hell out of her. She had a good heart. And she loved me. How can you not love someone who truly loves you back?" His words were genuine.

He meant them. I could see it in his eyes.

I'm not sure what that text message was about, but at that moment, I was convinced that Greg wouldn't have done anything to hurt Olivia. Nor would he have gotten someone else to do it.

"I loved her because she loved me. She loved me even though she knew…"

"Even though she knew what?"

He exhaled. "That I love you too."

"What? What the hell are you trying to say?"

"When you introduced me to Olivia, you said that you knew the perfect woman for me. I can see why you would think that. Olivia was amazing. We had a lot of the same goals, and dreams about the future. But she wasn't the perfect woman for me, Pep. The perfect woman for me was you."

No!

Honey was right.

"You didn't want me. I'm a man. I have my pride. I accepted that years ago. But though Olivia was a hell of a good woman…she wasn't you. After our first date, I would've married you the next day if I thought you'd say yes. You're edgy. Bold. Resilient. Tough, yet you have this softness about you. Genuine. And Unique. Olivia was a lot of great things, but everything I was looking for, in woman, in a lifetime partner, it was you."

My mouth was wide open.

I didn't know what to say.

"A man knows what he wants. He knows what he needs. He knows if he'll marry a woman or want to marry a woman, only a few days after meeting her. If it had been my choice…it would've been you, Pepper. After about six months of dating Olivia, I told her. I told her when you came around, even though we had shifted into being just friends, that I felt a connection to you. I told her that it was something about you that stirred things around inside of me. And guess what? Surprisingly, Olivia told me she understood. And then she asked me for one thing. She asked me to love her more. She asked me to love her more than I loved you. And I learned how to. I learned how to want her more than I wanted you; well, for the most part anyway."

My chest went up and down, faster and faster.

Greg stood up.

"I'm not asking you for anything Pepper. I just thought you should know."

Greg walked out of the living room, and he never returned. I didn't know what to say to him, so I didn't go after him. And once I was able to stand, I grabbed my purse and ran out the front door.

As I backed out of the driveway, I caught sight of Greg looking out his window. He just stood there, watching me.

Greg loves me?

He has always loved me?

And apparently, I was the only one that didn't have a clue!

And Olivia.

Her, Greg and Jai.

A threesome.

Jai was pregnant by Greg.

Olivia talked her into getting an abortion.

It was all a lot to drill into my head.

I sped past Kelli's house towards home. Her house was dark and her car was gone.

Pulling into my driveway, my automatic porch and garage lights popped on. Instead of pulling into the garage, with my house key in hand, I got out of my car and scurried to the front porch.

As I approached the steps, I noticed something small right in front of the door.

"What's that?"

I bent down and gasped once I saw what it was.

Hesitantly, I picked it up and then I peered around me in the dark.

It was a book of matches.

One identical to the one found at the scene of Olivia's death. Same color and everything.

With shaking hands, I opened it up.

All of the matches were inside.

Someone put this here.

Someone was at my house and left this here for me to find.

Rushing inside, with the matchbook still in my hand, I slammed the door shut, locked the door, and staring out the living room window, I faced a horrible truth.

Someone killed Olivia.

And though leaving this was their warning.

For me…it was proof.

****

CHAPTER SIX

Ding.

The doorbell chimed.

I struggled to open my eyes. Glancing at the clock, it was 5:42 a.m.

Instantly, my heart started to race. If someone was here this early in the morning, it must be an emergency.

Forcing myself from underneath the covers, I wrapped myself in my robe and headed for the front door.

"Who is it?"

I glanced out the peephole, but no one was there.

"Who is it?" I yelled from the other side of the door.

Still, no one answered.

I knew for a fact I'd heard the doorbell and that it wasn't a dream. With the chain still on the door, I unlocked the deadbolt and peered outside.

I didn't see anyone.

But...

Kneeling down, I stuck my hand through the space of the door and grabbed the envelope.

Just a few nights ago, I'd found a red book of matches on my porch, so I called the police.

The cops thought I was crazy. They couldn't understand why I would call them about a book of matches. I explained to them that they were the same, exact matches found at the scene of my sister's death, but I could tell that they thought I was concerned for nothing.

But I was convinced that they were left there as some kind of warning. I could only assume the same person left this too.

After locking the door, I inspected the small brown envelope. It was as light as a feather, so I ripped it open.

"What in the hell?"

It was a photo of me...

And of Greg.

Kissing.

Well, of me kissing him on mama's porch.

I flipped the photo over to see if there was anything on the back of it.

Nothing.

Who took this picture?

Nerves rustled around in my belly.

The cop was right.

Someone is watching me.

As soon as I reached the window, I peeked out of the blinds. It wasn't quite sunrise yet, but from what I could see, nothing was out of place. No one was out there. And if they were, they were hidden and couldn't be seen.

Without hesitating, I tore up the photo and rushed to my room to pack a few bags.

It wasn't safe for me to be here by myself.

After calling Kelli over and over again, finally, she answered her phone. And after telling her I thought someone might be out to get me, and that someone kept coming to my house, I asked her to drive down the street to watch me get into my car.

Beep. Beep.

At the sound of her horn, I grabbed my bags, and hesitantly, I made my way outside.

Kelli got out of her car.

"What the hell are you talking about? Someone is out to get you? What does that even mean?"

I paid very close attention to my surroundings as I placed the bags inside my car.

"Pepper?"

I heard her, but I was focused.

"Pepper!"

"What!"

Kelli looked annoyed.

"Someone has been watching me. Coming to my house. Leaving matches on my porch. And 5 o'clock this morning, someone decided to ring my doorbell, and leave a photo!"

"What photo?"

"Of me...doing something I shouldn't have been doing. Proving to me that someone is watching me."

"Why would someone be watching you, Pepper? Why would someone be doing all of this?"

"I don't know. Maybe I'm getting too close to the truth. Maybe someone wants me to stop looking into Olivia's death. I've been uncovering a lot of lies lately...including some of yours!"

The cat is out of the bag now! And what a relief it was.

"What? What lies have I told?"

"For starters, the other week when you told me you were still at work, I rode by your house and saw you getting into the car with Carlton! You lied for nothing! So, what...you're screwing him or something?"

"That's my business. And I didn't want anyone to know about Carlton until I was sure of where the whole thing is going. I have the right to keep shit to myself. So, yes. I lied about being with him."

"Answer this, we're y'all fooling around when Olivia died?"

"What? No. He approached me from behind days after we went back to the mansion. He remembered me. He asked for my name, and everything went from there. Whatever we have going on is new; so, you damn right I lied about where I was! So what!" Kelli defended herself.

"Why not try your luck with Brian? Instead of sending him my way?"

Kelli blinked.

"Yeah. He told me. He told me you that you set the whole thing up. But when I told you about him, you acted interested and pretended not to know who he was."

"I didn't pretend. I just didn't tell you that I knew him."

"It's the same thing! You told him that I was going through something and that I could use someone to help take my mind off things. Or was that your way of hoping I would be too preoccupied with some dick to look into Olivia's death? Huh? What are you hiding?"

"Okay, now you're reaching for something that isn't there, Pep! Yes, I set you up. Yes, I sent Brian your way! I didn't know he was fucking your sister!" Kelli yelled.

"That doesn't matter. What matters is all the secrecy. I never even knew you were in therapy!'

"You need to be in some too! And bitch everybody has issues! I have issues. You damn sure got issues! So what if I want to talk through mine? I don't have to tell you every single detail of my life! That doesn't make me a liar!"

"But lying about being outside that night at the mansion does!"

I might as well tell her everything I know.

"I asked everybody if they saw anything. If they were outside prior to Olivia being found on fire. You, along with everyone else, except for Coco, said no. But I found a piece your bachelorette party pin is the only one missing a piece of ribbon," I told a little white lie. I had no idea if she was the only one missing a ribbon, but I wanted to see how this played out. "I checked yours. Just like I checked everyone else's. I found the ribbon behind the garage. So, tell me, what were you doing outside that night, Kelli?"

"I was with you when Olivia was found," she defended herself.

"True. But at some point, you were outside. And all the way behind the garage. Why? Were you with Carlton?"

Kelli opened her mouth and then clamped it shut.

"Why were you behind the garage?"

"Pepper it's not..."

"Why were you behind the garage?"

"I didn't have anything to do with Olivia's death."

"WHY WERE YOU BEHIND THE GARAGE!"

I screamed at the top of my lungs. I was sure someone was going to hear me, but I didn't care.

Kelli opened her mouth, but still, she didn't answer my question.

"Get the fuck out of my face, Kelli! And until you can tell me what you were doing outside that night, stay the fuck away from me!"

I opened my car door and slammed it closed behind me. She knocked on my window, but instead of rolling it down, I started to beep my horn over and over again, until she got into her car and moved from behind me.

I couldn't believe that Kelli was hiding something from me. She was supposed to be one of my closest friends. If I couldn't trust her, I couldn't trust anyone.

Speeding, I arrived at mama's house about ten minutes faster than I was supposed to. Immediately, I noticed the white pickup truck on the side of the road in front of her house.

Using my key, I assumed she would still be asleep, so I tip-toed inside.

"OH...MY...GOD!"

I dropped my bags at the sight of mama on her knees, doggie-style, with some man's head in her ass.

Literally!

I'll never be able to "un-see" this shit!

I'll never look at sex the same again!

I gagged a little bit in my mouth as mama, and the man scrambled to cover up their old and wrinkled, naked bodies.

Wait a minute, I recognized his face.

"Bill?"

He was the last man I ever remember mama being with.

"Uh, hello, Pepper," His voice was scruffy.

"Mama?"

The living room smelled like *Bengay*, ass and corn chips, so I pinched my nose, and turned my back so that Bill could put on his pants.

"What are you doing here so early, Pepper?"

"Someone is trying to kill me."

"What!"

I probably shouldn't have said that. The way mama screamed; I probably almost gave her a heart attack.

"I mean, someone keeps messing around my house. So, I didn't feel safe anymore. I came to stay here for a little while, but..."

"Gal, I'll smack the hell out of you if you say something like that again and not mean it! And no buts...go on up there to your old bedroom. We'll talk about that...and this a little later."

I didn't even bother to say anything else. I walked up the stairs with my eyes closed, as though I could still see them.

Mama has a man.

That's what she's been hiding. I'm pretty sure on those days she was supposed to be at church, she was with Bill.

I shivered in disgust from the flashback of what I saw them doing.

Seriously...what's the age limit on fucking?

I mean after a certain age, it should be a health risk or something. And old men Bill's age damn sure shouldn't be doing those type of things with his mouth. I would never be able to look at him without wondering if his breath smelled like old people shit.

I felt like I was going to be sick.

I slammed the bedroom door closed behind me and flopped down on the bed.

Just wait until I tell Kelli this shit!

Wait...I forgot.

I'm not speaking to her.

I can't trust her.

Expectedly, I started to mentally replay everything she'd said to me.

Her and Carlton?

For some reason, I was under the impression that he was married. I was almost certain that his parents stated that he had a wife. I sure hope Kelli wasn't fooling around with someone else's husband. No good ever came out of those situations. And I knew that first hand.

In between dealing with Rodney, and before I was set up with Greg, I dealt with a guy named Rodriguez. He was Columbian and Black, and he had this little *swag* to him that I just couldn't get enough of.

Anyway, he was married.

At first, I didn't know. But once I found out, I kept screwing him anyway. I told myself that it was his responsibility to be faithful and committed to his wife.

Not mine.

Boy, did I learn my lesson!

Rodriguez's wife found out who I was and she and all her little friends jumped me. And they got me good too. They broke my wrist and my nose. One of them bitches even hit me in the head with a stick. I fought good and hard, but it was about five or six of them. Once they got me on the ground, I knew it was over for me.

I knew I was getting exactly what I deserved for sleeping with someone else's man. And that ass whooping taught me to never do it again.

Shifting my thoughts, I thought about Kelli's therapy comments. Hell, she was probably right. After all of this, I just might need therapy too. Still, it seemed strange for her not to mention that she was in therapy; especially after I told her about Honey's secret therapy sessions and her affair with Brian. And she damn sure should've mentioned the part about sending Brian in my direction.

But she didn't say a word.

Feeling somewhat safe, I closed my eyes, and just as I started to drool, my phone started to ring. With my eyes still closed, I pressed the button to silence it. It began to ring again. And again.

"Hello?"

"Pepper! Pepper! Somebody broke into the cleaners!" My employee, Jordan, screamed in my ear. My heart dropped into the pit of my belly, and with the phone still on my ear, I was up, down the stairs, out of the house and on the way to the cleaners in less than two minutes.

"When I got here, it was already like this."

The police and Jordan were on the scene.

The dry cleaners was completely destroyed.

The windows and glass door were shattered.

Most of the clothes were cut up and thrown all over the place. The equipment and machines were broken.

Yet, nothing was missing, and they left behind the cash register.

This wasn't a robbery.

No. This was another warning.

"It happened overnight. Probably late night, early morning, while everyone was long gone or at home fast asleep. Your front camera shows nothing, before going completely blank. They came in through the back door. And once they were inside, they disabled the camera equipment."

There are four businesses connected to each other. One long building that used to be owned by the same man. My dry-cleaning business was one of the buildings in the middle. There's no way someone randomly chose to destroy my business and leave the other three businesses untouched.

This was on purpose.

"There's nothing but dumpsters at the back of the building. Late at night, no one would've seen anyone. And as you can see, they came prepared. The glass on the backdoor was broken from the outside. They didn't bother to reach in and unlock the door. They just stepped in through the broken glass. But the windows were broken from the inside."

The cops continued to walk me through the scene, and all I wanted to do was cry. It had taken so much time and money to get this place to where I needed it to be. And now, it would take even more time and money to put it back together again. They asked me a few more questions before I told them I needed to step outside.

I just needed to breathe.

Whoever rang my doorbell this morning probably did this too; before coming to my house.

"Pepper! What happened?"

I looked up.

It was Coco.

At this time, it was about nine in the morning. Coco was fully dressed, wearing a blue and green summer dress. Her belly wasn't showing, but her chocolate skin was glowing.

"Someone broke in last night."

"Oh no! I'm so sorry, Pep! Did they take anything?"

"That's the thing. They took nothing but destroyed everything."

Coco shook her head. I stared at her.

The guilty always came back to the scene; at least that's what *they* said.

"What are you doing on this side of town this morning?"

"Well, I don't know if you've heard the news or not, but I'm pregnant!"

"I heard. Congratulations, Coco."

"Thank you. Anyway, all night I was craving one of those strawberry Danish things from the deli. As soon as I woke up this morning, I told Troy that I was going to get breakfast. I didn't care that I had to drive twenty-minutes. I want what I want! And then when I pulled up, I saw the police over here and realized that they were inside of the cleaners. So, I came to check on you. The last time I saw this many police lights..." Coco stopped. I'm sure she was referring to Olivia's *murder* scene.

Wow. I said murder. And I meant it.

Olivia was murdered. And I was sure of it.

More and more each day.

"Anyway. I just wanted to make sure that you were okay. I'm so sorry this happened. I hope they catch the bastard that did this," Coco touched her stomach. "Whoo, I better eat something. I'm gonna' go and get breakfast, and I'll come right back. Do you want something?"

"A coffee. Please."

"Oh, how I miss coffee. I've been trying not to drink it since finding out the news. One coffee, coming right up."

Coco smiled and headed back across the street.

I turned to face the cleaners.

Maybe I was getting too close to the truth. I could feel it. And the truth is that someone killed Olivia.

Maybe I'd asked the wrong question...or the right one.

I'd asked a question that made someone worry. One that made them dangerous. One that made them want to scare me.

It was someone I knew.

Someone I'd questioned or spoken to.

It had to be.

And they were trying to get me to back off.

For months, I'd come to terms that I was surrounded by a pool of liars, but now I had an even bigger concern.

In the deepest part of my heart, I knew that a killer was amongst us too.

~***~

"We heard about what happened to the cleaners. We went by your house and then stopped by Kelli's. She told us you were at your mama's house."

I haven't spoken to Kelli since she refused to tell me what she was hiding, so I figured that Coco told her about the cleaners and that I was staying at mama's.

Crystal and Jai both stared at me.

Their parents' house was a few houses down the street. We all practically grew up like sisters. We had some great times together, but these days, they were nothing more than distant memories.

Jai's vibe, was stand-offish, as usual, especially lately. And Crystal was all over the place like she'd taken a few shots of adrenalin; either that or high on laced crack.

"Do they know who messed it up like that? I rode by there, and it looks bad! Like, why would someone want to do that? What did you do?" Crystal asked.

"I didn't do anything."

"Well, you've pissed off somebody. That's for sure."

Crystal scratched her nose, bringing attention to the ring on her finger.

"I heard that Haji said you dumped him. That you two weren't getting married. Is that true?"

Crystal immediately frowned. Jai looked at her sister.

"Who said that? Who told you he said that?"

"That's just what I heard."

"Well, you heard a lie! I am getting married. I already have *the* dress. The cake. The flowers and all! I am definitely getting married!"

"Okay, okay, okay. Damn."

Jai shook her head.

Crystal rolled her eyes and looked down at her phone. "Speaking of wedding, I have an appointment. I gotta' go."

Crystal turned to leave.

"Jai, I need to talk to you about something," I blurted out, once she turned to walk away too.

Crystal said goodbye and walked down the street in a hurry, towards her parent's house.

Jai and I took a seat on the front porch.

"What's up?"

"Well..."

I wanted to know if what Greg told me about them was true. I wanted to know how mad she was about the situation and at Olivia for demanding her to get an abortion. I wanted to see if she'd been mad enough to kill her.

"Greg told me about that night."

"What night?" Jai pretended to be clueless.

"The uh, the threesome."

Once she realized that I actually knew something, she exhaled.

"He told you?"

"He told me everything."

"It was Olivia's idea. I was drunk. I mean, I was super-duper drunk. I would've never agreed to do something like that. And most definitely not with one of my friends and her man."

"You were too drunk to say no?"

"Honestly, yes. It was like I knew what I was doing. But in a way...I didn't. And I feel like..."

"You feel like what?"

"I feel like Olivia planned to get me super drunk and take me home with her all along."

Jai was definitely sexually attractive.

She oozed with sex appeal. She was sexy even when she wasn't trying to be. Big wide hips, with a big round ass. Jai had a small waist and a flat stomach, despite having three kids. And she had a nice set of boobs too. They were the perfect size. And they always have been.

"All night, she gave me drink after drink, and she kept slapping my ass. I don't know, maybe I'm overthinking it. I just never expected to do something like that."

"And Greg..."

"He didn't seem to want to do it either. It was all Olivia. It was like she barely wanted him to touch her. She wanted to watch him touch me."

"And you got pregnant?"

Jai looked at me as if she was shocked that Greg mentioned that part.

"Yes. I got pregnant. And that's when everything changed between Olivia and me."

The tone and her voice changed too.

"She didn't want me to have a baby by her man. But she'd wanted me to sleep with him. I told her that I would have the baby and take care of it by myself. But Olivia wasn't having that. She stayed on my case about having an abortion, even though I told her I didn't want one. I don't believe in abortions. I never have. And I never will."

"But you had one anyway?"

"Who told you that?"

"Greg. He said Olivia went with you to the clinic."

"That's what Olivia told him. And I guess that's the story he decided to tell you. I guess to spare your feelings about your sister. But the other day, I went to his house, and I told him the truth. I told him what Olivia did to me."

"What? What did she do?"

"That bitch...she made me lose the baby."

I was so confused.

"How?"

"She came over to my house. She offered to take me to the clinic. I told her that I wasn't going. She and I started to argue with each other. She said the threesome was a mistake and that we never should've gone that far. I agreed. But I told her I still wasn't getting an abortion. I'll admit, I got handsy first. Olivia jumped in my face, calling me a bad friend, bitches, and everything else. She told me that I was going to ruin her life and her relationship. She blurted out that she and Greg had decided to get married, and they wanted to start a family of their own. Still, I told her that I wasn't killing *my* baby. Olivia screamed and yelled in my face, and I got agitated. She was so close that spit was flying all over my face, and in the heat of the moment, I pushed her. So, she pushed me back. She pushed me, hard, causing me to trip over one of my kid's shoes, and I fell. I fell hard on my back. Olivia tried to help me up, but I swatted her away. Almost instantly, I started having back pains. I had a miscarriage later on that night. I lost the baby."

"Jai..."

"I know what you're going to say, but to me, it was her fault. And I hated her for it. I told her that I never wanted to speak to her again after I left the hospital. She told me that she wasn't going anywhere. She kept saying that no matter what, we were friends. We had a misunderstanding, and something unfortunate happened. She said there was no point in throwing away years of friendship behind it. She kept calling me, trying to force me to get over it, but I never did. I was angry with her up until the day she died. That's why I backed out of being a bridesmaid in her wedding. I didn't want to be a part of her day. I didn't want to be around her, and I didn't want to be at the bachelorette party either. I was planning not to come, but Crystal showed up, wanting to catch a ride with me. No one knew what Olivia and I were going through. Or what space we were in. It's sad to say that I never forgave her. And if she was alive, still, I don't think I ever would."

Jai exhaled, but I had to ask.

"Did you kill her? Did you set Olivia on fire?"

She looked at me. "No. But...I lied."

Here we go.

My breathing started to speed up as I waited for her next words.

"I was on my phone that night, watching videos and on social media. Again, I didn't want to be there. I didn't want to drink or even participate in the games. I was only there to let Crystal enjoy herself and to be her ride the next day. What I didn't mention was that I was sitting in one of the chairs next to the back window. When the cops asked me what I saw, and when you asked me what I saw…I lied. I said I didn't see anything before going outside. But I did."

I jumped to my feet.

"I saw Olivia on fire *before* Coco came inside to tell us. I was looking down at my phone, and I don't know. Maybe I can call it a glare, or maybe I should say out of my peripheral vision, I saw the flames. And so, I looked up and saw Olivia on fire; spinning around. I didn't see how the fire started, but I did see Coco running towards her. And then I saw her turn around and come back towards the house and…and…I just sat there."

What!

I wanted to smack the shit out of Jai!

I couldn't believe this shit!

"To be honest, I was partly in shock. I really was. It wasn't until Olivia fell to the ground that I realized what I'd just witnessed. I was mad at her, but I didn't want her to die. I remember seeing Kelli appear in the backyard. Remember, she's the one who answered Coco's scream. At least that's what she said. Honestly, although I was watching, I didn't hear the screams. I didn't hear anything. It was like I was under water for a few minutes or something. I couldn't hear anything. I didn't see anything or anyone around me. All I could do was stare outside at the flames. And then suddenly, out of nowhere, my hearing came back, and I heard Coco's announcement. Only then was I able to move. I was able to run outside to see about Olivia, just like everyone else."

Tears were streaming down my face. "You could've tried to help her! You could've told all of us what was going on, and we could've tried to save her!"

Jai sat emotionless. "I wanted to. I really believe in my heart that I wanted to. I was stuck. If I hadn't been so angry at her, I'm sure my first instinct would've been to help her. But for whatever reason, that wasn't my first instinct.

Anger had me frozen. Anger crippled me, and I ended up watching my "friend" die because of it."

Jai stood up.

"If someone else was out there, other than Olivia, Coco, or for a short moment, Kelli, then I didn't see them. If someone did that to her, as you seem to think they did, I swear I didn't see anyone. I swear I would've told you something like that. And whether you believe me or not, that's the truth. When I looked up, Olivia was already on fire."

Jai started to walk down the porch steps, as I tried to sort out my feelings about her.

"I told Greg everything I just told you when I stopped by his house. I told him about the miscarriage and about what I saw at the bachelorette party."

"Really? He didn't mention any of this."

Jai shrugged.

"He did mention that you tried to sleep with him and asked him to get you pregnant again."

"No. I didn't."

"You didn't? That's what he told me."

Jai looked me in the eyes. "Well…he lied."

~***~

"So, you and Bill?"

Mama sat down on the couch in front of me.

"We've been married for the past five years."

"Married!" I screamed at mama.

"Yes."

"Mama, why didn't you tell us?"

"It never seemed like the right time. When I left Bill all of those years ago, I dedicated my life to raising you girls the right way. I did that. Almost six years ago, we ran into each other. He was in town visiting his sister. We hadn't crossed paths in years because he'd moved to a different city. At the time, he was busy. He was the City Councilman, over in Mebane. When he saw me, he asked if he could take me to dinner. Dinner went well. And well, a few months later, he asked me to marry him."

I could tell that mama was relieved to finally be telling her truth.

"I told him that I wanted to find the right time to tell my girls. It never seemed like the right time."

"In five years? You couldn't tell us that you were married in five years?"

"After the first few years, I stopped trying to tell you. He just became my other life. He had his life as City Councilman, and I had all of you. And when we were together, we had each other. The older you get, the more important your own space becomes. It didn't bother either of us that we didn't live together. We just got used to a system. I would mostly go to him. And then, I would come back home."

"Ma, I just can't believe you're married."

"Remember that trip to Vegas? I told you girls that I was going with some ladies from the church. I was with Bill. We tied the knot in Vegas."

"Ma, church ladies ain't supposed to lie!"

"I know."

"Well, are you happy with him?"

"Very. Bill's reign as councilman came to an end, a while back, and I've needed to lean on him, a lot since Olivia died. He's been there for me to talk to and to hold me. He helped me through it. I wouldn't allow him to come to Olivia's memorial service because I hadn't told you or Honey. But Olivia knew about us."

"What? She knew? That you were married to Bill?"

"Not that we were married. But she caught us, once, a few weeks before she died. She came by here one-day, early morning, just as Bill was leaving. I didn't tell her that we were married, but I told her that he was my *old man*. I asked her not to tell you or Honey. I told her I was going to have a talk with all of you after her wedding."

I could tell that mama was trying to read my thoughts.

"I'm happy for you mama. If he makes you happy, then I'm happy."

"Thank you."

"I don't remember much about him. And what I do remember is that you were always fussing about him not coming home."

"Well, he used to drink back then. And if I'm being honest, baby, Bill was a *hoe*."

Mama chuckled as I gasped.

Hearing her say "hoe" cracked me up and for about two minutes, I couldn't stop laughing.

"What's so funny? That's how y'all say it these days, right? Not a whore. But a *hoe*? Chile, he was all that and then some. But time heals all wounds and age changes every man. And woman. He's better now," mama was beaming. "Well, I guess I'll tell your sister soon. Probably at Sunday dinner. That's if she comes. With her marriage in shambles, I'm not sure how she will feel about my news."

"Joe still hasn't come back home?"

"No. And honestly, I don't think he will come back. The affair was one thing. But another man's baby. That's a lot more difficult for a man to process."

"I'm sure it is."

"So, did they find anything out about who broke into your store?"

"No."

"And you think it has something to do with Olivia's death?"

"Ma, I've found out so many things. I've caught so many people in lies. And then all of a sudden, someone leaves a book of matches on my doorstep. The same matches that were found at the scene. That can't be a coincidence. And then they left a photo…"

"Yeah, you never told me about the photo. What was it of?"

I thought about lying to her, but I was so sick of lies at this point.

"It was of Greg and me. One night, I was all in my emotions…and I kissed him."

"Kissed him!" Mama's eyes almost popped out of her head.

"Yes. I kissed him. I don't know what I was thinking."

Mama didn't say anything. She just grinned at me.

"Apparently, someone was watching us, and they took a photo of the kiss. And then they printed it out and left the picture on my front porch."

"Baby, maybe you should call the police. I will not bury another daughter."

I continued to fill mama in. I told her about the ribbon I found at the scene; and the missing ribbon from Kelli's party pin. I told her about Kelli and Carlton. The cop pretending to be a bartender. Coco lying about what she was doing outside. Jai seeing Olivia on fire from the window and doing nothing. I left out the threesome and the baby part of the story. Mainly due to me wanting to talk to Greg again. I also didn't tell her about the strange text message on Greg's cell phone. But I did tell her that Crystal was trying to get with Greg, pretending to be Olivia, and lying about getting married.

Mama was just as confused as I was.

"You just gave me a headache," she said.

"Imagine how I've been feeling these past few months.

Mama shook her head. "Trust is a tricky thing. If you can't trust the people you love…then who can you trust?"

"Nobody," I answered her. "These days, you can't trust anyone."

"Now, there just may be some truth to that."

Once I was done talking to mama, I headed towards Greg's. It was Friday evening, and he should've been home from work by now. I didn't bother calling him before I went by.

And I'm glad that I didn't.

If I had, I'm sure the woman that was walking out of his house would've been gone by then.

Pulling into his driveway, immediately, I got out of the car. The woman looked at me and proceeded to walk towards her car that was parked on the side of the road.

I remember her.

And her car.

She was the woman that was sitting across the street from the church at Olivia's memorial service.

Greg stood on his front porch.

Both of us, watched her until she drove away.

"Who was that?"

Greg turned around and walked into his house.

I followed him.

"Who was that?"

Greg finally faced me.

"Who was that, Greg?"

"You want a drink?"

"No. I want to know who that was."

Greg walked over to the bar in his kitchen, grabbed a glass, and filled it up with vodka.

"Greg!"

"My wife. She was my wife."

What the hell did he just say?

"I married her in college. We met in high school. We didn't work out. After college, we went our separate ways. When I met you, remember I told you I was..."

"Divorced."

"Only, I wasn't. We were legally separated. And we had been for years. But my ex started traveling all over the world, as a flight attendant, and it was always hard to get in touch with her to get the divorce process going. So, for years, I just didn't worry about it. Olivia made it clear that she wasn't in a rush to get married. So, I would lay off on doing what needed to be done. And then, if Olivia and I happened to discuss marriage, I might try to reach out to my ex again, but it just never got done. Then, when Olivia told me that she was ready I knew I had to find her. I had to get a divorce, in order to marry Olivia. Finally, I got in contact with my ex, Shannon, that's her name, and she was being a bitch about the whole thing. She made the process more difficult than it had to be. But finally, we met with the lawyers and got the paperwork done; only I was cutting it close. The divorce wasn't final yet, and Olivia and I were scheduled to be married in only a few short weeks. Olivia was all over me about applying for the marriage license, and I kept giving her excuses because I knew that legally, I was still married to someone else. But my lawyer knew someone, who knew someone else, and for a not-so-small fee, they could speed up the process. I didn't care what I had to pay, I just didn't want Olivia to find out that I'd been married the whole time. And then, on the night of my bachelor party, a week or so before the wedding, I got confirmation that everything was done."

It's done.

The text message.

Is that what it was about?

"We were in the clear, and we could go Monday morning to get the marriage license. But...well...we never made it there."

Greg took a sip of his drink.

"Her coming by here was a total surprise. I didn't even know that she knew where I lived. She said she was just passing through here for a few days, before leaving back out from the airport in Raleigh. We reminisced about college days and about the time we spent together, but that's it."

Greg's phone was ringing off the hook. He glanced at it and rolled his eyes.

"Crystal."

"She's still reaching out to you?"

"She believes that Olivia would want us to be together."

"She's delusional. But speaking of Crystal, I spoke to Jai. I asked her about the threesome…"

"And the baby?"

"And the baby. Why did you lie to me? She told me that you knew she had a miscarriage, as a result of Olivia pushing her down."

"I don't know. Saying that they went to the clinic, sounded a lot better than the truth. I didn't want to say Jai had a miscarriage because of Olivia and because she pushed her down. Hell, I'd just been confronted by Deb about it too and…"

"Deb?"

"Yeah. Jai told her everything, apparently."

That's why Deb knew Greg wouldn't want Crystal. Because she knew he'd had a threesome with her sister. That's the secret she refused to share that night.

"She said that I should've been ashamed of myself for letting Olivia talk me into sleeping with Jai. She said I messed up their friendship. And that I should've been man enough to tell Olivia no. She's right."

At the conclusion of his statement, we heard the shattering of a windshield.

Both of us hurried towards the front door.

Crystal.

I had to blink twice before I could believe my eyes.

Crystal was standing there---in the wedding dress that was supposed to be Olivia's.

She was holding a crowbar in one hand and a bouquet of flowers in the other.

She had a short veil covering her face as she leaned up against Greg's car.

"Greg, it's our big day!"

Sadness tugged at my heart. It was painful to see Crystal acting this way. It was scary to see her being so crazy.

"Crystal, what are you doing?" I asked her.

"I came to get my husband."

"Crystal, Greg is not your husband."

"Not yet. But he's going to be."

Crystal inched towards the porch.

"I know you love him, but he's mine. Olivia would want me to have him!"

"Love him?"

"Oh, don't try to play me for a fool. I saw the two of you kissing. I took a picture."

"You left the picture on my front porch? It was you."

"Yep."

"And you left the matches too?"

"What matches?" Crystal asked. She shook her head. "I don't know anything about matches. I'm talking about you. You want him. I know you do. But I was her best friend. We shared everything. She would want me to make him happy. I know what he likes. Olivia told me everything about him. Come on, Greg. Let me make you happy."

Greg didn't say anything.

"Greg!"

"Crystal…you need help. You are not Olivia. And you never will be."

"Greg! We have a wedding to get to. The preacher is waiting!"

"You're not Olivia," I repeated to Crystal. "You're not Olivia."

"I know that, Pepper!" Crystal screamed. "I know that!"

She dropped her bouquet and placed her hand on her head. "I know that. I know I'm not Olivia. I know that. Olivia was my friend. She was my friend. She was my friend."

I started to cry so hard that I was sure I could be heard a mile away.

Grieving was different for everyone, but watching Crystal just broke my heart.

Greg rushed past me.

He walked towards Crystal.

She stared at him, as he removed the crowbar from her hands. And then, he pulled her close to him.

He held her and immediately, Crystal broke down.

She cried so loud that Greg's neighbors started to come outside.

"I miss her so much," Crystal sobbed. "I just miss her so much."

I couldn't move. All I could do was stand there and wipe my own tears.

"I don't know how to be here without her. It's not that I'm trying to be her. I'm just trying to keep her alive." Crystal explained herself,

And then suddenly, she pulled back from Greg and took the veil off her head. She found my eyes and looked directly into them.

"I saw Kelli, and the bartender go outside," she said.
Huh?

"I asked her about it, a long while ago. The bartender reached me the tray of Jell-O shots. Before drinking my first one, I went to the bathroom. I think two of those strippers from the party went in there after me. Anyway, as I made my way back to the bar, I noticed Kelli and the bartender going out the front door. They weren't out there long though. I'd only downed three Jell-O shots before they both came back in. He came back to his spot behind the bar, and she went over there to you. It was a good while before the fire, so I didn't think it was important. And when I asked Kelli about it, she said that it was a coincidence and that he'd stepped outside to get some fresh air the same time as she did."

That must've been when Kelli ended up behind the garage. She was with the bartender. And he was a cop.

Is she the "her" that he told me to ask?

"I didn't think anything of it until a few days ago, she called to ask me if I told you about her going outside that night. I told her no. And then I asked her why it was a big deal. She said that it wasn't, but she also asked me not to mention it. I'm sorry I lied to you before. I'm sorry I told you I didn't remember anything else. I guess, I didn't think it was important, but to Kelli, obviously, it is."

It may not have been important to Crystal.

But it was damn sure important to me!

And though she was in the house, right beside me, when Olivia was burning alive, something told me that there was something more to see.

Hmm...did you have my sister killed, Kelli?

****

CHAPTER SEVEN

Honey's family came inside.

"Good to see you, Joe," Mama smiled in surprise.

He kissed her cheek.

"Where's Honey?"

"She stopped to sit on the front porch."

We were at Mama's house for Sunday dinner. And she was going to tell Honey the news about her husband today.

I went outside to find Honey.

I couldn't explain it, but on the inside, I felt empty.

I felt drained.

These past few months had left me more confused, hurt, and drained than I'd ever been before.

It was sickening to think that someone in my inner circle could have either orchestrated, planned, or even executed something so vile as to killing someone we all loved. But that was looking more and more like the case, each and every day.

"Hey, sister."

"Hey, sister."

Honey's stomach was about to pop.

She had to be about due now. She didn't want a baby shower. Since Olivia left her all that money, she decided to buy everything herself. And though I'd finally cashed my insurance checks, I still hadn't touched or spent a dime.

"I'm so ready to have this baby."

"I'm glad Joe came back. I'm glad he will be there to help."

"And so will Brian."

I looked surprised.

"Joe said he wasn't keeping another man away from his child. So, we had this big, long talk about us and about everything. And then we had a talk with Brian. That talk didn't go so well…since Joe reported Brian for having *relations* with one of his clients."

"No, he didn't, girl."

"Yes, he did. For now, Brian is suspended, pending investigation. But there's no way around it. Not with a baby coming. He's going to lose his job. And possibly not be able to do what he loves, ever again. All because of me."

"No. It's because of himself. Brian is a grown ass man! He made a choice to sleep with you; whether he knew the whole truth about you or not. What he did know is that you were one of his clients. Someone he was in charge of helping to heal. He wasn't supposed to be screwing you. That's on him. Not you."

Honey was quiet for a while. "They both were so upset, but by the end of the conversation, Brian wants to be a father to the baby and Joe said that he wouldn't have it any other way. He still wants to be with me, Pep. I don't know why, but he does."

"Because you're freaking awesome! That's why. And like I told you…don't nobody want Joe."

Joe was only fifty, but to me, he looked about sixty-five. He looked like somebody's grandpa.

Honey smiled at me. "I had to tell him everything. I had to tell him some of my past issues too and some of my secrets. I had to tell him why I was going to therapy."

I didn't bother asking her why she was going to therapy again, because every time I asked her that question, she ignored me. But to my surprise, she kept talking, and she said:

"Pepper…I was molested when I was younger. A few times. And somehow, I forgot about it. It's like I blocked it out. And then one day, Neela came home after a sleepover and told me that her friend's brother touched her inappropriately. And right then and there, it all came rushing back to me."

"Honey! Oh, my God!"

Neela was Honey's daughter and my ten-year-old niece.

"Why didn't you tell me! About Neela? About you?"

"It was about a year and a half ago. Joe and I went to Neela's friend's house. The brother denied touching Neela inappropriately. He was about thirteen at the time. He says that he was playing with all of the girls, chasing them around, but Neela says that he touched her vagina, and tried to get her to touch his penis. I believe her. His parents believed him."

"I'm your sister! You should've told me!"

"I didn't want Neela to feel overwhelmed. Joe and I told her that we believed her, and we told her that it was wrong. Though their son continued to deny it, they told us that they were going to put him in therapy. That's where I got the idea that I might need to go to therapy. I was just a child when *someone* took advantage of me too."

I touched Honey's hand.

"What are sisters for, if you don't tell them stuff like this? Like what happened to you?"

"I was scared at the time. I didn't want to tell anyone. I didn't know what to say. At first, I'm not sure I knew it was wrong; especially the touching part. But when he started doing other things, like holding me down and..." Honey inhaled and exhaled. "Neela's situation caused me to feel so much anxiety. The memories became too much for me to handle some days. I knew then that I had to talk to someone. I had to deal with what happened to me. I had to tell someone, talk to someone, because it affected me more than I could've ever imagined. So, I started going to therapy. Joe had no idea that he'd married damaged goods."

"You are not damaged goods! You were a child!"

My blood was boiling.

"Yeah, well. Brian did help me in that area. He helped me see that it wasn't my fault. He helped me to forgive someone who took something from me. My innocence. My voice. Ooohhh…" Honey hissed. "Ooooh!" She hissed again.

"What? What is it?"

Honey continued to grunt.

"Joe! Joe!"

Joe and mama both came running.

"What is it, Honey? What is it?" He asked her.

"I think it's time!" Honey frowned as Joe helped her to her feet and liquid splattered against the porch from underneath her dress. Mama clapped her hands in excitement.

Just then, mama's surprised pulled into the driveway.

Joe helped Honey down the steps as mama smiled at Bill.

"Well, I guess there's no time like the present. Bill come here," Mama yelled at him. He headed in our direction. "Bill…Honey is in labor! Honey…do you remember Bill? We're married!" Mama screamed.

But Honey wasn't paying mama any attention.

So, Mama tried to tell Honey her news again, but Honey's screams interrupted her.

"Ahhhhhhhh! Ahhhhhhh!" Was all Honey said.

The baby is coming!

But her last words were still stuck in my head.

~***~

"Hey, mama," I said to her.

Honey and the baby were resting comfortably at the hospital. Mama left shortly after the baby's birth. She was supposed to be going to Honey's to get the baby items, but I found her at home.

"Are you okay?"

"Yes, baby, I'm fine. I just came home to sit for a while. I don't know why, but the birth made me think about…"

"Olivia?"

"Yes. And the fact that Honey is naming the baby after her. It just stirs up those feelings. But I'll be okay. How are you?"

"I'm fine. Honey told me something. She told me why she was going to therapy."

"Was it the incident with Neela?"

"She told you about that?"

"Of course. But she asked me not to tell her sisters."

Her statement caused me to stop and wonder if Honey told her about being molested.

"Is that why she was going to therapy?" Mama asked.

She doesn't know.

She doesn't know Honey's secret.

And it wasn't my place to tell her.

So, I lied.

"Yes. I guess that and other personal issues with herself."

"I just want my babies to be okay," Mama said. "You and Honey. And my grandbabies. I just want all of you to be okay."

"We're okay, mama. You don't have to worry. You worry about that man of yours," I smiled. "Excuse me, your husband. Where is Bill?"

"He's at home. Now, since I've told you two, we're trying to figure out if we should finally move in together. I don't know if he'll move here or if he will want me to move there."

"Mebane isn't that far away. I think you should. Really, I think you should move. You've been here since we were kids. You raised us. Now it's your turn to live."

"Oh, but Honey just had the baby and…"

"And she has a husband…and a baby's daddy that can help her with the new baby. And not to mention, she has me and all of our friends. Honey will be just fine. You go and just focus on you and your happiness for a change."

Mama smiled at me as she stood up.

"I love you baby girl," she said as she grabbed her purse and headed for the front door.

"I love you too, ma," I shouted behind her.

As soon as the door closed, I started to whimper.

This was the first time I was able to process what Honey told me. She went into labor on the front porch, and then she was in labor for thirty-eight hours with my new niece, so now, I could finally release.

I was always protecting Honey and Olivia, for as long as I could remember.

Where was I when she was getting molested?

I thought we told each other everything.

How could she keep something like being molested from me? From her sisters?

Who touched her?

And where I was?

I wondered how old Honey was when *it* happened to her. Maybe that's why she was the way that she was growing up. So quiet and sensitive. So passive and easy to get over on or take advantage of.

My heart was hurting.

I was so full of sorrow. Pain, worry, and anxiety.

I just needed a friend.

Continuing to weep, I pressed on Greg's name.

Though things were still weird and maybe even a little uncomfortable between us, if no one else, I knew that he would be there for me. And I needed someone. Someone to hold me. Someone to tell me that everything was going to be okay, even if it was a lie. Even if nothing would ever be okay again, I just needed to hear the words.

After telling Greg how I was feeling and what I needed, he was at mama's house in less than ten minutes.

"Everything is going to be okay," Greg said as I laid my head on his chest.

"No. It's not. Everything is broken. Everyone is broken. Nothing will ever be okay again. Nothing will ever be the same." I took a deep breath, and then I told Greg everything. I told him about Honey and made him promise to never tell a soul. I told him about the lies that everyone had told. I told him about the things that seemed suspicious, and the questionable things that had been happening to me. I told him about the *not-so-gay* bartender and about what was going on with Kelli. I told him why I thought she was hiding something and how disturbed I was by her secrecy. Literally, for almost an hour, I told Greg everything that I'd come across since trying to find out the truth about Olivia's death.

"And through all of that, I still don't know what really happened to her. All I know is what I've felt from the very beginning...her death wasn't an accident. I just know it wasn't. Someone did that to her. If it was just an accident, then why would someone leave the book of matches on my front porch? Or break into my cleaners, destroy it, and not take anything? We know that Crystal left the photo, but she wasn't responsible for the other things. And I know in my heart that it has something to do with me getting too close to the truth. Someone is worried about what I'll find out if I keep looking. If I keep asking questions."

"I'll have my inside source check on the cop that was pretending to be the bartender. I'll see if they can find out why he decided to play bartender that night and if he and Kelli have any connections. I believe you. If you believe something isn't right about Olivia's death, then I believe you."

Greg placed his hand underneath my chin and lifted my head. "Everything is going to be okay. You hear me?"

Tears timidly rolled down my face.

I was just so overwhelmed.

Suddenly, Greg leaned in close and kissed my cheek. And then from cheek to cheek, he kissed my tears, and then he pressed his nose up against mine.

We were both breathing so hard.

Heavy.

My good angel on my left shoulder started to speak to me.

This is too close. This is so wrong. On so many levels.

Greg had been engaged to my sister. He was going to marry her. They were in love.

And furthermore, he is my friend.

"Greg?" I whispered.

He didn't reply. He just stared deep into my eyes.

Now, my bad angel, on my right shoulder, was starting to speak up, and as much as I was trying not to listen, I couldn't seem to get the thoughts out of my head.

Olivia is gone.

She's dead.

Greg is here.

Right here.

And I need him.

I---I---I want him.

I want him?

Uh oh!

There it is!

I admitted it.

I want Greg...well, at least at the moment I do.

"Greg."

Still, he didn't respond. Instead, this time, he kissed my lips. And then he kissed them again. And again. Until finally, my lips kissed him back.

I tried to stop myself, but I couldn't.

For the life of me, as wrong as I felt deep down inside, and as much as my heart told me that this was the lowest of the low, I just couldn't pull away from him. Thoughts of Olivia somewhat suffocated me, and not to mention, the fact that he'd slept with Jai crossed my mind.

But none of it was enough.

None of it stopped me.

Greg kissed me, passionately, and it was as though my entire body wanted to submit to him. My body temperature started to rise, and there was so much chemistry, and desire in the room that I could barely breathe. It made the space feel so small. As though there was no escape. As though I didn't have a choice but to let Greg take me and have his way with me.

And so I did.

Greg had me out of every single piece of clothing in less than a minute. He eyed my naked frame, greedily. And once he undressed, I eyed his too.

I touched his visible abs, with tears still streaming down my face. I was convicted and confused, but it didn't stop me from opening my legs and welcoming him inside of me.

Greg looked into my eyes. He connected with me. He wanted me to see how much he wanted me.

He leaned in to kiss me as he pushed his *meat* deep inside me.

"Ahhh," as if it was a movie, I moaned at the exact same times as the thunder clapped outside.

Greg closed his eyes and moaned my name. As I waited for him to look at me again.

He did.

And right there, in mama's living room, on the same couch where I shared so many memories and conversations with my sister; I made love to the man of her dreams.

And suddenly I realized...

Greg was the man of my dreams too.

And I think he always has been.

~***~

"Hi, baby Olivia," I whispered.

Every time I said her name nowadays, I felt guilty.

Neither Greg nor I, knew what to say once we finished making love. That's exactly what we'd done. It'd been more than just sex. For him and for me; although I hated to admit it.

I asked him to leave as soon as we finished, and I haven't spoken to him since.

I realized that the older I became, with him around me as my friend, I was always looking for someone who was just like him. Or at least had most of the qualities that he possessed. I never considered myself to be jealous of what he and Olivia shared. But maybe a part of me regretted giving him to her, and I just refused to acknowledge it because I loved her. Or perhaps I didn't realize it until now.

"A penny for your thoughts?" Honey asked.

"Nothing. Just thinking. Baby Olivia looks just like Brian."

"A spitting image. She looks nothing like the other kids."

"And Joe…"

"Joe is amazing. He's been a lot more helpful than I thought he was going to be. He's acting as though she's his own. And watching him, with her, makes me love him even more. And it makes me so disappointed in myself for sleeping with Brian in the first place."

"I think everything is going to be okay. And God gave us another Olivia to love. So, that makes everything even better."

"That he did."

I placed the baby down in the bassinette.

"So, what do you think of mama being married, for five years? And now that she told us, can't you see how happy she is? Did she tell you she was thinking about moving?"

"Yes. She told me."

"And?"

"And they can stay in her house. Why she gotta' be the one to go?"

"Honey, if it makes her happy…"

"Yeah. Yeah. Yeah."

After sitting and talking with Honey for a little bit longer, she decided that she needed to nap while the baby was sleeping, so I told her that I would come back to visit her tomorrow.

In complete silence, I drove towards home.

I didn't plan on staying there, but I wanted to ride by just to make sure everything was intact and plus I needed to get more clothes.

There I was, lost inside of my own head when the flashing blue lights caused me to slam on my brakes.

They were at Kelli's house.

I couldn't get out of my car fast enough.

Running towards the yellow police tape, the officer grabbed me.

"What happened! What happened!"

Three black body bags were on the front lawn.

It was a cool and breezy day of Fall, but I was sweating as though it was a hundred degrees outside.

"Kelli! Kelli! Kelli!!!"

"Ma'am, please. Please!"

The officer let go of me and stood in front of me.

Placing my hands on my head, I questioned a bystander.

"What happened? Do you know what happened?"

"A wife shot her husband and his mistress. And then she turned the gun on herself."

No!

"No!" It wasn't until that moment that I noticed Carlton's truck.

I knew he was married!

Kelli!

Dropping to my knees, I felt as though I was about to lose my mind.

First, Olivia; and now Kelli.

Now, what I was mad about seemed so small.

She's gone.

My *best friend* is dead.

And she died with her secret too.

Before she could tell me her truth.

Bawling uncontrollably, I called all of our friends.

One by one, they arrived. And side by side, we all went through the pain together, again. Our bond of sisterhood had been broken again.

"You can't sleep either?"

I shook my head.

Deb sat down beside me on my front porch.

Deb, Crystal, Jai and her kids, Shakira and Brenda, were all sleeping over at my house. Coco had come by, but the pastor told her she couldn't stay and to come home.

"It's been a terrible year."

"Tell me about it."

"Did you know about her and Carlton?"

"Kind of. I spotted them together, so she didn't have a choice but to tell me."

"Oh."

We found out that Carlton was actually divorcing his wife. They'd already started the process before he and Kelli hooked up. Apparently, his wife still wanted to be with him. She wanted him back. She still loved him. She saw Carlton and Kelli together and followed him to Kelli's house. She approached them. She blamed Kelli for Carlton not wanting to work on their marriage. A witness said that his wife told Kelli that before he started seeing her, they were trying to work things out and things seemed to be getting better until she came into the picture.

Carlton told his soon-to-be ex-wife that he really liked Kelli and that he was going through with the divorce.

His wife made sure that he didn't.

If she couldn't have him, then Kelli couldn't have him either.

She shot both of them and then she turned the gun on herself.

"I still can't believe this happened. I still can't believe Kelli is dead."

"At least we know exactly what happened to her. And we don't have to wonder about it. We don't have to wonder about her death like we wonder about Olivia's."

I was mad at Kelli before she died, but I still loved her. I just wanted her to tell me what she was hiding.

"I drove by the dry cleaners. What are you going to do?"

"I don't know. With everything going on, I haven't really thought about it."

My business was still closed and boarded up.

I'd had the damages accessed.

$43,000.

Plus I had given refunds and damage costs back to customers. And though I had the money to get the cleaners up and running again, I wasn't sure that I wanted to.

"Greg told me you ripped him a new asshole…about the threesome," I changed the subject.

"Oh. So, he told you?"

"Yeah. He told me."

"That was a mess! We all know how sexual and adventurous Olivia was, but that's one situation Greg should've put his foot down and been man enough to tell her no. That threesome messed up their friendship. Big time. And then the miscarriage incident. It was going to take Jai a mighty long time to forgive Olivia. Especially after the doctors told her that most likely she wouldn't be able to carry a baby to term again. She already has three, but still. If she wanted another one, chances are she would have another miscarriage."

"Really? Jai didn't tell me that part."

"That's what she told me. And she hated Olivia for it too."

"Hated her enough to kill her?"

Deb looked at me. "Probably. But of course, she didn't."

"How can we be sure?"

"Because Olivia was *our* sister. Yes, we fight. And we argue. Some days we may even hate each other. And then the next day, we love each other again. But at the end of the day, all of us, have always been sisters. We're like family. And "family" just wouldn't do something like that; especially not like that. Do you know how heartless you have to be, or how hateful a person has to be to set someone on fire? On purpose? You can't honestly believe that any of us would be capable of doing something so cruel."

This is why everyone always talked to Deb.

She always made sense.

She always knew just what to say to make you believe her.

Still, we all know what happened to Olivia that night. We just had to figure out who did it.

"There's no way anyone of us had something to do with the fire that killed Olivia. I refuse to believe that," Deb said. "Oh, guess who I saw the other day?"

"Who?"

"Your ex-husband chile! He was with his wife and all they damn kids!"

"Rodney?"

"Yes. He was holding both babies in his arms, looking tired as fuck. As though he hadn't slept in days. His wife was chasing after the other kids. They were coming out of the grocery store. I was going in. His wife is cute, but she doesn't look better than you. Anyway, she and the other kids headed towards their car. Rodney lingered around, once he noticed me, and then he asked me about you."

"Me? Why?"

"He asked how you were doing since Olivia's death. I told him you were doing fine. And that was it."

I'm not fine.

And I haven't been for what seemed like a very long time.

Deb snuggled up close to me, and for a long time, we both just sat there in complete silence.

Maybe Deb is right.

Maybe I wanted the truth so bad that I was willing to turn everyone that I loved into a suspect.

And now, Kelli and I would never get the chance to make amends. I pushed her away because if she couldn't tell me what she was doing outside that night, then in my mind, she was guilty of something.

Was I that desperate for the truth that I really thought the women that I grew up with, laughed with, cried with, and loved…was I that crazy to think that it was one of them had something to do with Olivia's death?

To think that one of them could do something like that?

Have I been looking in the wrong place all along?

Or am I just wrong?

Wrong to think it was anything more than what the police says it was.

An accidental tragedy.

Could it be?

~***~

"Fuck them!"

Greg and I were finally going to talk.

It was early in the afternoon, and I was surprised when he called me to stop by.

I'd been helping Kelli's mother with arrangements for her funeral all morning. I'd seen Kelli's body at the funeral home. Dead and gone, Kelli was still so beautiful. She looked as though she was sleeping.

She looked as though she was at peace.

"Man, I gotta' go." Greg hung up his phone. "Hey," he said to me.

"Hey."

We both took a seat.

"How are you holding up?" Greg chuckled. "I'm sure we're both tired of having to ask each other that question."

"Yeah. But I'm doing okay. Better than I was."

Greg nodded.

We small talked about Kelli and the incident, and then he brought up a different conversation.

"My police contact found out what Dre---Officer Deondre Bell, was doing at the party. Pepper, who asked you to hire him?"

Um...I tried to think back.

It was my idea to have strippers and a bartender but..."Deb," I answered him. "Deb said she knew a good bartender for the party. She gave me his information, and I hired him. "

Greg nodded. "That's what he said. He says Deb knows his wife, Sarah. I think they used to work together. Anyway, he says Sarah told him that Deb wanted him to call her about a paid, off-duty gig. When he called her, at first, she asked him could he patrol the area and sit outside all night at the bachelorette party. He says Deb told him she felt like something bad was going to happen. She wouldn't say what, but she did seem worried. Deb told him that she didn't want to worry Olivia or the other girls, so she only wanted him to stay outside and patrol the area, but he had an even better idea. He told her about his bartending history. Deb thought it was the perfect cover-up. If he was inside the house, he could be closer if anything happened. So, she told him that she would get the sister of the bride to hire him as the bartender, and she would still pay him for his "protection" services too."

I was so confused.

Why did Deb think something bad was going to happen? How did she know that?

"I don't understand. So, Deb knew someone was going to hurt Olivia?"

"He couldn't answer that question. He said it was almost like Deb thought something bad was going to happen to her…not to Olivia. He says she didn't want to ruin the party and have everyone on edge, so she wanted to keep who he really was just between them."

Why didn't Deb tell me this?

"But Kelli recognized him."

"She recognized him?"

"Yes. He said he was fixing her a drink and that she kept staring at him. And then she told him that she recognized him, and she knew he was a cop. She also asked him why he was pretending to be gay. When he refused to answer her, she said she was going to tell you that something was wrong. That's when he asked to speak to her outside."

So, Kelli and the cop did go outside.

"He told her that he was "working" the party. Kelli wanted to know what that meant. He told her that he was hired to keep everyone safe. The officer said once he said that, Kelli started to panic, and he had to pull her from the porch to a more private area so no one could hear her."

"Behind the garage."

"Yes. He told her there wasn't anything to worry about. He says that Kelli assumed you or Olivia hired him. She didn't know that it was Deb."

"Well, technically, I did hire him."

"Yeah, but you know what I mean."

You know what…

I thought back to the bachelorette party.

Kelli and I were drinking, and she kept asking me if I was okay. She asked me the same thing, at least ten times. Maybe that's why. I thought she was asking me the question because I was drunk, but perhaps she was asking because of what the officer said to her.

"Well, if he was there to protect, he did a horrible job!"

"He thought he was protecting Deb. He said he didn't see the fire, or Olivia until everyone else did. He said when he saw her, he knew it was already too late. There was nothing he could do."

I didn't know what to say, so I didn't say anything.

"He says after he made the 9-1-1 call, he asked Deb how she knew something was going to happen, but Deb seemed confused. As though she didn't understand what was going on. He asked her if she knew anything about the fire and Olivia. She said no. She said she was the one in danger. Not Olivia."

"And he believed her?"

"Not at first. Officer Dre told his superiors that bartending was a hobby for him, and that one of the ladies at the party feared for her life. But that it wasn't the victim. He told them it was Deb. They conveniently left that part of his statement. They sent him to talk to Deb, again, in uniform. She told him the same thing. She didn't know what happened to Olivia. He was there because she thought something bad was going to happen to her. He asked her what it was and she told him she knew something about someone that she wasn't supposed to know, but that it didn't have anything to do with Olivia. And when all of the evidence pointed towards Olivia's death being an accident, and because there wasn't any foul play, he took her word for what it was. He told his superiors that there wasn't anything there."

I wasn't so sure.

Deb always knew something, about someone, or someone's secrets, so maybe she was telling the truth.

Then why hide that she hired the cop?

Why not mention it?

She had plenty of opportunities to say something about that night. She had something to say about everything else. Unless she truly believed that one didn't have anything to do with the other. Unless she really thought that Olivia's death wasn't related to whatever it was that she'd been scared of.

The "her" that the cop told me to ask wasn't Kelli.

It was Deb.

And the crazy thing is, I was there with Deb that night. She still pretended as though she didn't know him and as though she didn't know that he was a cop. And even once I came back inside and told her what he told me, she said nothing. She didn't say a word.

And I'm not sure why Kelli wouldn't have just told me that she was outside talking to the bartender---the cop.

I mean, what was so hard about that?

I asked Kelli to her face why she was outside. If she thought the cop was hired by Olivia or me, why not just say that? Or ask me?

Still, none of this makes much sense.

"If you ask me, none of it makes sense."

"I was just thinking the same thing. And it still doesn't explain what happened to Olivia. Why did Deb need protection? What does she know? Who left the book of matches on my porch? There are still so many unanswered questions."

Maybe Deb left the matches.

Maybe she was trying to scare me into leaving Olivia's case alone. But would she have broken into my business and destroyed it?

I don't think so.

I need to talk to Deb.

Again.

"They need to reopen Olivia's case. There's so much more here than they thought there was."

"Already on it. I'm going in to see the detective that was working the case tomorrow. I'm sure they'll have questions for you too."

"Kelli's funeral is tomorrow. And I'm going to talk to Deb. But I'll be ready to talk to them too. I'm ready to find out the truth and just…I'm just tired of all of this! I'm tired of the confusion and all of the secrecy! I'm tired of questioning everything and asking all these questions in my head. It's driving me crazy!"

I was mind boggled.

And I was sick of it!

Greg got up and came to sit next to me.

Hesitantly, he placed his hand on top of mine.

"We're gonna' get to the bottom of this. Together."

I hope so.

In a matter of seconds, mentally, I tried to recall everything that Deb, Kelli, and the officer had said to me.

"What about Olivia's phone records? Since you don't have her phone anymore, do you know her information to see who might've called her that night? Deb says that she saw her on her cell phone, not long before she died. Do you think her phone records are still available online or something? So we can see who she was talking to?"

"Our phones were on the same plan, and though her number is disconnected now, I can still check. If I can't see anything, I can get my buddy down at the station to work on getting her phone records."

"Please do. It's worth looking into."

Greg didn't say anything for a while, and neither did I. I could tell we were both in deep thought. We were both wondering, analyzing, and probably overthinking everything we'd just discussed. Finally, Greg started to speak.

"About the other night…"

"Greg. I can't think about the other night and Olivia at the same time. I just can't."

"Do you regret it?"

"Greg."

"Do you? Just answer that. Do you?"

Exhaling, "No, Greg. I don't regret it. I feel guilty and a little ashamed. But I don't regret it."

"Me either."

Greg stared into my eyes.

"I know the circumstances are crazy. I know that if Olivia were still alive, what happened between us never would've happened. No matter what I've always felt for you, I would've never acted on them. But she's gone now. And we're still here. It may not be right, it may be wrong, but I can't deny what I feel about you anymore, Pep. Once all of this is over. Finding the truth. Getting closure. Once it's all over...come with me. Come with me to Florida. You can reopen your cleaners there. We can get away from here. Or if you want me to stay...I'll stay here. I'll stay here with you."

"Greg."

Mama would have a heart attack if I popped up in a relationship with Greg. I'm positive that it wouldn't sit right with her. And for the record, it didn't sit right with me either.

"Just think about it. I can't imagine what our families will say. What our friends will think. But I don't care. Just think about it. Okay?"

Just to get him to shut up, I agreed.

"Okay."

~***~

The funeral was packed.

There were so many people there to say goodbye to Kelli. A lot of people from her job. And I noticed that Brian was there too. All of Kelli's closest friends sat on the same row.

Through my tears, I kept my eyes on Deb.

She was crying. And she sat next to Coco. Coco was crying dramatically, and her pregnancy had started to show. And she kept nodding her head to everything that her husband said about death and Kelli.

I was all in my feelings. I had so much rambling around inside my head.

There were so many unanswered questions. So many assumptions. So many worries and circumstances.

And not to mention, I received yet another "warning" last night. Since Kelli's death, I'd been staying at my house. When I got home last night, I checked my mailbox.

Inside of it, on top of my mail, was a cigarette.

The same brand of cigarette found at the scene with Olivia's DNA all over it.

At first, I started to panic.

Fear shot through my body like a speeding bullet, but it only lasted for a second. And then suddenly, my fear went away.

I wasn't scared anymore.

Whoever was leaving the warnings, if they wanted me, they would have to come and get me! I wasn't going to run away or back down, and I wasn't going to let anyone get away with my sister's murder!

I ended up staring at that cigarette all night.

And then a thought crossed my mind.

What if leaving these random things at my house wasn't a warning at all? What if they were trying to get me to see something else about that night?

Then again, that wouldn't explain the break-in at the dry cleaners.

I couldn't be sure, but I wouldn't find the answers to my questions by looking at a cigarette. But I was sure as hell going to get some answers from Deb today!

Once the funeral was over, and once Kelli was lowered into the ground, everyone was heading back to Kelli's house to mingle and eat with the family.

It was her mom's idea to have the repast there.

On purpose, I didn't drive.

And though I caught a ride to the funeral with Mama and Honey, I asked Deb if I could get in the car with her to go to Kelli's.

"It was a beautiful service."

"It was."

Deb's eyes were bloodshot red.

"Deb?"

"Yes?"

"Why did you hire the cop to watch over you at the bachelorette party?"

Deb almost ran the red light. She slammed down hard on the brakes.

"What?"

"You got me to hire him as a bartender. But he was really a cop. A cop that you hired because you said you felt like something was going to happen. What? Why? Why did you hire him? Why did you think something was going to happen? Something did happen. It happened to my sister."

"I didn't know that something would happen to Olivia!"

"Well, what did you know?"

Deb breathed slowly.

"I should've never opened my big mouth!"

"About what Deb. Tell me."

Deb pressed on the gas.

"I don't know what to think. I don't know if Olivia's death was because of me. Or if it had nothing to do with me at all."

"Deb. What are you talking about? And slow down."
She didn't.

Deb was driving way too fast and shaking her head at the same time.

"I was there that night."

"What? What night?"

Deb kept her eyes on the road.

"I saw what he did to her."

"What he did to who?"

"I asked her about it, and at first she tried to deny it, but she couldn't. When I saw him, I knew exactly what I saw, so she didn't have a choice but to admit it. She was so ashamed! And I was angry! And I opened my big mouth!"

"Deb! Deb! Slow down! Slow the fuck down!"

"I called him, and I told him that I knew what he did to my sister and I told him that I was going to expose him. I told him that I was going to tell everyone what he was. But then…right then and there…he threatened me. He told me I would never get to say a word. He said: "You'll be dead before then." His exact words. And his voice was so deep and so cold. I knew he meant it. I should've listened to her! I shouldn't have said anything! I shouldn't have opened my big mouth!"

"Deb!"

I gripped the handle on the door.

"I'm sorry if it's my fault that Olivia died! I'm not sure, but it might be all my fault! Oh God, it might be all my---"

BOOM!

Shatter.

BAM!

Crack.

The airbag slammed against my face, and then everything went black…

****

CHAPTER EIGHT

"Your *brother* is in love with you."

I struggled to open my eyes.

Mama.

Instantly, I recalled my last memories, and I gasped.

"Calm down, Pepper. You're okay."

I struggled to speak.

"D---D---Deb?"

"She's going to be okay too."

Mama patted my leg, motioning me to lie back and relax.

"How…"

"You've been out of it for about a day. You suffered a concussion. You have a broken arm and some bruises. But you're going to be okay. Baby, you're going to be okay."

I exhaled and then I looked around the room. It was filled with so many flowers.

Mama noticed me looking at them.

"More than half of those are from Greg. That's why I said your "brother" is in love with you. I could always see that he loved you more than he's supposed to."

"Apparently everybody could see it, but me. And when you say *brother* like that it makes me want to hurl."

Especially considering I'd had sex with him, but I dare not say that aloud.

Mama chuckled. "We can't always help who we love. We're just not made that way. I was never quite sure if my instincts were right, but they were. Greg loves you. As strange and somewhat disturbing, as it is to say. I had to threaten to beat him with a stick to get him to leave your side," she said. And then she changed the subject. "You scared me."

"I'm sorry, mama. I tried to tell Deb to slow down. She was so upset."

"Why?"

"I'm not 100% sure. She was rambling, and I was confused."

The doctor came into the room. After he examined me and asked me tons of questions, he told me that he was keeping me in the hospital for another night.

"Honey is going to stay with you tonight. Joe is out of town on a work trip, and I'm going to stay with the kids. My phone has been ringing off the hook. I promised to call everyone once you woke up. I guess I should get to it."

Mama started to make phone calls, and one by one, my friends started to arrive to check on both me and Deb.

I wanted to get to Deb so bad. I wanted to make sure she was okay. And I also wanted to hear the rest of her story. I wanted to hear what else she had to say.

Although she was rambling like a lunatic, I'd heard some things crystal clear.

She saw something.

She said something.

She felt like she was in danger and that something terrible was going to happen to her. Someone was out to get her.

That's pretty much all I heard.

My friends left, and the last to stop by was Greg.

He stared at me from the doorway.

"I'm going to go ahead and get out of here," Mama said at the sight of him. "I gotta' get to my grandbabies. Your sister will be on the way up here as soon as I get there," Mama grabbed her purse. She stopped in front of Greg. "Hey, son," she called him.

"Hey, ma," he answered her.

She stared at him for a while, and then she looked back at me.

"Have you always been in love with Pepper?"

"Mama," I groaned.

"Answer me, son," she ignored me and spoke again to Greg.

He looked at her, and then to me. And then back at her again.

"Yes," he answered her honestly.

"Then why on earth were you going to marry her sister?"

Greg shrugged. "Because I loved her too."

Mama looked disappointed in his answer, but she knew he was telling the truth.

"In love with two sisters. How about that?" Mama shook her head. "But in my opinion," mama studied him as he looked at me. "If you ask me...you were going to marry the wrong one," she said surprisingly. "It's always been Pepper. And it still is. It's always been in your eyes. It's in them now." Mama told me she loved me, and she was gone.

Greg inched closer to me.

"Why did you buy me all of these damn funeral flowers?" I forced myself to chuckle.

"Remember that time I asked you what your favorite flower was? You said, and I quote: 'Roses...no, wait lilies...no, I like sunflowers too.' Remember that?" Greg laughed. "You couldn't make up your mind. So, I got them all."

I said that to him about eight years ago on our first date.

"I thought I lost you. When I got the call..."

"I'm okay, Greg."

He nodded his head.

I stared into his eyes. I was looking for the love that everyone else saw so easily.

"Are we really going to do this? Are we really going to...be together? After Olivia? Are we really considering doing this?"

"Only if you want us to. If not, I'll always be here. We've been just friends this long. Nothing will change that."

I took a deep breath.

If Olivia *was* in a grave, and not in an urn on a shelf, I'm sure she would be turning over.

"Sit with me."

Greg took a seat beside the bed, and we both just sat there, quietly, looking at each other, until Honey walked in.

"Damn, y'all might as well kiss or something," Honey said.

Greg stood up and offered Honey his seat.

"I'll see y'all later," he cleared his throat, looked at me one last time, and then walked out of the room.

"Umph, I told you."

I knew that she was referring to what she'd said about Greg a while ago; about him loving me.

"But anyway, how are you feeling?"

"Like shit. How do I look?"

"Like shit," she chuckled. "I stopped by Deb's room before I came in here. She looks horrible. Her face and everything is 10x's worse than yours. And she's still out of it."

"She could've killed us."

"Why was she driving so fast in the first place?"

"Uh, she and I were having a conversation. I was asking her about some things, about the bachelorette party, and then she just went into this rant about something she saw. Something she knew. Something she said to someone. And then she said someone threatened to kill her."

Honey swallowed the lump in her throat.

"What? What is it?"

"What did she say she saw?"

"I don't know. She went on and on about something. I was trying to make sense of it, but I couldn't. Honey, I have to know what she was going to say."

"Well, first thing in the morning, let's go ask her. Hopefully, she'll be up and feeling a little better by then."

The tone in Honey's voice was alarming. And the sudden look on her face told me that she was worried.

But the conversation came to an end, just as a nurse came in to give me a shot of something to help me relax. And before I knew it, I was more than relaxed.

I was fast asleep.

"Overnight, she had some complications. We had to put her in a medically induced coma."

From the wheelchair, I stared at Deb.

"Will she be okay? When will she wake up?"

"We're going to monitor her very closely, for the next few days. Hopefully, we will know something soon."

We asked a few more questions, and then Honey rolled me out of the hospital.

Damn!

Come on, Deb!

You have to pull through!

None of us could handle another death.

And although I hated that it was even on my mind…I still need answers! I still need to know what she was going to say!

I had to know if what she was referring to was somehow tied into Olivia's death.

Honey helped me inside her car, and then we headed to mama's house.

"Aww, mommy missed you," Honey said to baby Olivia.

"She's probably hungry. You go take care of *yours*. And I'll take care of mine," Mama said, referring to me. "Are you hungry?"

"I'm starving."

She helped me into the kitchen. "Ms. Crystal and Jai came by earlier to see if you were here yet. I told them you should be here soon. I'm glad to see that Crystal is doing better. She isn't pretending to be Olivia anymore. That was crazy, wasn't it?"

"Yeah. It was. She's going to be okay." I looked around the kitchen. "You sure have a lot of packing to do."

"Well, after we talked about it, Bill is going to move here. After what happened to you, I want to be as close as possible to my daughters and my grandbabies. I know. Mebane is only about an hour away, but I can't move. And not to mention Bill just got some news too. He just found out that he may have an almost forty-year-old son in town. And grandbabies too."

"What?"

"Apparently, decades ago he was told that he wasn't the father of *her* child. She had the baby, married the other fellow, and they had a few more children too. The son recently became ill. He needs some kind of transplant, Bill said. The mother wasn't a match. And neither was the "father". And according to the doctor, if neither parent is a match then…his father *isn't* his father at all."

"Say what! Wow! That's some fu—," I cleared my throat instead of cursing. "That's some messed up stuff."

"Yes, it is. Bill doesn't know much else. He's just waiting to find out the truth. He's been keeping quiet about it. I don't really know what he's feeling."

"So, she's only telling him because she wants one of his body parts?"

"Hey, a mother does what she has to do. As a mother, you'll do just about anything to save your child. I'm more concerned if he isn't. That man is going to die if she can't figure out who his father is. And even if Bill is his father, Bill's age may come into play when it comes to a transplant. If he even wants to do it. I guess we shall see."

Mama placed the plate of food in front of me.

"Did Deb go home today too?"

"No. They had to put her in a medically induced coma."

"Oh, no! Why? When I saw her, she was resting, but they said she was going to be okay."

"I hope she is. I need her to be okay. And I need her to finish telling me what she was saying before the wreck."

"What do you mean? What was she saying?"

"All I know is that she said someone was trying to kill her."

"What!"

"The night of the bachelorette party she was afraid that something was going to happen. Someone threatened her. Something about something she knows."

"Does that mean…"

"I don't know mama," I answered her, knowing what she was thinking. "I don't know if any of it has to do with Olivia, or why she died. I need Deb to get better in order to find out."

I wasn't trying to sound so selfish. But saying it aloud, it sure did sound that way.

Taking the first bite of mama's meatloaf, I closed my eyes as I savored the taste.

"Um, it's so good mama."

"Thank you," Mama said.

"No. Thank you for this food."

"And thank you for the way you love your sister. Thank you for sticking to your gut feeling and trying to find the truth. No matter how many times we all told you to move on."

I smiled at her.

I hope trying to find the truth was the right decision. And most importantly…

I hope the truth doesn't get me killed.

~***~

"You sure this is what you want to do?"

I nodded.

I was letting go of my father's dream and starting the journey to figuring out my own. I was officially selling the dry cleaners. With all of the damage, I wasn't getting much, but that was okay.

I still had insurance money from Olivia, and after all that's happened, I was well overdue for a fresh start.

I shook the new owner's hand, with my good arm and hand, and then I walked away from the cleaners, without looking behind me.

Just as I pulled out into the street, I spotted Coco and Pastor Troy walking into the deli.

They were holding hands, smiling, and pregnant.

I beamed.

They reminded me that one day, I still wanted that too.

With Greg?

I still didn't know about that.

I headed towards the hospital.

Days were rolling by, and every day, I was waiting for Deb to be in a better condition for them to wake her up out of the coma.

My phone was connected to the Bluetooth in my car, and the sudden loud ringing startled me.

Surprisingly, it was Brian.

His contact was still saved. I should've deleted it a long time ago.

"Hello?"

"Hello, Pepper."

"Uh, hi. What's up?"

"I heard about your accident. I just wanted to make sure you were okay."

"I'm fine."

"And your friend? Deb? Is she okay too?"

"She's…"

Why was I so hesitant to tell him?

Not knowing what all Deb was going to say had me on edge. Hell, the last few months I've been on edge.

"Uh, yeah. She's going to be okay."

"Good. That's good to hear."

There was an awkward silence.

He was the father of my niece. There wasn't much else for us to talk about.

Ever.

"Well, take care of yourself."

And with that, Brian was gone.

After stopping at a red light, I picked up my phone and deleted his contact and then continued towards the hospital.

"She's awake. But..."

I brushed past the doctor.

"Hey, Deb. Welcome back. How are you?"

She stared at me. "Who are you?"

Huh?

I looked back at the doctor.

"She wasn't wearing her seatbelt during the accident, and the blow to her head may have caused more damage than we anticipated. She's suffering from memory loss."

"Memory loss?"

"It could be temporary. It's normal for it to be temporary. Or it could be..."

"Who are you?" Deb asked again. "Who is she?"

Saddened, I looked at her. "It's me, Deb. Pepper."

She was emotionless. She just stared at me.

"Does she remember anything?"

"We're not sure yet. She does remember her name. So, that's a good sign. But everything else so far has been a blank."

I was ashamed of myself. My friend and her health were more important than hearing her secrets. Still, I couldn't help but feel disappointed.

What if she never got her memory back?

What if she couldn't finish her story, her confession, or whatever it was?

In a strange way. I found the situation ironic.

The one person that everyone told their secrets to…no longer remembered them.

All day, I sat there and tried to help Deb with her memory. She looked at me like I was crazy for the most part. She had no clue as to who I was or what I was talking about.

A few of our friends ended up coming to visit her too, and none of them were able to get through to her either.

It was hard to be hopeful, but we all were trying to be.

Deb needs her memory.

Completely exhausted, finally, I left the hospital in pain. I'd been there all day, and I was pretty sure that I overdid it. I was tired, sore, and I needed to rest.

Not to mention that driving with one arm was extremely uncomfortable too.

Although I was supposed to go back to mama's house, it was already dark, and my house was closer. So, I headed in the direction of home instead.

What used to be Kelli's house, looked abandoned as I drove past it. Seeing her house caused me to think about her and the fact that she was really dead.

Finally, I pulled into my driveway.

"Ahhh! What the fuck!"

Dressed in all black, a figure shot from the side of my house, running full speed in front of my car, causing me to slam on brakes.

My chest was tight, my heart was pounding, and I was struggling to breathe. Panting, I looked for the figure.

Where did they go?

Which way did they go?

Wherever they'd gone, they were out of sight.

What were they doing at my house?

Were they waiting for me?

Did I come home before they could break-in?

There was no way in hell that I was going in there!

A nervous wreck, still paranoid, and watching my surroundings, finally I was able to put my car in reverse and so that I could get as far away from my house as I possibly could. The entire time, I kept my eyes open for the figure dressed in black. Once I turned onto the main street, instead of going to mama's house, I decided to head towards safety. Towards someone that I felt could protect me.

Greg.

"And you didn't see their face?"

"No. They were in all black."

"Wearing a mask?"

"I think so. Or maybe it was a black cap or something. I don't know. It happened so fast."

Greg had called over his officer buddy.

"Greg tells me that you've had some other issues."

"Someone has been coming around my house for a while now. They left a book of matches on my front porch and a cigarette in my mailbox. They were identical to the ones found at the scene of my sister's death."

"And you don't think her death was an accident?"

"No. And I never have. No one would listen to me, but I've always felt like something was missing. I never thought she set herself on fire."

After a few more questions, the officer told me to come down to the station the next day to fill him in on all of my thoughts, details, and things that I'd come across regarding Olivia. He also suggested that I stay away from my house for a while.

"Florida is looking more and more appealing these days," I said to Greg once he walked the officer to the door, and then sat down beside me.

"Does that mean you're coming with me?"

I shrugged.

"I hope Deb gets her memory back."

"Why?"

"Whatever she has to say is going to help me with finding out the truth about Olivia."

"You really think so?"

"I hope so."

"Is your arm okay?"

"Yes."

Greg's phone started to ring. He answered it and walked away.

Examining his coffee table, I picked up the stack of papers.

Going through them, I noticed that they were call logs from Olivia's old phone. A print out of all calls to and from her cellphone; all the way back to three months before her death.

With one hand, hurriedly, I rummaged through the pages of phone numbers. Finally, I got to the page of phone numbers from that night.

"Incoming…incoming…incoming…"

Huh?

I found my phone and checked the number. And then I moved my finger from the phone number to the other end of the page with the call time.

Why would he call her?

I need to know.

The person to call Olivia that night was Honey's husband…

Joe.

~***~

"Where's Joe?"

Honey shrugged.

"He should've been back a while ago. He's off today but had some running around to do."

Joe has been a part of the family for years.

He was a simple man. Good with his hands. Loved to eat, and he loved Honey.

He was indeed like a brother to me.

But like a brother…is *not* a brother. So, why in the hell did he call my sister?

Joe called Olivia that night, and they were on the phone for two minutes and twenty-four seconds.

He never so much as mentioned calling her, or that he was possibly the last person to speak to her alive.

Why?

And why would he call her, on the night of her bachelorette party?

What was it that couldn't wait?

Unless he was calling her, baiting her, to come outside.

Okay, Pepper. Don't get ahead of yourself.

I was trying not to jump to any conclusions.

"You know what crosses my mind all the time? I wonder if Olivia would still be alive if I'd never rented the mansion. If I'd had it at my house like you told me to."

"Yeah. But you wanted to be over the top."

"I wanted the night to be special," I mumbled. "I'm glad you don't have to carry the memory of seeing her like that. Not like I do."

"I wish I could. Maybe then I would be as adamant as you are about her death and whether or not it was really an accident."

I was trying to think of a way to ask her my next question, without making her feel like I was interrogating her. I didn't want her to know that I was trying to figure out what she and most importantly, what Joe, was doing that night.

"And y'all were asleep when I called you to tell you what happened to her?"

"I was. Joe wasn't. I wasn't asleep the first time you called, just like Joe said. I was right there. I was just in my feelings and didn't want to go. And after we ate and put the kids to bed, I took a long bath. I cried that night in the bathtub. I closed the door, and I just cried. I didn't want Joe to hear me. The baby kicked that night, and it made me sad. And I just started to cry. I was crying over Brian and the situation. And I think I might've been crying a little bit about Olivia too. The fact that we were arguing and in such a bad place. We were in so bad of a place that I didn't want to go to her bachelorette party. She was my sister. I was being overemotional and overdramatic."

I touched her hand.

"But seeing her like that probably would've killed me. You know how sensitive I can be. I guess, in a way, I'm glad Joe lied for me."

"Why didn't Joe go to Greg's bachelor party. He was invited, right?"

"Yeah. He said he didn't want to go, though. You know Joe. He's old. He would rather be at home watching one of those fishing or crime shows. And since I wasn't going, he didn't even pretend to be interested in going. I took a bath and fell asleep. I guess Joe was watching TV or doing whatever. All I remember is him shaking me, hard, telling me that you were on the phone and that something happened to Olivia." Honey exhaled.

Joe could've been doing anything that night, and she wouldn't have known it. And I'm sure she doesn't know that he called Olivia.

"So, any news on Deb?"

"Still no memory. Hell, my memory is somewhat fried too. I've been working my memory over time, trying to remember everything she said to me in the car that day. Wait a minute…" I paused, making sure that my thoughts were correct.

"Deb said: 'He did something to my sister' Yes. That's what she said. But she doesn't have a sister. But…"

The wheels inside my head were turning.

"She *does* call all of us her sisters. She said someone did something to her sister, and she confronted him about it."

Honey looked uncomfortable.

"Yes! That's exactly what she said. Okay. Okay! It's coming back to me. She had to be talking about one of us...right?"

Honey exhaled. "Pepper." She paused. "I think. Uh, I think she may have been talking about me."

"What?"

Honey and I were at her house. She sat in the single chair across from me, with baby Olivia wrapped in a blanket, in her arms.

"Pepper, I knew about mama and Bill about a week before the bachelorette party. I knew because Deb told me," Honey started.

I was all ears.

"She was showing a house in Mebane, and she saw them together. Literally, the day before Olivia and I got into our little argument, she stopped by the house, so that Joe could take a look at her car. It was running hot. You know, he thinks he can fix anything. Or at least he was hoping to tell her what the problem was. Deb and I were sitting on the front porch, and she mentioned that she saw mama with a man. She said she was sure that it was the man that mama used to date when we were little; although it was twenty years ago, I mean, he still looks the same. Just older. And remember mama didn't date anyone else but him, after Olivia's father. So, I knew it was him. I knew she'd seen mama with Bill. And mind you, I had already started therapy. I already remembered what happened to me; the touching. The molestation."

"Wait, what are you trying to say? Are you saying that Bill...Mama's Bill...molested you?"

Her chest went out and in, faster and faster as she breathed. "Yes, Pepper. It was Bill. He's the man that touched me."

I got hot.

I got REAL hot. And REAL fast!

"That motherfucker! That damn pervert! Oh God! And the pervert is mama's husband!"

I told myself to calm down. I needed to be here for Honey. She just told me her horrible secret, and she needed me to keep it together. She needed me to be the tough one. She needed me to be *me*.

"I started to shake that day, but Deb touched my leg and then…" Honey wanted to shut down, I could tell, but she kept talking. She forced herself to get it out. "And then Deb told me that she saw."

"She saw what?"

"Remember that sleepover we had, for my 9th birthday? All of us were there. We were all princesses for the night and slept downstairs on the living room floor?"

Vaguely.

If Honey was nine, I was only seven, so my memories from that night were limited.

"Everyone was asleep. Everyone but Bill. He woke me up and told me to come with him. I said no. And then he reminded me of what he would do to me if I said no again. He used to tell me that he would kill you, and Olivia, if I didn't let him touch me. And he told me if I told mama, he would deny it and kill one of you just because I told. I was young. I believed him. I was too young to know that he was just trying to scare me. He was manipulating me. All so that he could touch me. So, that night, he pulled me by the arm behind him. Deb says that she woke up and she saw him dragging me behind him. She got up."

"Why didn't Deb say anything?"

"She said she wasn't quite sure what she saw. At least not back then. Like me, she wasn't sure what it meant. But she heard him say he wanted to give me a birthday present. I told him I didn't want it. He told me to shut up and to touch *it*. And he touched me too."

Tears rolled down Honey's face.

"I won't go into details, but Deb saw what Bill did to me. She was a child. She didn't do anything. She didn't say anything. She didn't help me. And I was too afraid to help myself. That day on the porch, she told me she was sorry. She told me that she was sorry for not saying anything. And for not understanding what it was that she witnessed until she saw Bill's face. Until she seen him with mama. I opened up to her about it, cried to her, and like the shoulder that she so often is, she was there for me to lean on."

"Honey, I'm so, so sorry."

"Yeah. Me too. Deb wanted us to tell mama right then and there. She said that Bill and mama were kissing when she saw them. So, she wanted me to tell, and get him away from mama. I didn't know what to do. I told Brian about it. And he told me to follow my heart. My heart was confused. To learn that mama was with someone, again, after being alone for so many years. I guess I wanted her to have that. I wanted her to be happy. Mama has lived her entire life for us and through us. And now she has something that's just for her. And for mama's sake, I just wanted to forget it ever happened all over again. So, I told Deb to keep what I told her just between us. I didn't want anyone else to know. I definitely didn't want mama to find out. I didn't want her to think that somehow it was her fault. Deb didn't agree with me. She wanted me to go to the police. She told me that she knew a police officer, and she could help me. I told her to let it go. I just wanted her to let it go."

The baby started to whine. Honey popped her breast in her mouth.

"Deb became obsessed with finding out more information on Bill. She came back to my house, two days later and told me his life story. She told me that Bill used to be a City Councilman and that he'd done all of these great things. She told me that people adored him. And she told me that he was married...to Mama. She'd found a record of their marriage online."

"You knew they were married?"

"Yes. And after learning that, I knew for sure that I wasn't going to be able to say anything. I didn't know how I was going to be able to stay away or avoid him, whenever mama decided to share her news, but I didn't want to hurt her. And I knew that I would if I told her the truth about her secret husband. I was stuck between a rock and a hard place. I thought: What if she doesn't believe me? It was so long ago. I didn't have any proof. So, I choose to stay in the hard place. I chose mama's happiness over my pain. Deb didn't understand it, and I'm sure you probably don't either. But what else am I supposed to do?"

"Tell!"

Honey shook her head. "After that conversation, again, I told Deb to back off and let it go. She said she would. She never mentioned it to me again, so I assumed she did. So, maybe what she's talking about has nothing to do with me at all. Or maybe it does. I don't know. But it does feel good to finally tell you the truth."

Was Deb talking about Bill?

My head was throbbing. And so was my heart. I had to find a way to calm down.

"I mean, we are talking about Deb. She always knows something, about everybody, and everything. Maybe she was talking about something else. You, Me, Crystal, Jai, Shakira. Even Brenda or Valeria. She calls us all her sisters. I mean, Bill is what, in his sixties? You said she said someone threatened to kill her. Do you really think Bill would threaten her?" Honey said.

"I think if he'll touch a little girl, he'll do just about anything!"

I was trying to see how and where Olivia tied into all of this.

If Bill threatened Deb…why was Olivia the one dead? Was it safe to say that one didn't have anything to do with the other?

The cop was at the party for Deb.

All this happened right around the time of the bachelorette party. I'd hired the "bartender-cop" under Deb's request, just two days before the party.

She had to receive the threats before then.

That's for sure.

Why would she think that whoever was trying to kill her would do it at the party?

The mansion was about forty-five minutes away from where we lived. And even further away from where Bill lived. Still, there had to be something that made her think that whoever was out to get her had plans of getting her that night.

But nothing happened to Deb.

Was Olivia's death really just some drunken accident?

And if that's the case, who left the matches on my porch and the cigarette in my mailbox?

Why?

And who broke into the cleaners and who was that running away from my house?

If it was all an accident, why was someone taunting me?

I managed to squeeze in thoughts of mama.

Oh, mama!

She was going to be hurt, and she was going to be angry.

I spoke to her earlier. Bill was moving in, and they were getting everything settled.

She was so happy. Every day she had a glow and a look of pure happiness all over her face.

But we had to tell her the truth.

It's only right.

She deserved to know the truth about the man she's married to.

Honey's sacrifice was beyond me!

It was unbelievable!

She has always possessed a big heart. And to be willing to suffer in silence, so that your mama can have some piece of happiness was just like Honey.

Luckily…I was nothing like her.

If she couldn't do it, she could put the burden on me to tell mama.

Speaking of mama…

We both watched her pull into Honey's driveway.

"Don't say a word, Pepper. I mean it," Honey said through clenched teeth.

"Hey, girls! How are y'all doing today?" Mama said as soon as she entered the house.

"Good, " we both greeted her at the same time.

She looked at Honey. "Girl, it's too chilly to have that baby out here."

Honey reached the baby towards her.

"Where's Bill?"

"He's at home. Oh no, she needs her diaper changed. Come on, grandma's sweet baby. Let grandma get you out of this mess."

Coddling the baby, Mama disappeared.

Honey looked at me.

"No."

"What?"

"No, Pepper."

"But…"

"No. You will not tell her. Just let it go, Pepper. Lord knows I'm trying to. Just let her be. Let her be happy."

"She deserves to know."

"We all deserve a lot of things. Life isn't always so generous."

I rolled my eyes.

I was so upset that I didn't know what to do with myself.

How could she ask something like this of me?

"You better never take my nieces and nephew over there around that man!"

"He will never come near my kids!" Honey growled. "That's gonna' be the hard part. Keeping them away from him and keeping them from mama's house, without telling her the truth, is going to be hard. I don't know how I'm going to do it."

"You're going to have to tell her, Honey."

"No. I'm not. And I'll never forgive you if you do."

"You'll never forgive her if she does what?" Mama asked, walking back into the living room.

"What y'all talking about?" She smiled as she waited for an answer.

"It's a sister-secret mama. We can't tell you," Honey said.

"A sister-secret? But I'm the mama. You can tell me," mama looked at me as I looked at Honey with resentment.

Rolling my eyes at Honey, I replied.

"Sorry, mama. But these lips are sealed," I said, zipping my lips.

Maybe not today, or tomorrow, or even weeks from now. But I was going to tell mama the truth about Bill.

Someday.

Somehow.

****

CHAPTER NINE

"Ugh!"

I wiped my mouth with the back of my hand.

"It must be something that I ate," I said to Greg. He didn't respond. Silently, he sat on the edge of the bathtub, rubbing my back, while I leaned back over the toilet.

For over a week, I'd been sleeping at Greg's.

I was too scared to go home.

And too disgusted to sleep at mama's house.

Being around Bill was a definite no-no for me right now. I knew for a fact that if I saw him, I was going to demand him to admit what he did to Honey.

Hell, I might swing on him a few times too.

So, both Honey and I were staying as far away from mama's house as possible.

And mama noticed.

Neither of us showed up for Sunday dinner. She was used to the occasional one daughter not being able to make it, here and there. But for neither of us to show up---she was already asking if something was wrong.

She asked us if it was Bill. And if it was because he was living with her now. We both lied to her. We told her no. Honey used the baby as an excuse. I told her I wasn't feeling well.

Well, I guess I spoke this on myself.

After throwing up again, finally, I was able to pull myself off the bathroom floor.

"What did your friend say? Are they going to reopen Olivia's case?"

Both Greg and I had gone down to the police station. We talked for hours. In my opinion, I gave them tons of good reasons as to why they should reopen Olivia's case, and make it a murder investigation.

"He took it up with his lieutenant, but apparently, they still need more. Something more concrete. Everybody lying about something just isn't enough. And although someone left the same exact matchbook and cigarette at your house, from Olivia's death scene, only your fingerprints were on them. Just like with Olivia. He says they need more."

"Tssk." I sucked my teeth. "Bullshit! I can't even go home because someone was there and they were going to get me. They were going to do something to me."

"Then why did they run away? They could've easily stayed hidden, attacked you from behind, or broke inside while you were there."

"Really? Really Greg?"

"I'm just saying. They ran. If anything, I think they could've been looking for something."

"Looking for what? And at my house?"

"I don't know. It's just a thought. Or it could've just been someone trying to break in and steal, but you came home. You were in the hospital and then over at your moms. Maybe someone just noticed that you hadn't been home in a few days and saw an opportunity."

I rolled my eyes at him.

"I have to go out of town for a couple of days. I have to go to Florida."

"It's almost time."

"Yeah. It is. Do you want to fly down there with me? Or you can just stay here. You don't have to leave."

"Okay. I'll stay."

Greg and I haven't had sex again.

And we weren't sleeping in the same bed either. There was no way I was sleeping in the same bed with him that he used to share with Olivia. Nor was I going to fool around with him in this house.

After small talking for a few more minutes, Greg said that he had a flight to catch. He told me if I needed him, for anything, just to call, and with that, he was gone.

216

Since I hadn't slept much the night before, I stretched out on Greg's gray sofa and at some time or another, I dozed off.

I woke up to the sound of Greg's house phone.

He's the CEO of a company, so he always kept a house phone, just in case.

It stopped ringing and immediately started to ring again. Once the caller hung up and called back for the third time in a row, I forced myself to get up and answer it.

"Hello," I growled.

"Hello. I'm trying to get in touch with Greg. I tried his cell, but he's not answering. Is he home by any chance?"

"No. He's probably on the plane. He had to travel to Florida for work."

"Work?"

"Yes. The company he works for is opening a location in Florida. He's the CEO. I guess he's going down there to oversee the plans or something."

"Funny, I'm the owner of the company that Greg *was* the CEO for. And we aren't opening up another location in Florida."

"What?"

"I was calling Greg, personally, to beg him to come back to work. He resigned a while ago. After his fiancée passed away, he just wasn't himself. He came back to work and then out of the blue, put in his two weeks' notice. Two weeks later, he was gone. But the company just isn't the same without him there. We need him back. I'm willing to meet any demands that he has. I just need him back in that seat. So, when you see him, tell him to call Dan."

He said goodbye, and then he was gone.

Greg quit his job?

Why was he lying about it?

Why was he pretending to still be the CEO of the company, and as though he was moving to Florida for work?

Finding my cell phone, I called him, but he didn't answer for me either.

If he wasn't in Florida for work...then where was he?

Ugh! I'm sick and tired of people lying to me!

~***~

"I'm so sorry. I'm so, so sorry," Deb cried.

"You remember?"

"Yes. Well, some. Some things from a long time ago are still a blur, but I remember recent things. Recent years. And the accident. I'm so sorry, Pep. I could've killed you. I could've killed myself."

I sat down beside her bed.

"Come on now, don't get upset. Don't cry. You don't need any added stress on you right now. Not with the condition of your head. You don't want to lose your memory again. I'm fine. You're fine. It's all okay."

Deb squeezed my hand.

"I've been by here to see you almost every day. The others have been coming too. I'm just glad you're back."

Deb shook her head. "I was watching TV. On the movie I was watching, there was a car wreck. It was like as soon as the car slammed into the other one, tons of my memories came rushing back to me, all at once. Our car accident was the first thing I remembered."

"Yeah bitch, you blacked out or something. You were telling me..."

"I remember exactly what I was telling you."

All of a sudden, I felt nervous or scared. I couldn't tell the difference. I didn't plan on bringing up the conversation just yet. Not with her condition. But if she wanted to talk about it, then I sure as hell wasn't going to stop her.

"Bill..."

"So, Bill *is* who you were talking about?"

Deb nodded.

"When we were younger, I saw him..."

"You saw him molest Honey."

"Honey told you?"

"Yes."

"She didn't want to tell your mama or the police. I just didn't understand. I think I became obsessed with seeing all of the good things about him, all over the internet, yet knowing the monster that he was inside. Honey told me to leave the past in the past. That shit is easier said than done. I felt guilty. I saw him, and I didn't speak up back then. She was my friend. My sister. And if she couldn't tell, I should've been able to. I just pushed it to the back of my mind, just like Honey did, and made myself forget it."

Deb was staring off into the distance.

"But after seeing his face, I couldn't forget it. And knowing that he was with Mama Grace. I just wanted to do something about it. And I was going to. I figured Honey would be mad at me for a while, but eventually, she would get over it. I figured that in the long run, she would see it as justice. At least I was hoping that she would."

I couldn't be sure about that part. Even now, Honey didn't want me to say anything. She didn't want anyone else to know what happened to her or about Bill. Even Joe, she told him she was molested, but she didn't tell him by who.

She was protecting Bill.

And I didn't like it!

I didn't like it at all!

"I called him."

"Who? Bill?"

"Yes. I called him. Four days before the bachelorette party. I'd found his number off the internet, and I called him and told him that I was going to tell the police what he did. I was going to ruin his name and his legacy. No one would care about all the good things and the community work that he's done over the last few years. They were going to see him for the monster he is. I told him he was going to jail, where he belonged. And I told him that he had no right to do what he did to my sister!"

My eyes shifted to the machine attached to Deb.

"Deb, calm down. We can talk about this later."

Deb wasn't listening to me. I could tell that she was thinking about what she was going to say next.

"I said all of that and guess what he did? He laughed in my ear."

"Laughed?"

"Yes. It was like a crazy, psychotic type of laugh. He didn't seem afraid at all. And then in this deep, cold voice, he told me that I would be dead before I said a word to anyone. And then he hung up. And I don't know. Just from the way that he said it…I felt like he meant it."

I could tell that she was still shaken up by it.

"Honestly, he scared the shit out of me. Immediately, I wished I'd respected Honey's wishes and kept my mouth shut. I called her that night, but I didn't get to tell her that I called Bill. She was in a bad mood. I didn't want to piss her off any more than she already was. And being that she told me to mind my business from the very beginning, I just kept my mouth closed. And even with Bill, after the threat, I planned to keep my mouth closed about that too. Even though I didn't want to. I didn't want to die over it either."

"Do you really think Bill meant what he said?"

"I don't know. All I know is a day or two later, I kept getting the feeling like someone was watching and following me. Even when we met for lunch, at that restaurant, it felt like random people were staring at us or watching us. Hell, he was into politics, and you know how I feel about politicians. He could know somebody, that knows somebody else, that handles people like me; loose ends like me. Maybe I watch too much TV, but I'm telling you, when we left the restaurant that day, somebody was following me."

I could tell that she believed everything that she was saying.

And I believed her too.

I didn't know Bill. I didn't know what he was capable of. He was older, and just from looking at him, no, he didn't look like someone that would try to have someone killed. But then again, he didn't look like a lot of things.

"So, why would you think he would attack you, or send someone to attack you at the bachelorette party?"

"Honestly, I didn't know what he would do. Or if he was just threatening me to make sure I kept my mouth shut. All I know is that I was feeling watched, and if someone was watching me, then it was a possibility that they could follow me to the mansion and to the party. And I didn't want anything to happen to anyone else because of me. And because of the one time I opened my big mouth! I was a nervous wreck. Paranoid. And if I was going to be drinking, I couldn't watch my back. So, I needed someone else to do it for me. Initially, I was just going to have Dre patrol the area, but you texted me about needing a bartender while I was right in front of him. I read your text message aloud, he mentioned that he used to bartend and that he had his license. So, I figured he could make a little bit of money doing both jobs, and I would feel a lot more protected with him inside the house. But as it turns out, he should've patrolled outside all along. Maybe then he would've seen what happened to Olivia."

Olivia.

"And Olivia didn't know any of this? Not about Honey or what you saw? Or Bill?"

"Nope. If she did. I didn't tell her."

"And why couldn't you tell me all of this?"

"I don't know. I was trying to protect Honey's secret. It would've been hard trying to explain one part, without the other. So, I was trying not to mention it. And I definitely didn't want Honey to know that I said something to Bill. But then you questioned me about Officer Dre. So, I figured that he told you something. I never told him everything. I just told him I didn't feel safe and that I thought something bad was going to happen to me. I asked him not to tell you. After it all happened, I begged him not to tell you, if you came around asking questions. I guess he told you anyway."

Actually, he didn't.

At least he didn't tell me much.

"I could've just been paranoid. Like you said, Bill is an old man, and maybe he didn't mean what he said. But I didn't want to take any chances. It was just something about the way he said it. I can't explain it. You had to hear it for yourself. Something wicked was in his voice. Officer Dre was just there to keep me safe. If anything happened that night, I thought it would be to me. Not Olivia."

"And we still don't really know what happened to her. We still don't know how she ended up on fire. She didn't know about what Bill did. She didn't have any enemies. Yet, she's dead. At this point, I don't think I will ever find out what happened to my sister."

Deb's eyes grew wide, and then she sat up straight. "Sister. Sister. Hmmm," she said. "Unless…"

"Unless what?"

"Unless Bill thought…unless he thought *she* was me."

"What? Why would he think that? You and Olivia don't---didn't look anything alike."

"No. I'm saying unless he thought it was Olivia who called him. Or you."

I wasn't following her.

"When I called him, I called him from a private number, and I kept calling Honey my "sister". He hasn't been around you guys in what, twenty years? Well, until recently, I suppose. But he wouldn't have known what either of you sounded like over the phone. Perhaps he thought I was Honey's "actual" sister. Maybe he thought

Olivia called him, or that you called him, and not me. Maybe he sent someone after Honey's real sisters."

"Hmm...then why Olivia and not me?"

"I don't know. But I do know when I called Bill, I never said my name. The only name I said was Honey's. And I told him that I saw him. I said that I saw what he did to my sister."

I wasn't sure about what Deb was saying, but at this point, anything and everything was worth looking into.

After everything Deb just said, there was no way that I was going to be able to keep quiet. The truth about Bill must come out! And it was going to come out right now!

I'm sorry, Honey.

But this is something I have to do!

~***~

"Where did you go?"

"Hello to you too."

Greg had called me both days that he was gone, but I didn't mention that I knew he was lying. I wanted to look him in the face and have that conversation with him once he was back home.

"Dan...the owner of the company...the same company you quit as CEO...he called."

Greg exhaled.

"So...what are you lying about now, Greg? And why are you lying about moving to Florida?"

"I'm not lying about moving to Florida. I just lied about it solely being for a job."

"A job you no longer have."

"That's the thing. I'm taking a new position...in Florida...to be closer to my daughter."

"Say what?"

"Remember my buddy out in Miami? The one that got married like a year before Olivia and I decided that we were going to get married?"

"Yes."

"Well, the bachelor party got a little wild. Long story short, I cheated on Olivia that night. She knew about it. I told her the very next morning when I found the girl naked beside me. I didn't really remember any of it, but I mean, it was obvious we'd had sex."

"You cheated on Olivia?"

"In my defense, it wasn't on purpose. It wasn't intentional. Not like when Olivia did it. She cheated on me too. Twice. Whether you want to believe it or not, we were not a perfect couple. Not like everyone thought we were."

Olivia never told me that she cheated on Greg. And she never mentioned anything about Greg cheating on her either.

I felt deceived in some way. I spent years idolizing their relationship. I looked up to them and wanted whatever it was I thought they had.

It was all a lie.

"Olivia forgave the indiscretion after I explained the situation. And we never talked about it again. I didn't see the woman I cheated with, nor did I know that she'd gotten pregnant that night...until right before the wedding. She practically ran my homie down one day, back in Miami, and told him that she'd gotten pregnant at his bachelor party. She told him that she'd had a baby, and then she described the man she slept with. Me. He called me with her information, I called her, and then I flew out there to take the paternity test. She's mine. I have a daughter. Her name is Reagan. I couldn't believe it. And with the wedding only a month away, at the time, that was yet another thing that I couldn't tell Olivia. I decided to keep it to myself until after the wedding."

"That's a hell of a lie to start off a marriage with Greg!"

"I know. And technically, it wasn't a lie. Not yet. But I was going to pretend as though I didn't find out the possibility until after the wedding. I knew that was the only way. I also knew Olivia. She would've accepted it. Just like she accepted knowing that I was in love with you. For her, I was "it". She said it all the time. I know you're wondering, if she felt that way, then why did she cheat on me…twice? Your guess is as good as mine. I gave her everything she wanted. Since I couldn't have you, I made her my "it" too. I forgave her. She forgave me. And we always managed to move forward. And with all that had gone on with her and Jai, and that whole pregnancy situation…yeah, there was no way in hell that I was telling her about my daughter before the wedding. And shit at the time, I was on edge wondering if there would even be a wedding, with what my ex was taking me through."

Now that Olivia was dead, I realized that I didn't really know my sister at all. She had this whole side to her that she kept hidden. A side of her that she kept to herself. A side of her that she kept from me.

"Once Olivia died, and after talking to Jai that night, I confessed to her that I had a daughter. I told her I was thinking about moving to Florida. She told me it was the right thing to do and that Olivia was no longer around to try and control the situation or to stop me. And once this new position became available, I knew I had to go."

"You could've told me. You could've told me the truth."

"What would you have said?"

I looked at him. "The same thing that I'm going to tell you now. Florida is where you need to be. You need to be with your daughter."

"Will you be there with me?

I shook my head. "I don't know Greg. I don't know."

He looked at me, as though he was begging me with his eyes.

"Shit, you lie to damn much for me! I'll end up in jail fooling around with you!" I said to him.

Greg grabbed my hand. "I'll never lie to you again. I put that on everything I love. Never."

Instead of continuing the conversation with him, I told him that I would see him later.

There was something else that I had to do.

There was another liar that I had to call out today. And I was as nervous as a virgin waiting on a man to put *it in* for the first time.

It's Sunday, and I was on my way to mama's house. And though Honey wouldn't be there, I knew that it was going to be some backlash to what I was about to do.

It's time for everyone's secrets to come out. I just hated that mama had to get hurt in the process.

"Hey," mama said. "Your darn sister isn't coming again. She says that she's tired."

"She should be. She should be tired of lying."

Honey was going to hate me for this, but I had to get this off my chest. And it was time for Bill to confess.

Not to mention, what Deb said never left my mind.

Did he think that it was Olivia who called and threatened to expose him? Is that why Olivia is dead? If so, why did he think it was her and not me? Did he kill the wrong woman?

"What are you talking about, child of mine?" Mama said.

Bill walked into the kitchen.

I exhaled loudly.

I was standing right in front of the Devil.

"Do you want me to tell her? Or do you want to?"

Bill chuckled.

"Hello, Pepper. Last time…"

"Tell her!"

"Pepper, sweetie, what's going on?"

Mama touched my arm.

"Tell her, Bill!"

Bill didn't open his mouth. It was as though he was wondering if I knew what he didn't want anyone to know.

"Tell her what you did to Honey. Tell her what you did to her daughter."

Mama looked at Bill and then back at me. And then she looked at him again.

"What is she talking about, Bill?"

He looked at her, as though he was truly sorry for what he'd done. Still, he didn't open his mouth.

So, I did.

"Mama, Bill molested Honey.

"What!" Mama's voice cracked, and it was as though I could literally hear her heart shattering into a thousand pieces.

"Grace…"

"He did what?" Mama looked at Bill. "Is this true? Did you touch my daughter?"

Bill looked sympathetic, but he didn't answer her.

So, I answered for him.

"Yes! He did! He molested my sister! With your ole' 'come here and sit on my lap' perverted ass!" I yelled at him.

"Grace…" Bill spoke.

Mama started to shake. Hurriedly, she grabbed a knife from the kitchen counter and pointed it at Bill. "Get out! Get out! Get out!" She screamed.

"Baby, Grace look, I was a different man back then. I was a troubled man. I---I---I'm not that man anymore. I'm sorry. I swear, I am. I'm sorry."

"Get out!" Mama threw the knife in Bill's direction.

He dodged it. "Grace, I'm sorry."

"You damn right, you're sorry! A sorry piece of shit!" Mama examined the counter for another knife.

There was still something else I wanted to ask him.

"Did you kill Olivia?"

Mama's head whipped around so fast that she almost made me dizzy.

"What?"

"Did you kill Olivia?"

"No. No. Why would you think that? I didn't kill anyone."

"You told Deb that you were going to kill her."

"Who?"

"Who? Really? Deb! Our friend Deb! She saw what you did that night to Honey, and you threatened to kill her if she told. Did Olivia find out and threaten to tell on you too? Is that why you killed her? Or did you think she was the one who called you? Did you think that Olivia was Deb? Since Deb called Honey her "sister"? Admit it, it was you, wasn't it?"

My skin was burning.

My entire insides felt as though they were on fire.

"What? No. I didn't kill anyone. And no one called my cell phone threatening to *tell*."

What?

"Olivia died at her bachelorette party. I was with your mother all night. Wasn't I Grace? I was nowhere near that mansion. I didn't kill anyone."

Mama nodded her head to assure me that he was telling the truth about being with her.

Damn it!

Now I was even more confused.

Deb said she called him, and he threatened her.

Bill says that she didn't.

And he says that he didn't kill Olivia.

Mama is his alibi.

He's a pervert, but clearly, he isn't a killer.

Then…

Who threatened Deb?

~***~

"How dare you!" Honey screamed.

I wanted to be the first to tell her that I'd ignored her wishes and told mama the truth about Bill.

So, after mama chased Bill out of the house with another knife, and once she started to scream and cry, and told me not to touch her, I left her there.

I couldn't see her like that.

There wasn't going to be anything that I could do to comfort her. There was nothing I could do to ease her pain or make it go away. So, I gave her space. I was letting her have her moment. And came to face the music from my sister.

"I had to tell her."

"You didn't have to do a damn thing!" Honey yelled. She was so mad that she was turning red. "How could you? What did she say?"

"She tried to stab him."

"Oh, my God!" Honey screamed.

"And then she started crying. I've never seen her cry like that before."

Honey looked as though she was about to start crying too. She also looked as though she wanted to strangle me. "See, I told you to leave it alone. I told you to just let it be. It won't change what he did to me. It won't change anything. All you did was hurt mama!"

"She deserved to know, Honey. Come on. She deserved to know."

Honey steadied her breathing. "I know. I know."

Honey took a seat. "Honestly, I'd already told myself that I was going to have to tell her. I just didn't think she would have to be told today."

I took a seat beside her.

"Did he try to deny it?" Honey asked.

"No. He didn't."

In a way, I could tell that Honey was relieved.

"He didn't try to lie about it. He tried to explain. He said he was a different man back then. Of course, mama wasn't trying to hear that. But he tried to tell her anyway. He didn't lie about it. And I don't think he was lying about not threatening Deb either."

"What do you mean?"

"As you know, Deb got her memory back. Well, most of them. Anyway, she says she called Bill and told him that she was going to expose him. She was going to tell the police what he did to you."

"What! Are you freaking kidding me? I told her to mind her business! Both of you are so wrong! It wasn't your business or your place to say anything, to anyone! It happened to me! Not to you or to her…but to me!"

"I know, and I'm sorry, Honey. I really am. I'm sorry that it happened to you, and I'm sorry that I said something when you told me not to. And I'm sure Deb is sorry too. But she says that she called to confront Bill and that he laughed at her. And then he told her that she would be dead before she could tell anyone his secret. Deb says he threatened to kill her. But he says he didn't threaten her. As a matter of fact, he says he never spoke to her at all."

"That doesn't make any sense. If Deb didn't speak to him, then who did she speak to?"

I was wondering the same thing.

"Honey…is Joe here?"

"Joe!" She called to him.

I hadn't told Honey that Joe was the last person to talk to Olivia, but I was about to.

Enough is enough.

It's time for everybody to start telling the truth.

"Yes, babe," Joe said.

"Why did you call Olivia's phone the night of the bachelorette party?" I didn't waste any time.

"What? What are you talking about?" Honey asked.

Joe seemed unbothered.

"That night, Honey went into the bathroom, and I heard her crying. She was bawling like a newborn baby in there. I don't know what was going on between her and Olivia, but I knew whatever it was, it was hurting my wife. Once Honey fell asleep, I figured that maybe the bachelorette party was over. So, I called Olivia. I wanted to ask her what was going on between them. And I wanted to see if I could get them together to fix whatever it was that they were going through before the wedding. Honey would've had a fit about me getting in "sister business" but it was worth a try. It was a stupid idea. I mean, it was her bachelorette party. I don't know why it didn't cross my mind that Olivia would probably be drunk once it was over too. But I called her anyway. She could barely hear me. And from what I could hear, the party was still going on. Olivia kept screaming in my ear, and I could tell she was drunk. I told her that I would call her back, but she kept telling me to wait. She kept saying, 'Joe, wait a minute. Wait one minute'. As though she was going to go where it was quiet so that she could hear me. But she never did. So, I hung up on her. I figured I would try again the next day. You know, once she was sober and all. Unfortunately, she didn't make it to the next day."

He was so calm, and relaxed. So much so, that I knew he was telling the truth.

I believed him.

He called Olivia because his wife was hurting.

Just like he said he did.

Honey said a few words to her husband, and then he left the room.

"Pepper, I'm your sister. And Olivia was my sister too. So, I'm saying this with love. You're going to drive yourself and everyone else around you crazy, if you don't let this go. For months, you've been at this. For months you've been going around in circles, confused, and confusing everyone else too. So, sister, sure, go ahead and figure out who Deb called. Ask her again. But if that leads nowhere. If nothing comes out of it, Pepper, then…please, just let it go. Maybe it was an accident. Maybe it wasn't. But it's time for you, for me, for all of us to have peace. All I want after the year I've had is peace," Honey confessed.

And so did I.

As I waited for the doctors to finish examining Deb, I stood, watching small children play on the floor. I was back at the hospital. I was going to take Honey's advice. I was going to see if Deb had anything else to say and if she could figure out who she talked to and who threatened her. And if she couldn't, then I was throwing in the towel.

I tried.

I did everything I could.

I tried to find the truth.

I really did.

The children laughed loudly, and I couldn't help but smile. They seemed to be waiting to go into the room next to Deb's. The mother looked as though she was about to have a nervous breakdown. As though she'd received bad news and didn't know how to process it yet.

"Pep?"

Deb called out to me, and as the doctors walked out, I walked in.

The past two days have been rough.

Mama didn't want to be bothered. She told both Honey and me that she would be fine, and that she just needed some time. She needed a few days to process it all.

Honey wasn't mad at me anymore, and whether she wanted to admit it or not, I know in my heart that she's glad I told. She still didn't want to press any charges or anything against Bill, but I could tell that she was happy that he wasn't going to be around anymore.

A hundred-pound weight was now off her shoulders.

Thanks to me.

Mama was divorcing Bill. She also wanted Honey to seek some kind of justice, but she said she would respect

Honey's decision. Mama also said she wishes she could kill Bill and get away with it.

She wouldn't be that lucky.

She wouldn't be as lucky, and she wasn't as smart as Olivia's killer.

No one could tell me that Olivia wasn't murdered.

Not after all the crap that has come out. All of the lies and secrets. And even if I never found out who did it, I knew in my heart that I searched long and hard to bring my sister justice.

Now, just like Honey, more than anything else, I just wanted peace.

I just had one more thing to mention to Deb.

"Bill says that he never spoke to you. He says he never threatened you."

"That's a lie! He did threaten me! He said that he was going to kill me!"

I looked around to see if anyone else heard her comments since the room door was still open.

"I called his phone, and that's what he said to me. I swear. I wouldn't lie about something like that. You know what, give me your phone."

I reached her my phone.

She tapped on a few things. She was searching for something. Then she turned the phone towards me.

"William Leon Lineberger."

That's Bill's real name.

Bill was a strange nickname for William, for whatever reason.

"It has his Mebane address. And his phone number. It has a few numbers listed, but this one is the most recent. That's the phone number I called. I called him private. Ask your mama if that's his number," Deb suggested.

"Or…I can just call the number myself."

I pressed on the number.

It rang a few times and then someone picked up.

"Hello?" she said.

"It's a woman," I mouthed at Deb.

"Hello? Hello?"

Wait a minute…

"Hello?" She said again, as I inched towards the door. "Hello?"

She moved the phone away from her ear, just as I peeked into the hallway of the hospital.

It was the lady from the room next door.

Why was she answering Bill's phone?

"Keep an eye on them. I'm gonna' go outside for a minute," she said to a woman who was now outside the room that wasn't there before.

"What? What is it?" Deb asked.

"I don't know. But I'm going to find out."

In a hurry, I ran towards the elevator that the woman had just stepped onto.

"Whoops!" She stuck her arm out. "You almost missed it," she smiled at me.

I didn't know her.

I'd never seen her before.

I noticed that she was holding two phones in her hand, and a small wristlet with car keys attached to it on her left wrist.

"Visiting family?" I probed.

I mean, she did just answer a phone that was attached to Bill's name, with the same phone number that Deb swears that she called.

"Yes. My husband is ill. He isn't doing too well. He needs a transplant or…"

Wait…

Mama said something about a transplant.

Something about Bill's long-lost son.

I opened my mouth to say something else, but just then, the elevator doors opened.

She stepped off the elevator.

I did too.

"Excuse me," I said walking, behind her.

She stopped to look at me.

"By any chance are you related to Bill? Former Councilman William Lineberger?"

She observed me. And then almost running, she turned around and hurried away.

"Wait! Wait!"

She walked out of the hospital.

"Wait!"

Clearly frustrated, she turned around.

"Who are you?" I asked panting. "His daughter or something?"

"Who are you? And why are you asking me things about Bill?"

"So, you do know him? How?

"I don't have anything to say to you," she replied, walking further and further away from the hospital.

Her hands were shaking. She placed both phones in her back pockets.

"What is Bill to you?"

"Look, lady, I told you. I don't know what..."

"Look, Bitch, either you're going to answer my question, or there's going to be a problem!"

She chuckled and somewhat cocky-like, she answered me: "Trust me, Sweetie. You don't want these problems."

Her voice was completely different than it had been before.

Deep.

Evil.

Low.

The shit fucked me up!

It scared the hell out of me!

But I didn't show it. Instead, I pressed call on the phone number again, and her back pocket started to ring.

"Whose phone is that? Yours or your husband's?"

"Why?"

I shook my head. "Fine! You said your husband was ill and not doing too well. But I'm sure he can answer a question or two," I took a step back, towards the hospital, but suddenly, she started to speak.

"No. He needs his rest. He's dying. Let him…let him rest and die in peace."

"Your husband is dying? Who is your husband?"

She hastily answered me. "Rodney."

Rodney?

"Rodney who?"

"Mason. My last name is Mason."

Rodney Mason…my ex-husband Rodney Mason?

"Wait…wait…wait. It's Rodney in that room?"

"Yes. And to answer your question, Bill is his dad. Not mine."

"What? No. Rodney's dad is Mr. Earl."

She looked confused as to ask how I knew that. "No. It's not. Rodney is sick. Almost two years ago, his health started to decline. He had good days and bad days, for a while, but finally, they found the problem. He needs a kidney. Bad. His mother couldn't give one, but Mr. Earl was going to. But the truth came out, and Mr. Earl wasn't a match nor was he his father."

Well, I'll be damned!

I tried to think back to seeing Rodney a few months, after Olivia's memorial service. He looked good to me. He didn't look sick at all. Then again, I hadn't seen him in years, so maybe he was sick, and I just couldn't tell.

"The waiting list is years long. He doesn't have years. I'm not a match either. So, his mother had to cough up her secrets and tell who his real father is."

"Bill?"

"Yes."

I was flabbergasted.

"He just found out?"

"No. They've known for a while. Months."

Months? I thought mama said they weren't for sure yet?"

"Apparently, he lied to your mama."

"Wow. Thank God mama is divorcing his ass! That would've been one hell of a surprise. Bill invites his new son to dinner, and surprise…it's my ex-husband."

"Excuse me?"

"Yep. I'm Rodney's ex-wife and apparently his step-sister now…until mama divorces Bill!"

What a small world!

Bill was long gone before I met and married Rodney, so he knew nothing of him. And I never mentioned Bill to Rodney while we were together. I didn't have a reason to.

Bill couldn't have told Rodney about his marriage to Mama because if he had, I'm sure Rodney would've told him about our history.

"Rodney told me that he was never married before."

"For the record, it was a horrible marriage. If that makes you feel any better."

She shook her head. "That lying motherfucker!"

"It was a long time ago."

She still looked upset.

I got back to what mattered.

"So, the phone…"

"It's in Bill's name. We've been having a hard time lately since Rodney has been sick and out of work. Between bills, the older kids, the baby twins, and everything else, it was becoming hard to manage. Bill got these phones added to his plan for us."

If Deb called the phone number to one of the phones in the lady's back pocket then that means she spoke to Rodney and not Bill.

So, Rodney threatened her?

"Bill was going to give Rodney a kidney. At first, we were worried that his age might be a problem, but it wasn't.

But after testing, we found out that Bill basically needs a kidney too. His kidneys are in bad shape, and he can't spare either of them. " She looked disappointed. "I wish we'd known that before…" She clamped her mouth shut.

"Before what?"

She stared at me.

"What were you going to say? You wish you'd known Bill couldn't give Rodney a kidney before what?"

"Nothing. I told you what you wanted to know. Now if you'll excuse me."

She turned her back to me.

The wheels in my head started to turn. I tried to put together what Deb said, and what I now knew to be true.

"So, Rodney needed Bill's kidney," I started to talk aloud. "She calls Rodney's number, thinking it was Bill's. She calls him out on his actions and tells him that she knows the truth about him. She knows his secret. Only Rodney doesn't want his new daddy---Bill to go to jail. He needed him. He doesn't want to die. At the time, he was hoping to get one of his kidneys. So, he threatens Deb."

Rodney's wife looked at me with a strange smirk on her face. I could tell that there was something that she wasn't saying. Something that she was holding back. And call me crazy, but it seemed as though she was amused.

"What I still can't put together is…"

"Let it go…Pepper," she said in a low, deep tone.

Did this bitch just say my name?

"You know my name? I never told you my name."

She smirked at me.

So, this whole time, she knew exactly who I was?

I stepped back from her. We were outside, but I felt like I was suffocating.

"You know who I am?"

"Yes. I know exactly who you are. Pepper. Pepper. Pepper," she growled. "You just don't know how to let shit go, do you?" she asked harshly. "I didn't know that you were Rodney's ex-wife though. Now, I must admit, I didn't see that coming. I can't believe Bill didn't tell me. He told me everything else."

For whatever reason, though I wanted to speak, I couldn't seem to open my mouth. So, she continued.

"You said Deb. Who is that? I don't know anyone named "Deb". But it was me who answered Rodney's cell phone that night. He was in the bathroom, so I answered the phone. I put the phone on my ear, and that's when I heard her voice. *She* was raising all kinds of hell. She was screaming: 'Bill, I know what you did! I saw you! I know you touched my sister, Honey! And you're going down! You're going to lose everything.' That's all she kept screaming. She was really fucking annoying."

Now, Rodney's wife didn't seem as delicate. As fragile or flustered as she appeared to be in the hospital or at the beginning of our conversation.

She was different. Bolder. Devilish. She twirled her finger around the curls of her hair as she continued to speak.

"All I could think about was my husband. He needed Bill. At the time, we didn't know Bill wouldn't be able to help. Rodney is the only family I have…and the kids. No one was going to mess up his chance to live. So, I threatened her. I made my voice real low and deep, like this," she said in a deep, agonizing tone.

Damn!

She really does sound like a man!

"At the time, I didn't mean anything by it," she switched her voice back. "I just wanted her to back off. So, I told her that she would be dead before she could tell anyone the truth."

"So, you threatened Deb?"

"Again, who is Deb? No. I threatened Olivia."

Huh?

I was confused.

And then it hit me.

Deb was right.

Obviously, she thinks that Deb was Olivia. Because Deb referred to Honey as her sister.

"I asked Bill about it. Privately. I told him that Rodney didn't know anything about the phone call. I asked him if he molested some girl named Honey and I told him that her sister was threatening to turn him in. He asked me which sister...Olivia or Pepper."

Neither.

It was neither of us. It was Deb.

"Surprisingly, he told me the truth. He told me that if he could take it back, he would. He said he used to be a troubled man, and that he'd changed. I knew all about being troubled. Yet, I didn't have any sympathy for him. I don't have sympathy for anyone; except for my kids and Rodney. All I cared about was Rodney. And then Bill told me his other secret. After what he'd done, he'd had the audacity to marry Honey's mother. Your mother. He's a bold son of a bitch, ain't he? He told me that no one else knew about their marriage and that he'd actually been okay with things being a secret between them because he always knew in the back of his mind, that once their marriage came out...so would something else. So would the past. And his secret. He was stupid for marrying your mother in the first place. I mean, clearly, he'd gotten away with something horrid. Why go back? Why marry the girl's mother?"

Rodney's wife rolled her eyes. "After he told me his secret, he told me that Olivia was getting married soon. Olivia. Honey. Pepper. He'd given me all of your names. It wasn't hard to link you to each other on social media. I found all of you. I knew Honey wasn't the one who called him. It was one of her sisters. You or Olivia. I wanted to talk to you. To both of you. I wanted to ask if you could wait to expose Bill. Just wait until we got the kidney and then you could do whatever you wanted to do about him.

We just needed a little more time. I never told Rodney what I was doing. I have my own set of secrets and lies. He doesn't know my past. And apparently, you're proof that I don't know his."

She didn't really have to say anything else.

From the look on her face, I already knew.

This is her.

I don't know why yet. And I don't know how but...

This is the woman who killed my sister.

"Social media can be dangerous. We tend to tag everything. And everywhere. I didn't know which sister to approach, but it seems as though Olivia wasn't as accessible as you were. I saw you tagged in a post, and you were meeting someone for lunch. You were meeting someone with the name "Ms.D Real-Estate" or something like that."

Deb.

That's Deb's social media handle.

"I came to the restaurant. I watched the two of you. I wanted to approach you then, but you seemed to be in a bad mood. Or like you were in a panic. And the woman you were talking to, seemed nervous. She kept looking all over the restaurant. Like someone was after her or something. Anyway, you left in a hurry. By the time I got outside, you were gone. But I caught the woman you were with getting into her car. I tried to follow her. Once she stopped, I was going to approach her, and give her my information. I was going to tell her, to tell you, to call me. But it was like she was trying to lose me on purpose. She was driving all crazy through traffic, and I lost her at a red light. That lady was on edge."

Duh! Because you threatened to kill her!

Not Olivia!

It was Deb on the other end of the phone that night.

And the day that Rodney's wife is referring to had to be the same day I met Deb at the restaurant, only a few days before the bachelorette party. She said she felt like someone was watching her and that someone had followed her.

She was right.

It was Rodney's wife.

"The day of Olivia's bachelorette party was a bad day for Rodney; which made it a bad and sad day for me. He was in so much pain. He was so sick, and there was nothing I could do to make him feel better. I was anxious. I felt helpless. So, that evening, I rechecked social media. It was time for her party, and so many of you shared your locations. All I had to do was follow the GPS to the yard full of cars. Once the kids were in bed, and Rodney was knocked out on pills, I got all dolled up. And since wigs seemed to be the theme, from the pictures that were being posted, I threw on a blonde wig, a short leather dress, fishnet stockings, heels, and a pair of leather gloves. I didn't plan to crash the party. Well, I guess in a way I did. I just wanted to talk. Sure, there's a time and place for everything. It was probably crazy of me to come there. But I don't really think like everyone else. And I was desperate. All I knew was that at the time, Bill was still out of jail, and I wanted to keep it that way. My husband was sick and slowly dying. Bill was our only hope, at least we thought he was. I still had time to reason with Honey's sisters. To get whichever one of you, or both of you to hold off until we could get the surgery. That's all that really mattered to me. You just don't understand. Rodney saved me. And I was trying to save him. That's all I was trying to do."

The palms of my hands were sweaty, and I kept glancing at the cop next to the hospital entrance.

"I knocked on the door of the mansion. No one answered. I turned the doorknob, it was unlocked, so…I walked right inside. No one even noticed that I didn't belong."

"What? You were there that night? Inside of the house? At Olivia's bachelorette party?"

"Yes. I was late to the party, I should say. Mostly everyone was drunk, or completely in their own little worlds. No one noticed me. Some of the heavily intoxicated women even spoke to me. I'd dressed like a stripper on purpose. I could see in the photos and videos posted online, that a few strippers were in attendance. I simply planned to say that I was sent for additional entertainment if I was asked. I used to dance, back in the day, so I was prepared to shake a little ass if that would get me close to one of you. But I didn't have to. No one cared who I was. And then I saw her; Olivia. I recognized her face from her online photos. She was by the back door. At first, she seemed to be on her phone. She kept looking at it and yelling into it. Finally, tripping all over the place, she made her way to a small table, rumbled around in a purse for something, dropped her phone, and after figuring out how to open the backdoor, finally, she made her way outside. Casually, I followed her."

I can't believe this shit!

A whole person was there, that wasn't supposed to be...and nobody noticed?

So much for Deb's cop friend and his protection!

Unless he was outside, behind the garage with Kelli when this lady came in!

I couldn't stop moving.

The sound of my heartbeat was thumping in my ears. I was sweating and wondering what she was about to say next.

Yet, she was calm.

"When I approached her, she was walking along the edge of the pool. She was so drunk. I walked right up to her, and said, "Hello, Olivia." She asked me who I was. I said entertainment. She laughed and said Pepper overdid it with the strippers. She was all over the place. She tripped over her own feet and dropped her glass of vodka all over herself. The glass shattered to the ground. She laughed."

My heart was racing. I was panting, but Rodney's wife ignored my fright and continued. I got the feeling that she was excited to share what she'd done. As though she wasn't worried about the consequences.

"She was holding a cigarette and a book of matches. She told me not to tell anyone that she was smoking and then she said: "Smoking can kill you." She gave this whole big speech about how she stops at the store near her house just to buy one, single cigarette every day. It wasn't until I moved to the South that I discovered that some stores sell single cigarettes. It's a good thing when cash is low. Anyway, she said something about her father having lung cancer, and that her fiancé hated women who smoke, but that it helped her take the edge off. I wasn't one to judge. I pulled out my lighter and cigarette too. Olivia placed her cigarette between her lips, but she never bothered to light it. She just kept rambling."

At that moment, I realized that sometimes wanting to know the truth can do more damage than good. I knew that whatever she was about to say was going to change my life forever.

And I wasn't sure if I could handle it.

For the first time, since Olivia died, I didn't want to know what happened to her that night. I didn't want to know the truth.

Still, I stood there.

Still, I listened.

"I asked her if she was the sister that knew about Bill. Her response was: "Yes…Yes. I know ." So, I knew I was talking to the right one."

I shook my head.

Olivia must've misunderstood her question.

Yes. According to mama, Olivia knew that she and Bill were seeing each other. So, Bill lied when he told Rodney's wife that no one else knew about their relationship. Unless he meant that no one knew they were married; at least that's what he thought. Deb and Honey knew beforehand too. And Honey assured me that Olivia didn't know that Bill touched her.

So, Olivia must've thought that Rodney's wife was asking her if she knew that Bill and Mama were together. Not if she knew that Bill was a pervert!

"As drunk as she was, I knew explaining to her why I needed her to keep her mouth shut about Bill was pointless. But I tried anyway. I attempted to get through to her. I told her that my husband was Bill's son and that we'd just had twins. I told her that he needed a kidney from Bill, and I asked her if she could please hold off on exposing Bill. I told her that I would greatly appreciate it. Olivia laughed in my face as though I was a joke. And then she asked me who I was again. She dropped her cigarette out of her mouth, but she didn't bother to pick it up. Frustrated, I placed the flame from the lighter to my cigarette and took a puff."

I stepped back from her just a little more.

"I mentioned Bill again. And she snapped. She said she didn't want to talk about Bill and she didn't want to talk to me anymore either. I was just going to leave. I figured that I would try talking to her again when she was sober, and that coming there wasn't a complete waste of my time. Now, I knew which sister I had to get through to. Her. But as I walked away, she asked me a question. She asked me if I was married. Even though I'd already told her that I was, I turned around, and answered her anyway. I said yes. She asked me what kind of man marries a stripper. I ignored her. I knew I wasn't a stripper, even if I looked like one. Since she wanted to talk, I came closer to her, and asked her again to keep what she knows about Bill to herself until Bill saved my husband. And after she giggled, she responded. "Fuck Bill. And fuck your husband.""

Olivia was as sweet as pecan pie, but I always told her that she wasn't a "nice" drunk. She was aggressive, bossy, rude, and demanding whenever she had too much alcohol in her system. And she was snappy too.

"She kept blurting random, rude remarks at me. She was a mean drunk. Just like my mother. And I hated my mother," Rodney's wife confessed. "She said fuck my husband, over and over again. I didn't like that. Rodney is the best thing that has ever happened to me. He keeps me grounded. He's the first man that ever really loved me. I would die for him. And I would kill for him too," she said coldly.

Breathe, Pepper! Breathe!

"At that moment, your sister's comments, and how erratic and childish she was, made me think that I would never be able to get through to her. She was going to keep her word and expose Bill. Bill was going to go to jail. And Rodney was going to die. I mean, if Bill got locked up, and was awaiting trial, I'm sure what my husband needed from him wouldn't have mattered to the courts. My husband needed his kidney. But like I said before, I wish I'd known that Bill couldn't help Rodney that night. It would've been a good thing to know…for Olivia."

She was emotionless, as she prepared to confess.

"Olivia continued to laugh, and nag. And I think she slightly came *on* to me. I just wanted her to be quiet. I just wanted her to be quiet about everything, and about Bill…forever."

She killed my sister!

"She was wearing this ribbon. I still had my lighter in my hand. It all happened so fast, really. Nothing like the first time…"

The first time?

"She was still laughing. She didn't even notice that I'd flicked on the lighter and set the ribbon on fire. She didn't realize it until it was too late. She tried to pat it, and while she was doing that, I set fire to another piece of her pretty white dress. And again to another piece; the string that was in a bow, at the bottom of her back. She had flames growing in three different places. She couldn't say anything, to anyone about Bill…if she was dead. She started to spin around as I backed away from her. And then she started to scream. I dashed towards the patio area and hid. There was a fence there, but if I backed up far enough, into the corner, I knew that no one would be able to see me. Olivia screamed again, and again, and finally, I saw some lady come running towards her, just as I relaxed behind the grill. They both were screaming, but no one could hear them. No one but me. I watched the flames consume her. The pool was right there. The woman was trying to tell her to jump in. She wasn't listening. She wasn't a very good listener. All she had to do was listen. She should've listened to me. Just like my best friend…all she had to do was listen."

This lunatic!

She killed my sister for nothing!

She killed the wrong woman!

My mind told me to attack her, but the way she smirked at me, it was clear that she was ready for whatever I was thinking of doing. And with my arm still not in the best condition, she would surely get the best of me.

"Once Olivia fell, the other woman ran to the house for help. Another lady came out, and then together, they went to get everyone else. A swarm of intoxicated people flooded out of the house and with all eyes on Olivia, easily, I made my way over to the crowd and blended in. I even screamed a little bit, just to make sure my lack of reacting wasn't noticeable. And slowly, I backed away. I backed away from the scene. Still, no one noticed me. No one was paying attention. All eyes were on her. And with the flames still blazing, I made my way back into the house and back outside to my car. And just as the sirens drew near, I sped down the long, dark narrow road."

My mouth was dry.

Tears were streaming down my face.

"If it's the last thing that I do bitch, I'm taking you down for this! Do you hear me? Your murdering ass is going to jail! You killed my sister! And for nothing!"

Rodney's wife waited for me to explain.

I wanted to move, run, or lunge at her, but my feet were heavy, as though they were buried in cement.

I couldn't move.

I couldn't do anything that I wanted to do.

But I could speak.

"She wasn't the one to call Rodney's phone! Neither of us knew about what happened to Honey. The woman you spoke to, wasn't one of Honey's sisters. Not by blood anyway. She's one of our friends."

My sister died for nothing.

I was so heartbroken by the truth.

She was taken from us for no reason at all.

"I asked her if she knew about Bill…"

"She knew that Bill and Mama were secretly together! Not that he was a goddamn child molester!"

I checked for the officer at the entrance of the hospital door again. He wasn't there.

"Oops," Rodney's wife said.

"Oops? Bitch, did you just say oops? You killed my sister, and all you can say is oops?"

"Accidents happen," she smirked. "Olivia's death was an "accident". Just like my friend Nora's death was an "accident". Accidents happen all the time. Pepper."

"It wasn't an accident! Help! This woman killed my sister!" I started to scream.

"Prove it. There's no proof. You won't be able to prove anything because there's nothing there. Bill told me that you were looking for proof about your sister's death.

He doesn't know that I was responsible for it. He just said that Pepper was hellbent on finding out the truth about that night. At least that's what your mother told him. Anything you told her, she told him. And he told me. For what it's worth, I'm not as heartless as you may think. If I wanted to do something to you *too*, I could have a long time ago. I've known where you live for a while. Yet, I decided to try and scare you to back off. The matches. The cigarette. Breaking into your dry cleaners..."

"That was you?"

"Yes."

"And was that you at my house that night? Wearing all black?"

"Yep. Your mother told Bill about a folder you had. Something with evidence from that night. He told me that your mother talked about an accident you were in and that Olivia's *old* fiancé told her that he gave you a folder. And that he wished he hadn't. He wished that he would've just helped you to let go. Instead of feeding into your suspicions. I'm sure there's no proof; but curiosity got the best of me, and I was trying to get into your house to get the folder. You surprised me when you came home."

Whoever said that the truth would set you free was telling a bald-faced lie!

Just like everyone else!

I didn't feel free.

I felt empty, broken, and angry!

All at the same damn time!

"You just wouldn't let it go. So---now you know."

"And now you're going to jail! Help! Help somebody help me! This woman killed my sister!" I screamed again.

People started to look at me.

Rodney's wife chuckled. "There's no proof."

"You just gave me all the proof I need! You gave me a confession!"

"Confession?" She started to walk towards the hospital. "What confession? What did I confess to? Tell me, because I don't remember. Maybe everything I just said was untrue. Maybe I lied. *Everybody lies*, Pepper. Don't you?"

~***~

"I'm just happy she's dead," I said as I finished taping the flaps of the box together.

Things didn't go how I expected them to go with Rodney's wife.

Wanda had been her name.

I told the police everything she told me.

And she denied it.

Instead of admitting that she'd killed Olivia, she blamed it on her dead husband.

Rodney died that day.

And when she was pulled in for questioning, she somewhat told them what she told me, but she explained the occurrences and the murder as if Rodney had done them. She told the police that Rodney confessed Olivia's murder to her on his death bed.

She lied.

And just like she said…there wasn't any proof.

There was nothing that could pin her to Olivia's death. And Rodney wasn't alive to defend himself.

She basically made Rodney out to be desperate.

Desperate for life and willing to do anything to keep on living.

The police took the time to interview everyone from that night, again, and just like she said, no one noticed or remembered her. Not one person noticed that she didn't belong there.

When they saw her picture, no one even recognized her, except for Deb. And it wasn't from that night. It was from her running into her and Rodney at the grocery store.

And she did say that the more she stared at her photo, she may have seen her at the restaurant that day. But she couldn't be sure. There was no way of knowing who the ladies were that Rodney's wife said spoke to her that night. It didn't matter anyway. Apparently, they were too drunk to even remember.

The police looked up Nora's death; the lady who used to be Rodney's wife best friend. Nora's death was listed as "accidental" too, but there was nothing to connect her death to Wanda either.

So, Olivia's killer was free.

But her freedom didn't last long.

After it was all said and done, Rodney's wife, Wanda, went into a store late one night, a few weeks ago.

And she never came back home.

There was a robbery, and she was one of the two victims killed in the attack.

She was there to buy cigarettes. She died with them in her hand.

Olivia tried to warn her.

"Cigarettes will kill you."

And literally…they did.

It wasn't the justice that I'd wanted, but it would have to do. The truth was out, Olivia's killer was dead, and finally, I could breathe.

And it was time for me to leave.

I was selling my house and moving to Florida.

I was moving there with Greg.

He left for Florida weeks ago. And I finally made up my mind to join him.

No. I still wasn't completely sure about this whole Greg thing, but after talking to my family and my friends, I decided that I needed a fresh start. And what better way to start over than on a beach, in Miami weather, with a man who apparently has loved me since the very beginning.

And no one thought I was in the wrong.

Everyone reminded me that Olivia was gone.

Though I made it clear to Greg that still, I wasn't exactly comfortable with what we were about to do.

I asked him if we could take things one day at a time.

And he was okay with that.

So, I guess we will see.

"Hey y'all!"

My friends, my *sisters*, flooded through the front door. They were all there to finish helping me pack.

We were two sisters short; Olivia and Kelli, but the truth about Olivia, somehow made us closer than we'd ever been before.

"Hey baby, I'm Auntie Pepper," I said to Coco's stomach. She was huge and would be having the baby soon. Rubbing her belly almost made me regret my decision.

Not long after finding out who Olivia's killer was, I found out that I was pregnant by Greg. I didn't tell anyone. Not him. Not mama. Not Honey or any of my friends.

I made the decision to get rid of the baby.

At the time, it was the best thing for me to do. But one day, hopefully, babies and a husband were somewhere in the cards for me.

"I can't wait to come and visit," Deb said.

Everyone, except for Honey, agreed.

"I'm going to miss you," she pouted.

"Aww. I don't know if this is a forever thing. Who knows, I might be back within the next year. I just need to get away from here. I'll come home to visit all the time."

Everyone nodded and stated that they understood.

I'd tried to get mama to move to Florida with me.

She and Bill were done, and they'd started the process of separation. She was definitely getting a divorce.

I told her that she needed a fresh start, and that Greg and I would take care of her. Still, she refused. She said that Honey needed her here. And she wasn't the happiest about me moving either.

"We're going to miss you," Crystal said.

She was back to her usual self, and back with her long-time boyfriend, Haji. They were all in love again, and her sister Jai was in a new relationship too.

Deb passed out a glass to everyone, except for Coco.

I didn't blame her for what happened to Olivia.

None of us did. Not even Honey.

Deb was trying to be a good friend. Sure, if she hadn't opened her mouth, none of it would've ever happened. But she isn't the one who killed my sister.

Wanda did.

And she got what she deserved.

Glass by glass, Deb filled them with wine. Once everyone's glass was full, she held her glass in the air.

"We wish you happiness, peace, closure...oh and good dick," Deb laughed.

We all raised our glasses.

"To Kelli and Olivia," I smiled.

"To Kelli and Olivia," everyone chimed.

And for a moment, everything felt normal.

And for the first time, in a long time...everything was fine.

~***~

"I can get used to this," I said behind Greg.

I'd just arrived in Florida, and found Greg standing in his backyard; which was technically the beach.

He'd purchased a condo and a beach house, and I must say, it was everything that a house was supposed to be.

"Hi."

"Hey."

I stood close to him, and he grabbed my hand.

"So, this is happening," I said.

"Yeah. This is happening."

The wind started to blow, just as Greg turned to face me. He touched my soft curls and then he caressed the side of my face.

"Remember I said I would never lie to you again?"

Man, come on! I just got here!

"Yes."

Greg stared at me. "I killed Rodney's wife."

My heart dropped into the pit of my belly.

"The robbery, wasn't really a robbery. Once I saw that she was going to get away with killing Olivia, I took matters into my own hands. I didn't literally kill her. But I paid the man who did. He was only supposed to kill her. No one else. But the other bystander got in the way."

I exhaled loudly.

"Say something, Pep."

"Why? Why did you do it?"

"For you. For me. For Olivia."

I smiled at him. "That's the nicest thing anyone has ever done for me," I replied.

And I meant every word I said.

Wanda got what she deserved.

Plain and simple.

Greg exhaled, relieved. "I love you, Pepper. And just like I knew from the first moment I saw you, you're going to be my wife someday."

And though this love was unconventional.

And though I never saw things ending up this way.

"Dear Olivia, I'll love him enough for the both of us…okay?"

****

The END

Check Out these books next:
Give Him Back: https://amzn.to/2PFBU0f
Give Him Back 2: https://amzn.to/2OTcve4
Once Upon A Crime: A Black Girl Magical Suspense:
https://amzn.to/2DwpGj7

For autographed paperbacks visit: www.authorbmhardin.com

To contact Author: E-mail: bmhardinbooks@gmail.com

Made in the
USA
Middletown, DE